DUE DILIGENCE

Also by RW Wells

Crime X Three: A Trilogy
The Saint and the Soul Slayer
War
Surrogate

DUE
DILIGENCE

RW WELLS

A STAND ON GUARD NOVEL

BLACK
CAT
BOOKS

Due Diligence
Copyright © 2019 by RW Wells

Published by Black Cat Books, Cranbrook, BC

First edition

ISBN 978-0-9950072-4-6

Produced by Behind the Book (behindthebook.ca)
Cover design: Sean Thompson (seanthompson.crevado.com)
Typesetting: SpicaBookDesign (spicabookdesign.com)

Namaste

Printed and bound in Canada by Island Blue Book Printing

FSC

A NOTE ON THE NOVEL

A certain amount of artistic licence has been taken in the novel when it comes to spelling and syntax, particularly in dialogue. This is intentional. It is meant to capture the nuances of English as a second language and the grittiness of the setting in general.

Let the adventure begin. *Carpe diem.*

PART ONE

There shrines, and palaces, and towers
Are — not like any thing of ours —
O! no — O! no — *ours* never loom
To heaven with that ungodly gloom!
Time-eaten towers that tremble not!
Around, by lifting winds forgot,
Resignedly beneath the sky
The melancholy waters lie.

— "The Doomed City," Edgar Allan Poe

CHAPTER ONE

He stood quietly in the doorway of the sunroom for a moment and watched her as she lay upon the the chaise lounge. The sun pierced the double-paned glass and fed the exotic plants that grew in profusion around the large glass-encased room with only the odd, few antique bamboo chairs or lounges placed here and there within the jungle of plants. Off to one side of the planetarium there was a ancient statue of Buddha sitting in the midst of a small rock pond choked with lotus flowers. There was a tiny fountain in amongst vines above where the Buddha's hands were held out and the clear, fountain water trickled between the fingers of the sacred one and fell into the pond, creating a sound that enhanced the silence, the peace within the room.

He heard her sigh.

"I sense that you did not come to share the peace of this room with me, my son."

A slight smile lifted the corners of his mouth as he thought of how he had never been able to hide anything from her. Even when he was a child, she had always been able to perceive his mood when he was close.

"How do you do that, mother?"

"What?" she returned.

"Know what I'm thinking, feeling? I do want to talk to you, but in the library, rather than in this peaceful place."

"I'm your mother and a mother's love is a bond with her child, sharpened by perception and intuition for the one she has loved since birth. And now you want to go into the library? This must indeed be serious," Martha Wellworth-Campbell said in a soft, well-bred voice that was intermixed with the Canadian drawl of one who spoke several different languages.

Her son, Raphael, who owned the part of her heart not taken up by her husband, simply shook his head as he stepped forward and offered her his hand as she looked up at him. The sun filtered through the thick glass and seemed to form a halo of light around his head as he stood above her, preventing her from seeing the expression on his face. As she accepted his proffered hand, she felt the subdued strength within it, almost as much as Stuart's, but then no one had as much strength as her husband, Stuart James Campbell. The very thought of him brought a flush of heat to her cheeks.

As she stood she actually had to look up into the face of her son. When had he grown so tall? She was startled by how fast time had flown by. It seemed only yesterday that she had been looking down at his small, sturdy body running around in the compound of whatever diplomatic posting they were at, and now he was suddenly grown into a man, stretched up perhaps even taller than Stuart. Where had the time flown? And then their eyes met, grey on grey, except his looked the grey of a storm-tossed sea that matched the earnest, solemn set of his face at this moment, and she felt a sudden alarm. Something was wrong or at the very least was worrying him.

"Don't worry, Mother, it's nothing serious, just a change in plans ... my plans, that is," he responded to her look as he put his arm around her shoulders and gave her a reassuring squeeze. The fact that he had to reach down to make that gesture mixed in with her sense of time somehow being lost.

They walked out of the sunroom and through the great room with its massive fireplace. Above the mantel was a huge shield of cast silver with the coat of arms of the Campbell clan engraved upon its surface. Beneath it were two broadswords crossed and draped in the Campbell tartan. There were deep tufted leather sofas, settees and the odd large armchair arranged about the room. To one side there was a huge mullioned, leaded-glass window, the top of which was arched and contained a stained-glass window dispicting the bloody battle of Bannockburn. It was afternoon and the sun shone through that window. As the light entered through the stained glass, it lit up the interior of the great room, and the leather of the deep burgundy chairs were touched by sunlight and enhanced by the red in the stained glass in such a way that they looked like pools of blood. The ancient carpet, woven of silk and wool, with red around the edges and a blue design in the middle, almost looked like a wash of blood running down to the sea.

"I hate being in this room at this time of day. It's just so war-like, and I swear there are times when I can hear the war cries of the Scots and the shouts of despair of the English," Martha said with a slight shudder.

He turned and looked at his mother and grinned before saying, "Really? I hear the shouts of the Scots alright, but it's in victory. I loved playing in here when I was growing up ... I still love it."

"Yes, you and your father both belong in this room. Although, I must admit, this room at night with the fire going was and is beautiful," Martha returned.

"Oh, come on, Mother. I can see you as a shield-maiden wielding a broadsword." Martha looked at her son as a slight flush touched her ivory cheeks and suddenly she burst into laughter. Her son joined in, and they were still laughing as they entered the library.

"You and your father really are incorrigible," Martha said once she got her laughter under control.

"Who's incorrigible?" a deep voice returned from the depths of a chair.

Martha immediately recognized her husband's voice and said, "Do I sense some sort of collusion between my husband and my son?"

"Not at all, my love. I, too, have been summoned. I suspect to hear some sort of pronouncement by our son, although I do have my suspicion of what it might be," Stuart James Campbell said as he looked towards his wife, with a slight shrug of his broad shoulders.

Martha looked between her husband and her son and thought yet again that there could be no doubt that they were related except that now her son was the taller of the two, where her husband was broader across the shoulders and the eyes were different. Stuart's eyes were the blue of a brilliant summer day while her son's were the changeable grey of liquid mercury similar to her side of the family.

Raphael looked at both of them and it suddenly struck him that his parents were getting older. When he had lived with them abroad and here in the massive stone house which had always been called "Campbell's Keep," they had always seemed the same exciting, brillant, funny parents who had taught him about the world and acceptance of the cultures that lived within it as they travelled between various diplomatic postings. They had always encouraged him to learn the language of the area they were posted to, to make friends amongst the local people, to learn the local customs, and when he was old enough, to attend the various dinners and social events of the gentry and government officials that the diplomatic ambassador must attend. He had learned diplomacy at the knees of his parents. At times though, even as a child, he had said what he thought without using the filter of diplomacy, to the dismay of his parents.

He looked at them and all that they had always been and meant to him was still there. The brilliance was still there reflecting off both of them, but there were small signs that he had not noticed when he had still lived with them—the odd laugh line, small wrinkles around the eyes and silver dusting the hairline of his father's thick, ginger-coloured hair while silver strands twisted through his mother's long, blue-black hair like festive tinsel.

"Well, get on with it, son," his father said, breaking his contemplation of the two people in the world he was closest to.

"Alright," he said with an internal shrug. *Now or never*, he thought, and without the preamble he had planned, he stated plainly, "I have joined the police force."

"What?" his mother said faintly before abruptly sitting down on a side chair.

"RCMP? Now that might be alright, Martha. I know the commisioner. Raphael could get a plum job in the intelligence division with his knowledge of language and different cultures and not only that ...," Stuart managed to say before Raphael put his hand up and shook his head. His father's voice faded away and a puzzled looked replaced the smile that had started to form on his face.

"Mom ... Mother, Dad, I have joined the city police force, my last semester of university after I had completed all my international government studies, journalism courses. I was at a bit of loose ends, so out of a sense of curiosity I took a couple of criminal justice courses. I found them fascinating, so I did a little investigating of my own and talked to some police officers I had come to know who were taking courses at the university. Even went out on a couple of ride-alongs—talk about exciting! At times you have to make instant decisions, your mind is always working, you're always watching and the characters you meet, from all sections of society. I felt comfortable. It felt right, like I could belong.

I knew I could do it, and I think I could do a good job. I know, I know, you wanted me to do some sort of diplomatic service, and there is my writing, but when you think of it, police work is diplomacy at a very basic level. I just won't be on the other side of the world. Of course I can write wherever I am, when I'm ready to write that is," Raphael returned in a voice that grew more excited the longer he talked about police work.

There was a silence in the room as Raphael sputtered to a stop as he looked between his mother and father. His father was standing beside his mother's chair and he held her left hand while his mother fondled the heavy gold and jade pendant she always wore, with her other hand. Both wore the polite expressions of experienced diplomats when faced with a crisis. His mother spoke first.

"Raphael, this change in plans is so unexpected and the last thing I would expect for you with all your experience, intellect and training, to say nothing of your ability and knowledge of several different languages. I ... I just don't know what to say ... to say yea or nay to this ... this sudden change of career choice."

The mask of a diplomat had slipped slightly and he could read the disappointment showing faintly on her face. He felt small tendrils of not so much anger, but frustration winding their way up from the pit of his stomach. He knew he could have stayed at home and lived off his trust fund while he went to university. He had always felt there was a part of his parents that wished he had stayed with them. He understood how it had always been the three of them together wherever they were assigned, and he had been home schooled. If he stayed at home now, he would always be there. He wanted to have adventures of his own choosing, not just riding on the back of theirs. He had deliberately picked a university a few hours away in another city and lived the dorm life as he went through school, just another student struggling to get by. He had worked hard and even won certain scholarships and although he had accepted the accolades, he had quietly made sure the money went to a student that was equally deserving but was struggling financially, and he did it in such a way that no one would know of his altruistic gesture including the recipient of the money ... or so he thought.

Stuart Campbell watched his son's face and observed the excitement and the beginnings of frustration written there. He had watched discreetly as his son made his way into the world of academics and had pulled slightly away from them. He had been proud of how well his son melded into the student's life, his high marks, his popularity, not because he was flashy but because he was funny and a good friend to those he liked and hung around with at the university. He also was aware that his son was helping others with money from scholarships that he had won. Raphael had been canny with his trust fund and only used a small portion, just enough to get by. Stuart Campbell also knew the courses his son was taking and when Raphael had started explaining why he wanted to become a city police officer, the father felt a sudden longing to be young again and find that kind of excitement. Yes, he understood why his son wanted to join the police force and make it on his own. He also knew that soon he and Martha would be going back to the Middle East, their last posting and potentially the most dangerous one. It would be better if their son was here to watch over his grandparents and their holdings. At least if he was here in the Canadian city where he and Martha had met and fallen in love, Raphael would be relatively safe while they went overseas again. He felt both his wife and his son's eyes on him.

Stuart first met his wife's eyes and saw the worry for their son as well as her puzzlement at their son's eagerness to step out of the diplomatic circle they had been so imbedded in, and he shook his head slightly. Then he turned and matched looks with Raphael, his son. He felt the pride and love for his son welling up in his chest. Maybe this particular career might curb the wildness, the taste for the "damn the torpedoes, full speed ahead" reckless adventurer that lay just below the surface. This very wildness is what his astute wife had always claimed Raphael had inherited from him although Raphael had also inherited his wife's ability to focus and remain calm in a crisis, which had helped him rein in, somewhat, the clan Campbell's notoriously wild, dangerous ways and quick temper. All the high clans had that intrinsic trait that was part of their very survival as they battled other clans to protect their historic holdings and, of course, to battle the British—it was imbedded in their DNA.

Over the years Stuart had had to work hard to contain that particular trait and even formed a thin veneer of civilization, certainly joining the diplomatic service and falling in love and marrying Martha Wellworth had helped. But it still lingered just below the surface of civil, calm, charming diplomacy.

Life took odd turns every once in a while he reflected, as his thoughts turned to their posting to the embassy in Kabul. That was when, in fact, those wild war-like traits had stood him in good stead when the Afghan War had broken out, with its attendant terrorists, al Qaeda and the Taliban, hunting out those they considered not of their faith. He, his wife, their son and diplomatic aides had had to flee through Afghanistan.

It had been a running skirmish to get out of Kabul with al Qaeda and Taliban soldiers hunting them. At one point he and two of the Canadian soldiers assigned to them had had to set up an ambush to delay the terrorists while Martha and Raphael, along with a wounded diplomatic aide, had sped ahead. He remembered Martha, in ripped trousers and an old shirt, with an AK-47 slung over one shoulder, while his son, at eleven years old, had a semi-automatic handgun, which he knew how to use, tucked into the back of his pants as they had helped the wounded aide. He had known that both could handle the weapons adeptly, thanks to lessons both he and the soldiers had given them. But still, he felt the wretching guilt at not getting them out of the country before the insanity of killing for a religion exploded once again upon that unhappy land.

The memory of looking at their faces, for what might could have been the last time, was still etched in his mind. His wife had smiled resolutely up at him, her creamy complexion soiled with dirt while she tucked a long tendril of her hair behind her ear. He even remembered her words ... firm, low and quick ... "If you're not caught up with us in thirty minutes, I will be back to get you!" He knew she would do it too. The look on his young son's face was equally as unwavering ... no tears, and although he could see the barest edge of fright written in those grey eyes, his son's face only showed dogged determination. And then they were gone.

The ambush was a success and he and the soldiers had managed to dodge back and forth through the bombed out buildings and flying bullets to the meeting place just as his wife and son had been getting ready to go back for him. His wife had merely smiled as if she had expected no less from him as he had pulled her to him with one arm. When he turned to look at his son, he was met with a savage grin that aged Raphael's face into that of a man for a brief moment, a baptism of fire, he had thought at the time. Then that awful moment when he had heard the whine of incoming ordnance and he grabbed them both, pushed them down and covered their bodies with his as he felt the hot push of the explosion of air going over them and one of the soldiers behind them disappearing into bits of nothing within the ugly roar. Then they were getting up ... the running ... the pulling of the wounded aide with them as the one Canadian soldier remained a short distance behind them, covering their retreat.

Once out of Kabul, they had fled into the lower foothills of the Himalayas, the area known as the Hindu Kush. It was there that they had run into some of the men-warriors of the Kalash tribe who had guided them to their village hidden away in a secret valley.

Their sojourn amongst the Kalash tribe had been a time of anxiety for the adults and magic for Raphael. He had found a friend, Shandi Cershi, son of the chief, his first friend of his own age. After a time none could tell them apart, for Raphael, with his dark hair and grey eyes, looked just like any other village child, plus he had a talent for languages. Soon he and Shandi were inseparable, always together talking, laughing as the they ran about the village playing with the other children. Raphael had attended the Falash school with Shandi and they, along with other boys of their age who were considered at the edge of manhood, were taught by the warriors how to fight the al Qaeda and Taliban ... the terrorists who had sworn a fatwah against the Falash. They were taught how to disappear amongst the rocks and hillocks like wisps of smoke, to be completely still, to find the inner stillness, the calmness within, to feel at one with their surroundings, to see through the eyes of the eagle over-head, to let go of panic and fear that could blind them. For both Raphael and Shandi, trying to find the inner stillness had been the most difficult, for they were of an age when the energy of youth surged through them. They wanted to run and yell. Finally though, and after many disappointed looks and words from the warriors, they learned. Raphael found that focussing on and praying to the gods that resided on top of Tirich Mir, the highest peak that loomed over the hidden valley, he could send his energy up to its rugged, snowbound tip. He would feel a still calmness slow his breathing, his heartbeat would quiet and become regular and yet his vision would be even sharper as his eyes roved the surrounding hills looking for danger. Finding the inner stillness was difficult to do, but every once in a while he would succeed. The warriors who taught them seemed to know when they had found their inner stillness, and when they came in from the hills they would smile at them and nod.

The time came when it was finally safe to leave the village. Raphael had initially refused to go. Only a talk with Shandi's father and Shandi, both of whom had firmly pointed out that he must always honour his parents and elders, had convinced him to leave.

Just before they were about to depart, Raphael went for a final walk with Shandi. It was then that Shandi had told him that he had, after the sacrifice of a small goat, consulted with the gods that resided on Tirich Mir and they had whispered from within the winds that Raphael would return to them after a passage of time. Raphael had managed a weak smile, and then Shandi had pulled out a knife with a long, shining blade that looked very sharp. The handle was of polished bone with the image of a flame carved into it and a red woven rope with a tassel tied around the top of the handle. Shandi had held his own hand out flat and sliced the palm open and then had given the knife to Raphael and indicated that he should do the same. Once that was done, Shandi grasped his bloodied palm to Raphael's in a tight grip as they looked into each other's face. Raphael had gripped Shandi's hand like he would never let it go, the forlorn look upon his face finally stiffening into a fierce expression as he pulled his hand away, nodded as he tucked the knife into his belt as he said, "I will return this to you," before stepping apart. Shandi turned and walked away. When he was alone, Raphael had cried bitter tears at the loss of his friend.

Raphael had never spoken of it again, but his father knew his son's time amongst the Falash had been special. Shortly after they had arrived in the village, the chief, Shandi's father, had come to him and asked if Raphael could attend school with Shandi. Stuart had, after serious thought, acquiesced. He had known a part of their schooling was the way of the warrior. It had left its mark upon Raphael and perhaps pushed him into manhood too quickly. Every once in a while, Stuart, after they had arrived back in Canada, caught a flash of an intractable nature, the steel of a warrior who knew what needed to be done and intended to do it. There were other times when he would find Raphael sitting quietly staring out at the mountains, and there had been an absolute stillness about him. It had grown in him from their time with the Falash, reinforcing the wildness, or so Stuart thought. What he didn't know was that his son was controlling that certain trait.

Those thoughts had flashed through Stuart's mind before suddenly grinning at Raphael and saying, "Martha, I think, at this time, this is the perfect career choice for our son. He needs to be on his own and make his own decisions. And, Raphael, remember with choice comes consequence ... some good, some bad, or at least that is what I have always found. Martha, think on it. If he were to stay with us, it would curb his free will and he would feel duty bound."

"Yes, yes, I understand," Martha abruptly interjected, comprehending that her husband was about to refer to their travel plans.

Raphael was puzzled by the brief, obtuse exchange between his parents but that was soon forgotten in the joy and relief at their acceptance of his choice of a career. The way ahead, for him, suddenly seemed paved in the golden light. The tentative smile upon his face turned into a large grin that encompassed his parents. The "job" lay ahead. His choice, his consequence.

CHAPTER TWO

The first day at the police college almost felt like his first day in an actual school environment after Raphael and his parents had finally arrived back in Canada after all the years spent abroad at various diplomatic postings. He corrected himself—almost the same feeling except now he was an adult like everybody else, and he, along with his other classmates in the room, was a university graduate with some worldly experiences. They all had been put through the same physical, mental and emotional tests to even make it this far.

Everything was so new, different, and although he and the other applicants or rookies were for the most part subdued, there was a spark of passionate enthusiasm in their eyes, and one could almost smell the adrenalin surging through the room. They all fumbled around picking desks to settle into and tenative smiles were exchanged. They were wearing uniforms that were still stiff, scratchy and ill-fitting even though they had all tried their new uniforms on secretly at home, looking in a mirror at least a dozen times, staring at the uncomfortable stranger that stared back at them. The most gregarious had started to exchange names with others while some remained silent, shy perhaps or wondering, maybe, just what they had gotten themselves into.

Finally the door to the classroom opened and two obvious veterans of the police force, both sergeants, entered the room. Their very demeanour, the aura of self-assurance the two sergeants exuded, caused those in the room to rise and stand at attention. Both walked to the front of the class, turned and smiled. Both sergeants wore their uniforms like they were born to them—there were no awkward wrinkles, shirts that gaped open inconveniently, pants that were too long or too short.

"Thank you, you may be seated," the taller sergeant said.

There was a rustle as the rookies complied.

"I am Sergeant Gary Travers and this is Sergeant Cynthia Michaels, and we will be your main course instructors."

Raphael had entered the police college with far more excitement than he had entered university. University and getting good grades had been expected of him, and he had dutifully fufilled those requirements, as with most things— getting good grades had been easy for him.

Now, though, he was entering a setting in which he had little more than a very basic idea of what the standards for good grades and good behavior was or meant. Oh, he had learned some things from the military guards that were always posted at the embassies where they had been, and he had learned certain things from the warriors within the Falash tribe where he and his parents had hidden for almost a year. He also came from a clan where much was expected of the younger members, indeed the Campbell clan was Scottish royalty. Having travelled all over the world with his parents, seeing the things that he had seen and the situations that he and his parents had at times barely scraped out of, had taught him how quick thinking, talking and a certain amount of cunning could get one out of some very dangerous spots. He also had come to understand that deceit was something that one should rarely or never use unless it was a last resort, for if the deceit or falsehood is found out, trust was likely lost forever and anyway, the truth was always easier to remember.

And now this new adventure, this new beginning. When he had been applying for and filling out the copious forms to even start the process of entering the police college,

Raphael had decided not to devulge his vast knowledge of certain languages and cultures. He had simply stated that he spoke French as a second language and had taken journalism courses and criminal justice courses in university. He thought to level the playing field. He had often seen that, at times, saying too much could be far worse than saying too little. Better to let things unfold naturally.

He studied the two sergeants standing at the front of the class. Both had remained standing after telling the class to be seated. Sergeant Michaels started telling them about the courses they would be taking, expectations gradewise and the physical aspects of training while Sergeant Travers leaned against the front of a heavy desk with his arms crossed, casually watching the class. Raphael's eyes locked with Travers' for a fleeting moment, and Raphael got a sudden feeling that Travers was waiting for something to happen.

Suddenly there was a large bang, almost like an explosion, and the door to the classroom was kicked open with a huge whumping sound and some grubby, unshaven men burst in yelling! Two more bangs like gunfire! A scream ... cursing, and then they started to run right past Raphael. Without even thinking, he tripped one of the apparent bad guys, grabbed one of his flailing arms, twisted it to put him flat down on the floor and disarmed him as the bad guy groaned in pain at the rough arm bar that held him flat and helpless on the floor. The female classmate across from him had the same idea at the same time and put down the other bad guy with a brutal sack to the nuts, causing him to go into the fetal position on the floor while she ripped the gun from his now limp hand.

Raphael and his classmate looked at each other and grinned savagely until they had a closer look at the "hand-guns" they had torn from the bad guys and realized they were replicas.

"What the fuck!" they both said at once as the rest of their classmate remained frozen in various positions of diving under their respective desks or still sitting with looks of indecisiveness or shock written on their faces.

CHAPTER THREE

"Ok! Ok! You two heroes can release the two undercover members and then come to my office with me. Cynthia could you explain the 'test' to the rest of the class and then have a couple of the class members help the undercover who got nutted get up and to the washroom where he can regain his dignity as the pain dies down."

As they left the classroom, following behind Sergeant Travers, Raphael glanced over and said his name in an undertone.

"Lula's the name." His classmate returned a small smile that showed off her dimples; her hazel-green eyes sparkled.

"In here," Sergeant Travers said abruptly as he opened the door to his office and walked in. He sat behind his desk and reached for some files that were stacked neatly on one side of his desk.

Both Raphael and Lula sensed that for the time being they should be standing at attention on the other side of the desk with their mouths closed until they found out what exactly was going on. They watched as Travers shifted through the files until he found the two he was looking for; the rest of the files were put back. Raphael had no doubt that those were their personnel files. He watched as Travers flipped through each one in turn. Obviously he was looking for something. At a guess, probably some sort of indication of previous training in the military or some such, he thought.

The silence in the room was becoming deafening, with only the faint crinkle of pages being turned to break the silence. Both of them continued to stand at attention.

Raphael's thoughts turned inward. He had learned how to stay motionless, to blend in; he slowed his breathing as he focussed inward. While one part of his mind stayed atuned to Travers, the rest reviewed his actions in the classroom. He could find no fault with those, although the brief look he had exchanged with Travers, prior to the incident, should have warned him that something was going to happen. And then there was Lula. He had felt an instant, dynamic connection with her when she had put the other bad guy down. The grin they had shared was a part of the very thought between them … it felt like he knew her already.

He heard the paper stop rustling, and he refocused on Travers.

"Nice take down, both of you, although I think it's going to be a while before Brad has anymore amorous adventures. That's alright. He's a little too much of a swordsman anyway," Travers said with a slight smirk before the look on his face settled back into a grim line as he continued to speak.

"I would like to know what the hell was … is going on? We always check personnel files of new recruits before using that particular scenario to make sure that we don't have any ex-military or mountie types or those with certain martial arts with skills and quick reaction time to do a take down under those types of conditions. Having said that, the sin of omission is still a lie of sorts. All the files for this particular class were gone over several times by both our psychology team and class instructors to make sure, as much as is humanly possible of course, that the recruits in a class are similar in nature, schooling and background. There is nothing in your files, aside from some time spent overseas when you both were young, to indicate any type of training—military or otherwise. As you both know, deceit is grounds for dismisal, so you both best tell me now what is going on and just what it is that you are hiding, or at the very least haven't told us."

Raphael had heard Lula's shocked inward gasp of air at the word "deceit" was flung at her, and he spoke up.

"Sergeant Travers, I can assure you that nothing has been hidden from you. When I was young, between the ages of two and about eleven or twelve, I travelled with my parents to whatever embassy posting they were assigned to. The last three or four were in the Middle East when the tensions were starting to rev up and the military assigned to protect us began to teach some of the staff and children, such as myself, at those postings, various moves to protect ourselves should anything happen. They used to make a game of it, a way of passing time for myself and the few other children in the embassy, or so I thought at the time. My parents' last posting was in Afghanistan just before the al Qaeda and Taliban started to take control. They were about to send me home when the bombings started, and then the whole country blew up, so to speak.

I was ten ... eleven. We ended up having to fight our way out of Kabul with our military escorts and spent almost a year hidden amongst the Falash tribe, who hated the Taliban. The Falash warriors also taught me how to fight as part of my schooling when we were with them.

We finally managed to make it out of there and returned to Canada when I was around thirteen. Back in Canada I was just another kid going to school, and I honestly thought no more about it, although I did take boxing and wrestling in high school, did quite well too," Rapeal finished. His eyes had never left Travers' during his explanation.

"I imagine you did—do that well, that is. My only question is, why is none of that in the file?"

"Oh, but it is, sir. I listed that I travelled with my parents during their diplomatic postings. I didn't think the details were important as I was still a child when we returned to Canada," Raphael returned, a look of puzzled equanimity on his face.

"I see. Yes, that does make a certain amount of sense. You seem to have a highly developed sense of danger and how to react to it. Now, I'm interested in Recruit Murphy's explanation of how she took down the other undercover operative in such a brutal but effective manner. Were you at an embassy as well?" Travers said in a quiet, slightly acerbic voice.

"No, sir. My dad and mom were military for the first few years of my life. My brothers, sister and I did travel with them. Then they retired and my dad, because of certain skills he had, was hired by a security firm to protect their upper management while they were overseas. My dad always said that no child of his was going to die because they were too weak-kneed to take care of themselves, and if we did end up dying, then the asshole that got us better be lying dead beside us. So he taught us a few moves so we could take care of ourselves. Sir, I just don't know how to write that on an application form since he taught us those moves as we were growing up," Lula said with a wide-eyed, innocent look on her face.

Sergeant Travers closed his eyes, a pained look on his face as he heard a soft, short snort of laughter coming from the direction of recruit Campbell's direction. "Campbell that better not be laughter I hear or you're going to be doing sit-ups and push-ups in the gym from now 'til next fuckin' Tuesday.

"No ... uh, I mean yes, sir," Raphael said in a low, strangled voice.

Now what was he, or rather what were they *going to do?* he thought. These two standing before him were the ones from the class who really stood out, and it was felt that they had great potential as police officers, both having graduated from university with GPAs of 4.0. From all the interviews with family and friends, they were well liked and respected. And they had done well on the psychological and physical test. Shit! These two shouldn't be in this class. It was almost like putting two well-trained German shepherds amongst a bunch of half-grown puppies.

Gary Travers had spent ten years, his best years as a police officer, he thought, working in the K-9 unit, and he often thought of recruits and other police officers in terms of German shepherds, "Malimois," and K-9 officers and how they fit together, how they worked. He thought right now that he had two really well-trained shepherds, with the hunter-killer instinct, on his hands. Did they want to throw them back in with the puppies? He had already seen from the scenario, before it ended so abruptly, that some of the puppies were gun shy and probably wouldn't make it as police officers. He was going to have to talk this over with Cynthia, and not only that but obviously they were going to have to go through other recruit files to check for similar upbringings. He sighed and suddenly realized that he had left Campbell and Murphy standing at attention while he had had his internal dialogue about them.

"I'm sorry ... sit, sit. I was lost in thought," he said as he looked at them, really looked at them for the first time. The male, Raphael Campbell ... interesting combination of first and last name ... Arch Angel and High-Clan Scottish, and the female, Lula Murphy ... different yet quite beautiful first name and, wouldn't you know, another Scot or perhaps Irish, by her last name. Both were tall and on the slender side although Campbell's big shoulders gave promise that he hadn't completely filled in yet, and again he met those grey eyes that held a look of speculation in them. Murphy's looks gave every indication of her living up to her first name. The shining auburn hair, tied back in a bun right now, those moss-green-coloured eyes with long lashes beneath swallow-winged shaped eyebrows and those dimples at each corner of her mouth, no doubt added a wondrous dimension when she smiled, although she wasn't smiling right now.

"It would seem that we have put you in with the wrong set of puppies ... uh ... uh, I mean recruits," Travers blurted, a red flush surging across his face at his blunder.

He saw the worry mixed with confusion and disappointment seep into the look they both gave him.

"Look, we made the error, not you. Neither of you is in trouble; in fact we, that being Sergeant Michaels and I, are going to have to discuss whether we are going to keep you in this class or put you both in another more advanced class," Travers said and saw relief in the loosening of the stiffness in their bodies and the tension written on their faces.

"Tomorrow is another day, and we will have this sorted out by then. For now, you two are dismissed for the day, and we will see you tomorrow. Oh, and you better come in an hour early."

"Yes, Sergeant," they both returned at the same time as they got up and fled with as much dignity as they could put in a quick march.

CHAPTER FOUR

Neither of them said anything as they exited the office, turned and walked down a hallway in the opposite direction from the classroom and Travers' office. After what seemed like a long hike down a seemingly endless hallway, they found an opening and turned into what appeared to be a casual lounge area. Both of them leaned against a wall.

"Well, wasn't that an interesting morning. I thought we were about to be fired when he ordered us to the office and I didn't honestly know why. I'm still not exactly clear on what's going on? Are you?" Lula muttered in a voice that was still a little breathless from the whole morning's events in the classroom, Travers' office and finally the long walk.

Raphael shook his head and then looked over at Lula. Their eyes met and held for a moment before broad smiles appeared on both their faces.

"Listen, before anybody sees us, let's get changed out of these uniforms and go somewhere else, away from this building and grab some lunch and a beer, then try to figure this whole situation out," Raphael said.

"You're on. I'll meet you by the west exit. That's where my car is parked," Lula returned.

"Me too. See you there in ten."

They separated and went to the changing rooms.

The men's changing room was empty, much to the relief of Raphael, who didn't want to answer inquisitive questions and feel the curious stares. He changed quickly but even then his mind kept going over what had happened. He knew they hadn't done anything wrong in the literal sense, but perhaps, in the figurative sense, in that they weren't supposed to be able to do takedowns or react quickly to dynamic situations. Maybe what he and Lula had done, in a way, had taken the wind out of the instructor's sails? He grinned to himself as he had that thought—maybe that was it. He looked forward to discussing that with Lula. It was unexpected but pleasant to have someone who thought the same way he did, at least as far as takedowns were concerned. He hoped they ended up in the same class. He finished changing and headed out to meet her, not knowing that she had been having very similar thoughts about him.

They walked out to their cars together, spoke briefly about where to meet, then got into their respective vehicles and drove away unaware that they were being watched by sergeants Travers and Michaels from Travers' office window.

"I'm thinking the objects of our conversation are going to meet somewhere ... perhaps for lunch, in order to discuss us, the class and what happened this morning," Cynthia Michaels said as she stood close beside Travers looking out the window, their hands touching below the level of the desk so no one casually walking by would notice the intimate gesture.

"No doubt. That's what I would be doing if that had happened to me this morning," Travers returned.

"Still think we should keep them together as partners?" She asked, her one eyebrow quirked up as she turned to look at him.

"Yes, I do. I agree that we put them in the accelerated class. They both have the I.Q. for it, and if they are partners they won't damage any of the others in that class and none of the others can damage them. I have already talked with Jim Bilidou about the two of them and he is quite eager to have them in his class. You have any problem with meeting with him and Carstairs, the other instructor in that class, after work?"

"Not at all. Gary, you know we have to go through all these files again to make sure we haven't missed any other surprises?"

"I know, but I think we've found all the surprises. Think about that whole incident, Cynthia. The rest of the class acted precisely as we thought they would."

"Their palms met and their fingers intertwined gently, briefly, as they contemplated the view outside the window for a few moments more before they freed their respective hands and moved around to opposite sides of the desk.

CHAPTER FIVE

Raphael and Lula met for lunch at a restaurant across the city from the college. They both agreed that the last thing either of them needed were classmates or instuctors stopping for a quick lunch and recognizing them. They both had had enough of questions and implied disapproval for one day. They had found a quiet, dark corner where they could talk, with only the waiter providing a few discreet interruptions.

The afternoon flew by with each talking, their words swirling around each other, creating a type of magic that rarely happens between two humans who were of such similar nature, that their understanding of each other went beyond the redundancy of mere words. In the end, there was a silence that spoke of everything they needed to know about each other. They both smiled as they stood up.

"'Til tomorrow then?" he said.

"Yes, 'til then," she replied faintly.

They got into their respective cars and went their separate ways, yet Raphael did not feel separated from Lula. There was some part of him that would always be connected to her, just as he knew she felt the same about him. He did not remember driving home and suddenly he truly understood what the phrase auto-pilot meant. He thought about tomorrow; he would see her then, and a warmth started in his belly and worked its way up. There would many, many tomorrows and at the right time there would be nights to go with the tomorrows. All in good time.

He slept well that night and the next morning he met her in the parking lot of the police college. All they needed was an exchange of warm looks before they walked into the building, changed and went down to Sergeant Travers' office.

Travers watched them as they entered his office. Both Campbell and Murphy seemed relaxed and somehow content ... interesting, he thought, not the content of a night spent in each other's arms like he had thought might happen, but the serenity of knowing everything was going to be alright. Just as that random thought had crossed his mind, Cynthia, the woman he had spent the night with, entered the office.

"Alright then, let's get this party started. After you two were dismissed yesterday we had a conference with sergeants Bilidou and Carstairs and it was agreed that you two would be a better fit in their class. I should warn you both that their class is an advanced class in many ways," Travers said and then looked to Michaels, who continued.

"Yes, that particular class is strictly ex-mounties and military types and believe me when I say that the particular scenario that we ran yesterday we would not even consider running in that class. Everybody in that class has been overseas, has seen fighting against insurgents and also worked in various intelligent units within either the RCMP or the military. We think you two will do well there. However, you will have to stay up with them both physically and in the other courses that sergeants Bilidou and Carstairs will be giving instructions in. With that thought in mind, we are going to keep you two together as partners as that class has already picked partners and we are not going to disrupt what has already been started. Any questions, thoughts or worries?" Sergeant Michaels asked them with a quick smile.

Both Raphael and Lula shook their heads and returned her smile.

"Alright, let's take you down and make some introductions.

CHAPTER SIX

In the days, weeks and months ahead Raphael had had the odd inner thought about how he had believed it would be better to level out the playing field by not mentioning all he had gone through, when in fact he need not have worried for his classmates in this class had all had similar experiences. His classmates were every bit as knowledgeable and conversant as he was in languages, especially the different dialects and cultures of the countries around the Hindu Kush.

Then there was Lula, his partner in every way but one. Instinctively, they both knew that there was a line they should not, could not step over while in class, for it would've changed the dynamic of their relationships within the class. For now they were accepted as partners and friends and in turn they both developed friends within the class.

This particular class became particularly close because most were older and had similar backgrounds including enduring and surviving wars with all the the attendant horror which went along with them. None spoke of what they had seen or done, but every once in awhile, perhaps while doing the obstacle course on a wet, cold, stormy day, someone would slip and fall into the mud and start swearing in Farsi or Urdu and suddenly three others would join in cursing and swearing, then laughing at the misery of it all and the fact that here they were doing it all again. And then someone would throw in a curse involving camels, fleas and their growth in the sergeant's armpits. This would immediately cause the rest of them to start laughing and trading insults in various languages. The sergeant, who had been so throughly insulted, would simply turn away as he smiled to himself, this was part of his job of making them a team.

There were several other classes in the police college at the time, but they stayed away from the class that Raphael and Lula were in. Everybody knew that class was different in many ways. Initially, there had been games of soccer and murder ball between the classes; however, those had to be stopped because of the injuries sustained by the other classes. Not only was that class older but they played to win at any cost.

Usually, every Friday, the class went out for dinner and a few beers. Some brought their wives or respective mates, and it was a comfortable time where everybody relaxed. Stories were shared around the table about the daring, head-boned stunts that had been pulled off during class. And when they were prohibited from playing field sports with the other classes because of all the damage they had done, it had been recounted to wives and girlfriends, with great hilarity, over a particularly beer-sodden Friday night down at the Police Association Club.

Time, within that particular class, seemed to fly by. At the outset the subjects they studied were what he expected. Weeks with a traffic officer going over traffic scenarios, proper charging sections under the Criminal Code, High-way Traffic Act and Motor Vehicle Administration Act. Then there were the more commonly used sections of the Criminal Code like assault, theft under and or over, drugs and the various sections for those. Of course there were various scenarios for those as well, with some hilarious, although unintended, results because most who joined the job also had to develop one of their most important tools, and that was their voice, learning to project their voice to provide a implacable calmness that would hopefully make an agitated situation more relaxed.

Then gradually and in some cases, almost imperceptively, some of the subjects, seminars, tutorials and courses they took began to change, to differ from what the other classes were taking. For instance, Raphael was sure that none of the other classes had a course on how to make and disarm bombs or I.E.D.'s, given by one of his classmates. There were seminars on doing proper warrants for and running wire [wiretaps] and working informants.

There were times when he and Lula would look up at each with wondering curiosity. Raphael had overheard, while changing in the men's shower and changing room, recruits from other classes talking about what they were doing in class, and it was nowhere near what their class was doing. In fact, he had caught the end of one conversation between recruits about informants and how their sergeant had said informants were a subject learned on the street and most didn't get or start working their first informants 'til they had been on the street at least five years. All the bits of information and the things that Raphael had seen and heard didn't add up or fit together in what he considered would be even an advanced class of police training ... unless ... unless there was something more going on. For now, best to keep his mouth shut and his eyes and ears open, and he advised Lula to do the same. She had simply nodded—best not to even discuss it at all.

Whatever the course, it was not that they didn't or couldn't keep up; on the contrary, in some things they were ahead of others in the class, and although Lula coud speak several European lanuages, she only had a rough idea about the languages of the Middle East, so Raphael had been teaching her some of the basics and how to swear in Farsi and Urdu.

They both still laughed about the time another member of the class thought to take her on in a hand-to-hand combat exercise. That particular person, Jacob by name, had seemed to resent having a woman in the class, and there had been numerous grumblings from his corner of the room since the class had started. They had all been in the gym and Lula had looked at Raphael with a big shit-eating grin on her face. Raphael had simply shrugged, as a side of his mouth had lifted in a slight sneer, as he thought there always seemed to be one misogynist in any group. Well, maybe it was time to put the asshole in his place. Their gym time in class had been mainly specific takedowns with the whole class, nothing too aggressive as most, if not all of the class, were trained in various, specialized techniques that could be extremely brutal. The two sergeants were standing to the side, watching to see what would happen. This class, due to its personnel make-up, had been fairly calm except for the one, so maybe it was time to settle this one down. They sensed that both Raphael and Lula could handle themselves, and normally they would not have allowed this, but maybe it was time. They both nodded.

"Come on, little girl, time for you to be put in your place. Then maybe time for your little boyfriend to go, eh? Jacob muttered as he crouched and sidestepped around her.

"Typical, all mouth and dance with no balls," Lula said with a slight smirk.

Jacob growled, reddened and rushed in. Lula ducked and swept sideways, one leg extended in a move designed to knock Jacob's legs out from under him. At the last moment, Jacob managed to dodge the leg sweep and swung his arm in a feint to cause her move to his left. Lula instead moved to his right, causing Jacob to swing his right fist too fast, and all he hit was a bit of her shoulder as she swirled by. She stood up for a brief moment, and he thought he saw an opening and started to step in as she took a running step and then scissor-kicked up with one foot, smashing into his face while the other landed at the side of his throat. Jacob went down as blood gushed from his nose, and Lula stood over him, one foot poised over his neck, ready to drive the toe of her foot into his throat for the fatal crushing blow. She stood over him with a small, ominous smile on her face.

"Just so you understand, worm, it would not bother me to finish you, but alas there are too many around. You name the time and place!" she whispered as he groaned and held his bleeding, broken nose.

"Enough! Step back, Lula," Sergeant Bilidou said as he moved foreward to check Jacob's nose and help him to his feet.

"Go down to the medical office and have that checked," he added, and they all watched Jacob go, his head back slightly to stop the bleeding.

"That has been coming for a long time. Is there anybody else in this group who has problems with someone else? Now is the time to speak out. There is a reason that we have not done the physical takedowns that other classes practise so constantly, and that is because we know all of you have had all sorts of physical training from Savante," Sergeant Carstairs said with a nod at Lula, "To a mixture of many fighting styles."

"Lula could have very easily killed Jacob, and then we would have had to find a way to dispose of the body."

There was feeble laughter amongst the group and they all went back to what they were doing, but each had understood the unspoken message completely—they were a team. There was a new closeness within the group and even when Jacob returned, he apologized to Lula. She accepted with a smile and life went on, class went on.

Like the other classes they spent two weeks out at the TAC firing range, but where the others learned the rudiments of using handguns and sawed-off shotguns, two classes at a time, they went out alone. Their team were run through courses on semi and full automatic handguns, AK-15's, AK-47's and other types of assult weapons, as well as the various types of silencers and a number of different plastiques and C-4 explosives. Another fragment of the puzzle, bit by bit, was coming together, but it was all engrossing. There was a certain unique, extraordinary feeling about this class. It reminded Raphael of something, somewhere. At first he couldn't think of it, a faint memory just beyond reach, and then it hit him like the bomb that they had just exploded on the military grounds! Of course, the Falash tribe ... Shandi ... the warriors ... the Falash school! It was, in a way, training to be a warrior! At that thought his heart began pounding and his blood surging and immediately he forced himself to think of the inner stillness ... the quiet mind. Find the core of stillness, let it radiate out, picture Tirich Mir, its snow bound peak. And he touched the calmness, felt the inner stillness. And within the stillness he fit the final piece into place.

CHAPTER SEVEN

Time, fluid, flowing and yet seemingly, at intervals, fickle like holding a piece of ice that for a few moments was frozen to a stop. But all too soon it changed back into water and flowed on, carrying him with it. Smooth and deep the current when he was with Lula, only to speed up when they were in the class. Now they were all in the midst of the rapids that marked the coming to the end of this part of life where learning, listening and gaining knowledge were everything.

The last week before graduation had been been almost as tension filled as the first week. Written tests on all the arcane subjects that a police officer must know had been completed. Now came the interviews with and without partners. Raphael and Lula had discussed these so-called interviews—conferences in privacy—away from class. They both felt a certain amount of trepidation about them as they knew other classes didn't do interviews; mind you, this class had been unlike any of the other classes. They had talked it over and over and thought about what might be asked, like a child picking at a scab to see what lay beneath, 'til finally they could talk no more about it. As Raphael had said, it was like beating a dead horse. They had looked at each other at that point and burst out laughing.

"How is it we both think so much alike?" Lula had asked after they had both simmered down to a chuckle.

"I don't know. I do know I wouldn't be the same without you. It would be like a winter turning into summer without the fresh green of spring. They say that somewhere on earth everybody has the perfect partner, a match in every way. It's a karma thing. I have faith in the saying because I have felt it," Raphael said as they matched looks, liquid grey to moss green.

"It is what it is," she said softly.

"Yes."

The last week had been slow torture to them as they watched other members of the class get called in to the offices of their sergeants. Some had returned after what seemed like hours, their faces grey and beaded with sweat. Jacob had been one of those who looked like he had been through a wringer-washer of grey water, and he had shot an angry look their way when he returned, while others had been gone for a short time and returned with smiles on their faces.

Finally, they were called in. They looked at each other as smiles flickered across their faces, and Lula shrugged slightly as they walked out of the class.

They walked down the hallway, and Raphael's hand fleetingly touched hers just as they stepped in front of their sergeant's office. He knocked on the door and a brusque voice from inside invited them in. *Said the spider to the fly*, Lula thought, and she felt the slightest snort like someone choking off a gasp of laughter.

Raphael opened the door and ushered her in first and she sensed he did that, not only to be polite, but to pull himself together.

Both sergeants Bilidou and Carstairs were sitting behind a large desk. There was a window behind them with the sun shining in, so they could not see the sergeants' faces.

"Sit down, you two," Bilidou directed.

After they had complied and settled into the old-fashioned wooden chairs, there were a few moments of silence as both sergents appeared to be flipping through their files again.

Christ, they must have those files memorized by now, Raphael thought with annoyance, although he knew it was a ploy. *Just like them sitting with their backs to the window so we can't see their facial expressions. All part of the game played to throw us off, make us nervous so we answer them without thinking clearly about what we should be saying. Now there will be something else that will be said that is so outrageous it will bring on shock and anger and will really disrupt our thinking.*

Sergeant Carstairs gave a polite cough.

"There has been an allegation ... so just how long have you two been sleeping together? Has it been since the beginning of the class as alleged?"

CHAPTER EIGHT

Even though Raphael had known that they would try to throw them off with some kind of outrageous, despicable statement, the tone of it caught him off guard.

Raphael felt like he had been punched in the guts and then kicked in the head! *What the fuck!* he thought as searing, bitter anger raged in his stomach like a fireball and started to shoot up towards his mouth. That mendacious statement said with such disrespectful, scathing sarcasm, that seemed to disavow all the important hard work that had been done in class, was very nearly his undoing. But at the very last moment he managed to grasp onto the inner stillness. At first his grip was feeble, and then he forced himself to stop and think, push back the anger, forcing it back down ... down. And calmness filled the gap. It was only a nano moment in time, but it was enough. He felt Lula sitting beside him, waiting quietly. He started thinking clearly again, and it showed when he spoke.

"I don't know, nor do I particularly care what anyone has supposed, thought or assumed. I do know that if you had even one scintilla of a notion that Lula and I were sleeping together, we would both have been dismissed from this class. We are the best of friends and partners, and I have been teaching her some Middle Eastern languages when not here. That is it. We would never consider throwing out our careers for the simple act of sex. That physical act under the right circumstances may happen at sometime in the future but certainly not now. We have too much respect for each other, the team, and the job," Raphael replied quietly as he looked at the two silhouettes. He sensed them turning their attention to Lula.

Lula sat quietly looking at them briefly before she added, "In my own way, at this time, I do love Raphael like I love my brothers, and as with them, I stand with him; he is my partner. Whoever would try to do him harm would have to go through me—kill me—in order to harm him. And I know he would do the same for me. I feel sorry for whoever made this allegation, if in fact he or they actually said what you have claimed. But I also know that this class is different than the others, just like these interviews aren't done in the other classes. You want to see if we will stand together, because it is crucial in a team. A team or squad is stronger when working together. They are more valuable in certain instances than the individual, stronger than just the one. Sex is not a consideration within a good crew, supporting each other is. Sex is just a physical act, and yet it can pull a crew apart with jealousy. There is a saying, an adage, 'Jealousy is all the fun you think they had.' I think Erica Jong said that and it's so true. Jealousy has ruined many a good friendship. There must be virtue within the confines of a good team. It is the skills within the squad, the synergy, the collaboration and how they blend together that is paramount."

There was silence in the room once Lula was finished.

Jim Bilidou stood up, turned and looked out the window and appeared to be in deep thought. Then he nodded to himself and without turning he began to speak. "I threw that allegation out there to see how the two of you would react. I already knew it was not true. We wanted to see how you would react and you passed that test. You should also know, if you don't know already, that we did have lengthy interviews with those who know you best in order to get a complete profile of the both of you before we allowed you into this class. We learned that your experiences in life were every bit as stressful and traumatic as those already in class although experienced at a younger age. What you had learned as a youth you seemed to have retained into adulthood. Now do you have any questions for us?"

Raphael was the first to respond. "First off, I think this has all been a test, all these months, both for Lula and me, but also for the rest of the team."

Bilidou's and Carstairs' faces remained impassive as Carstairs spoke in an expressionless voice, "Go on."

"Alright, I suspect that since we came into this particular class two days after it started that the rest of the class had already been briefed about what the class's main goal was. Then we upset the typical first day of a very normal police class. When sergeants Michaels and Travers spoke to you, both of you thought what an excellent test it would be for your class and Lula and me. The rest of the class would say nothing or indicate in any other way what the 'advanced class' really was. That was the test for them, while Lula and I, our test was to see if we could figure it out and if we would say anything to the other class members. Even Lula's fight with Jacob was a set-up and another test."

Bilido and Carstairs said nothing although a subtle smile barely grazed Bilido's face. He watched them intently as he stood to the side of the window where Raphael could see his face.

"I've had time to watch, evaluate and consider all the specialized training we have had in class. Given what I learned and heard when I was with my parents, moving from posting to posting through countless embassies, mostly in the Middle East, during their years as diplomats, both in times of peace or teetering on the verge of war or caught in the middle of a conflict, even though I was young, I grew to know just how dangerous the area was by the number of soldiers guarding the consulate. Almost by osmosis I learned by the very way my parents and the soldiers acted, just how dangerous or safe the mission was, like developing a sensitivity to certain aspects of life. That sensitivity, or awareness, once learned has never left me.

I think that this class was put together partly because, although our country is respected, even loved by some, we bend over backwards in an attempt to be fair to everybody. When you look at what happened in Rwanda and Birindi, sometimes I think our policies have had the headings of "Shoulda, Coulda, Woulda," but by then it is too late for those poor people who were consumed by a genocide. Think on our poor immigration laws and lack of enough immigration officers to even enforce those laws. Think on certain wealthy families from Saudi Arabia and Yemen who were known to be sympathizers and adherents of al Qaeda and the Taliban who, when banished from their own countries, were allowed to enter Canada and reside here while they were still sending money and their children back to the Middle East to aid these terrorist. Canada was warned about these individuals and their families and chose to welcome them in anyway. As a result of the aforesaid laws, Canada has allowed terrorists from the Middle East, Pakistan and Africa to enter this and other port cities, like rats or cockroaches strolling through the holes in the sieve, and then spreading out into the rest of Canada and from there into the United States. It is a running, very unfunny, joke especially in the U.S. who has picked off several high-level terrorists whose first point of entry onto North American soil was through Canada, and we all know about 911 and how those particular terrorists entered through Canada. I think our intelligence agency has stumbled and fumbled right from the get-go. Look at what happened with the whole Air India debacle.

But I digress, I think that certain high-placed officers amongst the military, mounties and city police have seen what has been going on and decided to put a crew or teams together that have particular skills under the guise of being local gendarmes. What could be more innocuous than just another bunch of rookies going through police college? When in fact you have some highly trained officers who already speak the languages of terrorism, and have learned even more intricate skills such as the making then dismantling of IED's [Improvised Explosive Device]. And here's the kicker—those particular officers have their own hierarchy that has nothing to do with the Canadian Intelligence Agency. Initially they work as normal police officers as they develop informants, learn about terrorist cells within the city, possibly work with trusted, tested, tried and true immigration officers, run wire with the idea that once the bad-guy terrorists are identified, round-ups are done. Using certain laws that we actually have on the books, they are shipped back to their country of origin after, of course, they are printed, photographed, etc., and we start plugging up the holes. How am I doing so far?

CHAPTER NINE

"Very good, you have gotten most of it right. In fact, some of what you have said is alarmingly right, details and all. I find that concerning and disconcerting. I have to wonder who you have been speaking to? If someone is talking to you, they are probably talking to others and that could jeopardize the whole operation!" Bilidou responded in a tight, tense voice.

Raphael's face flushed red in ire at what had just been said to him, and he partially rose from his chair then thought better of it and sat back down before he spoke with hard, brutal detachment. "First, let me make it perfectly clear that I have not talked to anyone, not even to Lula about what I've garnered as we went through class. Number two, you might want to think on how you have presented yourselves since this class started. From the very first you sergeants have quantified and stated that this class was an advanced class that was only accepting ex-mounties and retired military police. That statement, in and of itself, is enough to get the least curious of people interested. And think on this: By their very nature, a good police officer is always curious, plus there is the ego thing. In other words, they wonder why they aren't in the advanced class. Secondly, you said that you interviewed those who knew us best, meaning, I'm assuming, our parents. My parents are diplomats who worked extensively in the Middle East when I was a child and travelling with them. I learned several different languages and in fact lived with a tribe in the Hindu Kush for a year. Also Lula grew up in a military family that travelled extensively throughout Europe. Finally, while I was still in university taking some criminal justice courses, I was lucky enough to meet some immigration officers who were also taking the same courses. We spent many a happy hour drinking beer after a day of schooling, dicussing ... guess what ... yes, immigration laws, the Taliban and other terrorists, what they, the immigration officers, could but mostly couldn't do to get rid of terrorists, gang-bangers, murderers and their ilk who had entered our country under the guise of immigrants and refugees mixing amongst the legitimate ones who were fleeing war and famine.

Of course Canada had opened wide her arms to succour all those who had suffered beneath the terrible cloud of starvation and persecution of governments, warlords and dictators that had considered their own citizens mere cannon fodder and test cases for their latest experiments with lethal gases. In recent years most of these poor people have been from the Middle East, Syria, Afghanistan, Pakistan, Iran and some out of Africa—the Sudan, Nigeria. Of course a considerable number of those who ended up on Canada's doorstep had fled with, in some cases, barely the clothes on their back, never mind any paperwork such as passports or other papers stating who exactly they were. Amongst the desperate were those whose only God was terror and jihad against the infidel and the nonbeliever. They had money and contacts here and soon slipped through the cracks in the immigration and refugee process and vanished.

After 911, our dialogues over beers became more and more serious especially when it was learned that those who flew the planes into the buildings in the U.S. had entered through Canada and then crossed the border into the States. I also know from listening to my parents, over the years, talk about our intelligence agency and the problems within it. Believe me it hasn't been too hard to put two and two together based on what I have seen and heard in class and what I have heard and experienced out in the world, so to speak. Mind you, most of it has been sheer happenstance or serendipity on my part—and putting it together." Raphael finished talking, leaned back in his chair and waited, his face calm.

Silence engulfed the room.

CHAPTER TEN

Bilidou and Carstairs glanced at each other and Trey Carstairs began to tap his pen on the desk in agitation, breaking apart the quiet with the annoying beat.

Bilidou turned and gave Raphael a stoney look before asking in a low, hard voice, "And just who have you been dicussing your theory with?" Officer Murphy perhaps?"

"Officer Murphy can answer for herself. As for me, I have simply watched and listened then put my theory, as you put it, together myself without talking to anybody else," Raphael said in a voice equally tense as he stuggled to keep the resentment out of his voice.

"Officer Murphy, would you care to enlighten us as to your thoughts and who you have been talking to? Carstairs asked as he continued to tap his pen on the desk.

Lula nodded her head before looking directly at the pen that Carstairs was tapping. She said nothing, just kept looking at the continually moving pen.

"Oh, for God's sake, Trey, put that fucking pen down!" Bilidou said in a exasperated voice.

The tapping stuttered unevenly, then stopped. "Uh, sorry. Could you answer my question now, Officer Murphy?"

Lula smiled politely as she thought, *Now the power has shifted in the room*, and she sensed Raphael's acknowledgement.

"Raphael has made a few observations when we have been alone. Having said that, I, too, have seen certain things within the class that concerned me, given the fact I grew up on military bases all over the world. I have drawn my own conclusions about what has been going on, and for the most part I agree with the sentiment behind it. However, my concern is for the hierarchy behind it. I have said nothing about what I've seen or thought, not even to Officer Campbell. Certainly I have felt 'the elephant' in the room and this whole test with the rest of the class and the two of us explains that feeling. Would it not have been simpler to explain it to all of us? The way you did it smacks of game playing at its worst. Having said that, what's done is done. There is just one more thing that has occurred to me, and at the risk of sounding over dramatic, this plan sounds a little like that T.V. show and movie Mission Impossible. You know the part where the voice on the tape says 'should you be captured or killed the director will disavow your actions.' This plan of yours is not like that ... is it?" Lula observed as she looked between the two sergeants, her eyes slightly narrowed in suspicion.

For the first time since the interview began, a grin broke out on Jim Bilidou's face and a slight chuckle mixed in with his words as he returned, "Lula, have you forgotten we are Canadian and Canadians just don't do things like those south of the border. As you pointed out before, we do have a hierarchy. What you don't know is it goes right up to the Minister of Defence. But we are police officers first and foremost. We will be following our laws to the letter. Even better though, we will be following the spirit with which they were written as will the immigration officers who will be working with us. That means those who can be deported will be deported immediately instead of being dragged before a judge only to be released back into the city and vanish again. Those who have been financing terrorists will have their assets frozen immediately. We will be using the hate laws which have been in the Canadian Criminal Code for some time but rarely used before, and we are not going anywhere near our own Intelligence Agency for reason you both already know. We are going to be up close and personal with these bad guys, working the very best undercover, if you think on it, as uniformed police officers. Who blends in better than the local police officer doing his or her normal routine on the streets of our fair city?

As Bilidou finished speaking he could see Raphael's and Lula's faces suddenly start to light up with smiles as they began to understand the outrageous, brillant plan.

Carstairs saw the understanding in both their faces and picked up where Bilidou left off.

"I ... we can see your point, to a degree. We did create the elephant as you so eloquently put it. Having said that though, I think, in one way, our thought was it was a way of forcing all of you to think, or be cognizant of what was going on before blurting something out that would endanger the plan."

There was a brief moment of quiet as if all within the room needed time to digest all that had been said.

"So what now?" Raphael asked, cracking open the quiet that had fallen upon the occupants of the room.

"You two have passed all the tests. In fact, you certainly have exceeded all our expectations. It's now your turn to decide what you want to do. Become, as you put it, innocuous gendarmes, or stay with the team and be prepared for a wild ride? Of course, at first you will be rookies on the street with an officer-coach just like everybody else. The officer-coach will have no idea what other talents you have. First you continue to learn how to be a police officer and then your real job begins. After the officer-coach phase is completed, you will be placed in certain areas of the city that have been identified as having the highest concentration of immigrants from terrorist countries. Most, of course, are simple immigrants and refugees who have fled from war. However, we have identified certain individuals who are connected to the Taliban and al Qaeda, and now a new group known as Isis is rearing its ugly head.

That is when your real job within the job begins.

PART TWO

Within those ancient walls
A Darkness of Souls looms tall.
The blackness of the Fanatic, always right,
Ready to pour forth and rip apart
those in the Light.
Jihad is might! Jihad is right!
Upon the sand Unbeliever's blood lies bright.

— "The Secrets of the Night," RW Wells

CHAPTER ELEVEN

The graduation ceremonies went well. Everybody's parents, wives, children or significant others attended with the usual flashes of cameras, the police chief shaking the hands of those who had graduated as he handed them their badges, with a stiff smile. The graduation party after the ceremonies was fun and, although there was an open bar, the members of the graduating class drank very little, but a few of their family members were not so hesitant.

Raphael felt a restless prickling of his skin as the day moved into the night of the party. All he wanted to do was get started, get through all the nonsense of graduation and get down to being a police officer. He sensed the others felt the same. Even though they all smiled for photos, he could almost see and certainly feel the tension, the stress in their voices and stances as they talked with all the family entourage each had brought with them.

There was a live band and all took the prescribed turn about the floor with mothers, wives and girlfriends. Raphael had finally managed to get a dance with his mother, and as he had swirled her about the room he thought how beautiful she was, and that came as a surprise to him. He had always thought of her as his mother who could be and was tough, strong and warm, caring and understanding. Depending on how he had needed her, she was there. She was his mother. Now amongst all these people he saw how others saw her, the long slender neck that set off beautiful blue-black hair that curled with a life of its own no matter how she pinned it down, the lovely face with the most astonishing, glowing, mercury-grey eyes, the creamy skin and the smiling lips, the slender, supple body that bent and swayed to the music, and he understood in part why his father loved her so.

The music ended. Somehow they had ended up by the patio doors to the balcony. His mother beckoned to him as she said, "Let's go out here for a moment while I catch my breath, and I also have something I want to discuss with you."

Raphael smiled down at her before he ushered her out onto the large balcony of the community centre.

Martha Wellworth-Campbell sat down on a woven, rattan armchair and for a moment gazed up at her son. Yes, he was her son although he had gone on to be so much more than her child. He was a man and she could see how his choices had changed him, hardened him. Yet the very best of him was still there and perhaps sharpened by what he had learned.

Raphael gazed down at her and suddenly gave her the old grin, the same grin that her husband always gave her just before he had taken some risk, like the time they had been about to battle their way out of Kabul. At some point during the day she had heard the phrase 'adrenalin junkie' during a conversation with the parents of one of Raphael's classmates whose son had fought overseas and had always seemed to be in the thick of the action. She had been stunned at how that phrase could describe her husband and her son. She returned his grin with a small smile before she turned for a moment to gaze at the glorious sunset of brilliant yellow-orange that tinted the underside of the clouds with a reddish purple tinge and painted the distant mountains a dark lilac. *Should I tell him now, or leave it lie for another time?* she thought to herself as she sighed.

"What's wrong mother? You seem pensive. You and Father have seemed unusually quiet today," Raphael asked as he watched her silhouette and heard the whisper of a sigh.

Martha Wellworth-Campbell, who had never dodged or avoided an uncomfortable situation in her life, even if it was painful, gave a mental shrug and turned completely so she was facing him and gestured for him to sit down on a chair facing the one she was sitting in.

Once he was settled he looked directly at her. She could see concern had taken hold of his handsome face, erasing the merry grin that had been there moments ago.

"It is nothing so serious, my son. We are so proud of you for what you have accomplished here. You are settled with your work and your friends, and of course there is Lula and, well, there are your grandparents to keep an eye on. They are not so young now, you know." She sputtered to a stop for a moment.

"A-a-a-a-nd what, Mother? What is going on?!" Suddenly he straightened, and his face took on the rigidity of a certain realization. "Oohhh no, you and Father have taken another diplomatic posting, haven't you?" Raphael demanded in a low voice, and as he looked at her face comprehension struck him almost as if he had been slapped. "Oh my God, you're going back to Afghanistan!"

Martha had been watching his face and even in the dwindling sunset she could see how his face had blanched and grim lines had sharpened his features 'til it was as if she was looking at a death mask of her son's face.

There was an almost roaring silence that surrounded them, blocking out the gentle murmurs of the party going on inside.

The unbearable quiet spoke volumes about his shock and forced her to speak in a voice barely above a whisper. "Raphael, it is our final posting and we will not be there for so very long. Afghanistan is at peace for now and we go simply to help supervise their first democratic vote and ...

and there is word that the Falash Tribe is having some minor problems. So we will hopefully help them resolve the situation, and then we will be back home. It will not be so very long although I must admit it will not be the same without you," she said with a tentative smile.

Raphael had watched her, and as she spoke his eyes slightly narrowed and said nothing. Martha felt a flush climbing up from her neck to spread across her cheeks and exasperation began to form like a small dark cloud in her mind. And then the storm broke, "Oh, for God's sake, Raphael, quit looking at me like I was some kind of mouse you have stalked. It should come as no surprise to you that we got another posting—we are diplomats, and this is what we do. As to where it is, we were asked because we know the land so well. We held off 'til you were finished and graduated from the police college, to make sure you were settled. You must go your own way, Raphael, as we must go ours, but with love, always with love." Her words were met by a stiff silence.

She realized there would be no more words spoken this night by her son. He would have to come to the acceptance of their decision in his own time. With understanding, she stood up and reached out to touch his shoulder as he stared out at the fading sunset. But at the last moment she dropped her hand and without further ado swept back into the party, her head held high, her light green dress swirling about her, leaving him to his thoughts.

CHAPTER TWELVE

He had stood up as he sensed his mother leave the balcony and leaned against the balustrade, staring out at the last of the sunset as the cloak of night began to tighten its folds about the ocean and the mountains, the last of pinkish light fading behind the dark purple peaks.

Damn it, he hated it when his mother was right. There was a part of him that hungered to go with them, but the other part of him wanted to stay here, to fight the good fight that was going on here. A bitter little chuckle escaped him as he thought of the arrogance, the overweening conceit he had shown his mother. She had been right—they had to go on with their lives just as he was about to start his own adventure. Odd, he thought, in a way they were doing the same type of work.

"A quarter for your thoughts," a throaty voice behind him asked.

A slow smile touched his lips as normal colour started to return to his face. "I thought it was a penny for one's thoughts," he returned without turning. He knew the owner of that particular voice. She always seemed to know when he was troubled.

She gave him her slow, molasses-sweetened laugh before replying, "What with inflation and the look on your mother's face as she came in from the balcony, I thought you might need someone to talk to." Lula walked up and leaned against the banister next to him.

He could smell the rich, earthy perfume she was wearing and the slight pressure of her shoulder against his. He felt like he could stand like this with her forever, the comfort of her presence, the understanding, and beneath all the sexual tension building slowly, slowly until there would come a time finally for the denouement and the start of a new aspect of their relationship.

Finally, reluctantly, Lula broke the quiet. "I take it your mother told you about the new diplomatic posting?"

"What the ... how the hell did you know? Why didn't you tell me?" Raphael asked abruptly as he turned towards her, and she felt what had been so warm a moment before turn chill.

"Raphael, think about it, your parents are diplomats ... your father an ambassador. When you introduced me to them, and they are lovely people, I sensed something, almost like they were waiting on something. Plus your mother has dropped a few tiny hints perhaps without realizing it. I guessed that they were waiting for you to graduate, to have your own life so they could go back to the work they seemed to love. I didn't tell you because it was not my business, and I wasn't completely sure. You should have sensed it as well—at least I thought you would."

"You have no idea how much I hate it when my mother and now you are right and I'm way off base," Raphael muttered in a low voice as his mouth lifted in a sardonic, self-mocking smile.

Lula caught the tone of his voice and could see the smile and gave a slight shrug as she added in a whispery voice, "It's always a bit shocking when we realize our parents have their own lives they must live after we have left the nest while we carry on with our own destiny that is sometimes mutually exclusive. Although in this case it's not so much given where they are going and what you are going to be doing."

Raphael sighed in agreement as he gazed out at the unfolding night. They both stood in a comfortable silence for a time, listening as the night insects fluttered about the one lamp on the balcony. They were so still they heard the leathery whoosh of the bat wings as the little creatures swooped and twisted above them in search of the insects that would be their dinner.

Finally, Raphael broke the silence. "Can you feel it, Lula? Can you feel the excitement, the tension? Everybody has been trying to hold it in, in front of their relatives, girl-friends and whomever else they invited. Everybody wants this day, this night to be over so they can begin. I can feel it, almost smell it, taste it ... the beginning of the chase, the investigation. It almost makes the hairs on my arms stand up and my stomach churn in exhilaration. I've noticed that none in our class has had more than one drink all night. They don't need it. They just want to get out and do the job. Both the job as a police officer and the other job as a type of agent provocateur, only in the sense we will be stirring up and outing the terrorists and shining the light on them.

Raphael felt a slight shiver in Lula just as he had felt the ripple of anticipation ride up his own spine, like thorough-breds born, bred and trained to race. And the initial race was before them—their time had come.

CHAPTER THIRTEEN

The next few days after the graduation and graduation party turned out to be crazy busy. Raphael's parents had asked him to move back into "Campbell's Keep" while they were away on diplomatic duties, and Raphael had reluctantly agreed. He was still slightly mortified by his childish behavior towards his mother at the dance and was eager to make it up to her, and although moving back into the Keep was not exactly what he had planned, it would have to do. It was a rush of a move because he was due to start out on the street in two days and he had yet to meet his first officer-coach.

He saw his parents off on the day before he started his own new job. Just before they were to leave the Keep for the airport, his father had called him into the study and sat down across from him at the huge, aged, antique desk. His father sat and leaned against the desk, considering him, his elbows resting on the desk while his forearms were raised and his fingers were steepled against his chin. Raphael met his gaze and suddenly had a feeling, a sense of impending ... what? Doom? No, not that exactly that ... something inimical, or pernicious, or malevolent seemed to hover over his father ... this posting, something felt wrong or was going to go wrong.

Raphael suddenly, urgently leaned forward and spoke in a low, resolute voice. "Father, don't go! This posting, this timing is off. Something is going to happen and this time you and Mom will not be so lucky to escape! Don't do it, Dad!"

Raphael's stormy grey eyes met his father's sky-blue ones, their gazes locked for what seemed like an eon but only lasted a few moments in time, and comprehension hit Raphael like a hard punch to the solar plexis that took his breath away. All of his father's reckless, devil-may-care and cavalier attitude was gone, and he saw his father for what he really was, a highly trained intelligence agent who had been sent into areas of the world where trouble was brewing or had already started. Travelling in the guise of a diplomat and an ambassador, he could look into the truly dark corners of the world and find out what was really happening. And perhaps there were times where he could drop a word here or there or his very presence could expose those doing the harm, or he could calm the situation that was about to explode into war or a jihad. The very best part of an agent provocateur—not to stir up but to calm down, to warn, to advise.

Raphael felt a sudden pride, although he had always felt pride when it came to his mother and his father. They were the largest part of his life until now. This was the understanding of one man for another. Then he had another thought.

"But surely you can't take mother with you this time!" he stuttered.

"Have you ever tried to stop your mother from doing anything? I don't know how ... woman's intuition, a woman's sense of when her mate is up to something. She seems to sense when I'm planning something, and you've got to know Raphael, she is an agent and every bit as involved as I am," Stuart Campbell said with a laugh as Raphael joined in with a broken chuckle.

Suddenly, Raphael's eyes opened wide as a thought came to him. "It was you!"

Stuart Campbell greeted that sudden statement with a slow and surreptitious smile before adding, "I was wondering when you would get it. But ultimately, finally, you figured it out and you gave your instructors a hard time, as you should … that's my boy! Your mother and I will be fine. However, should something untoward happen, as you seem to think, look to the Kalash." With that, Stuart Campbell looked at his watch and then nodded at his son.

"Time for us to go."

They both stood and Stuart came around the desk and looked at his son, his devil-may-care guise firmly back in place, and Raphael threw his arms around his father in a bear hug that his father returned with equal enthusiasm. They broke apart at last with each giving the other an embarrassed grin men give each other when they have just had an emotional and physical moment.

Raphael went to the airport departure gate with them and stood waving as they walked away. Finally, after they had disappeared from sight, he turned and began the walk towards the exit with the shadowy, pensive thought worrying him, like a dog worrying a bone … he would not see them together again.

CHAPTER FOURTEEN

Right from the first day on the street, Raphael knew this was where he belonged. His officer-coach was slightly crusty, very senior and Raphael could feel his devotion to working the street.

The police vehicle was loaded with all the accoutrements needed for a day on the streets of a large western Canadian city. All the ordnance required in a large city that had never really gotten away from its logging and cowboy origins were loaded into spaces alotted to them, including the sawed-off shotgun which was loaded and locked into the space between them. Raphael's officer-coach was a senior officer by the name of Wilmer Das-Groot, who, in appearance, lived up to his ancient Germanic name with his flaxen, almost ash-coloured hair. His eyes, when he looked in Raphael's direction, were the colour of the ice-blue of a glacier on the high mountains around the Eiger Peak. And he was tall, taller even than Raphael by a good inch, with broad shoulders that tapered down to a slim waist. He looked like he had been born in the uniform. At their intital meeting that first morning, he had barely grunted at Raphael when they were introduced and had said nothing since then.

Raphael had felt his stomach tighten with nervousness as he wondered how he was going to learn if his officer-coach refused or was incapable of speech. Raphael had, like any good rookie, researched his first officer-coach to see what he was getting into. By all accounts, Wilmer Das-Groot was an outstanding, stellar police officer who loved working patrol, didn't want to play the promotion game, just wanted to work the streets. There were plenty of stories about informants, fights with bad guys and even a nasty shooting from which Das-Groot emerged relatively unscathed with just a nasty scar on the side of his neck while the bad guy ended up in the morgue. Beyond that, those who knew him said he was an investigator who never gave up. If he got a bad guy in his sights, generally that particular bad guy was going to jail.

Raphael sat slumped in the passenger seat wondering what or how he was going to get his officer-coach talking. This was not how he had planned for this day to go; he had been so hyped when he found out who was going to be his officer-coach and now this. He felt like there was an icy wall between them, and it was slowly choking off his excitement.

They pulled into the drive-through of a Tim Horton's and Das-Groot ordered two double-doubles to go. When the clerk refused to take his money, Das-Groot dropped the money into the Plexiglas container for a children's charity. Das-Groot put the cardboard tray containing the coffees on a small shelf between them, and Raphael wondered to himself if Das-Groot was going to drink both double-doubles.

Raphael ended up staring glumly out the passenger side window and noted the change in scenery from high-rise buildings and businesses of the downtown area to forest-green parkland where he could smell the ocean. Das-Groot pulled into a small, shaded parking lot with no other cars around and parked in the shadiest spot where no one could see them from the road.

Without a word, Das-Groot handed Raphael a coffee and took a large drink from his own coffee cup before sighing with obvious pleasure. He then turned to Raphael and finally spoke.

"You must excuse my initial lack of words. I find this early in the morning, when working with a new partner, I need a coffee to help me gather my thoughts together, especially when my partner is a rookie coming from a class there has been much speculation about," Das-Groot said in a low, gruff, slightly acerbic voice.

Raphael straightened to accept the offered coffee, and his eyes narrowed as he heard what his officer-coach was saying, especially the last few words.

He matched Das-Groot's hard gaze before he responded. "I don't know what you mean exactly, and the only honest thing I can say in return is this is my first day out on the street and on the job. I've never been so excited, anxious, nervous and wanting to impress you, my first officer-coach. My first day as a police officer. Man, what a feeling, but I also feel like the village idiot because the dispatch sounds like a slightly garbled foreign language, and when I finished classes I actually thought I knew it all, and it has suddenly dawned on me that I barely know anything, and yet here I am out working as a police officer!" Raphael said with such exuberance and a big goofy grin that Das-Groot had to sit back and chuckle. Raphael joined him in the chuckle as he hoped his little speech had distracted Das-Groot enough so that he had, at least for the time being, forgotten about certain speculation.

As they drank their double-doubles, Das-Groot laid out what he expected of Raphael but also emphasized Raphael was his partner and would be treated as such. When a hot call came in, though, he expected Raphael to follow his directions exactly. Raphael nodded his agreement while in the background he could here dispatch calling various codes and car numbers. But her voice was a fast monotone that he could not yet interpret or translate into anything he could understand, and it sunk into a pleasant background noise as his officer-coach talked on about certain things he must be on guard for and watch out for. Of course Das-Groot mixed in war stories to underscore proper police procedure, and Raphael felt like he was learning more while drinking the double-double than he had in a month in classes.

Just as they were finishing their coffee, Das-Groot muttered an "Aw, shit," as he reached for the radio.

"Delta Two-Three, go ahead, dispatch," he said into the mic.

A calm, detached voice responded, "Can you respond to a 10-14, possible O.D. on Victor Street by 14th Avenue?"

"10-4."

"That address is flagged on your computer."

"10-4, I know it well."

"Thought you might. I will send backup when available."

"10-4," Das-Groot, whose voice had been flat and disinterested throughout the conversation, returned as he put his empty cup in the garbage, put the vehicle in gear and pulled out of the parking lot.

"Raphael, read what is on the screen of the computer out loud to me, and then I will tell you how we are going to handle this call."

"10-4, ur ... yes ... Ok, it's a drug house, uh, 2401 Victor Street, right on the corner. It looks like ... Holy shit! There was a shooting there a week ago ... one dead, one wounded. Looks like today someone, possibly a female, has called about an O.D., maybe crank ... maybe crack. Anyway, the guy is going nuts ... throwing things around and screaming about killing the glass spiders ... must be crack. That hallucination is usually hooked in with over-consumption of crack ... Fuck!!!" Raphael yelled the last expletive as they very nearly hit a fuckin' knuckle-head who didn't know how to drive.

"Ok, we will worry about what caused him to hallucinate later. It sounds like a black guy I know by the name of 'Itchy.' So we both know that pepper spray doesn't work well on those of the darker-skinned persuasion, and from the sound of it none of our tools are going to work that well except maybe our guns, and those are only a last resort so ... what are we going to do ... quick, we are getting close?" Das-Groot asked as he took a corner on two wheels.

"Well, sounds like trying to wrestle him to the ground is not going to be easy ... a sweaty black guy high on crack, suicidal, maybe homicidal ... call in an ambulance and 'drop and drool' him, I'd say!!! Raphael said as he tried to hold on as they drove the Beltway at a high rate of speed. Cars all around them played bumper cars to get out of their way. A few froze at the siren sound and seemed almost incapable of any kind of movement while Das-Grout was driving like he was in the Daytona 500 and death only inches away. Raphael could almost feel the cold breath of death as the police-car-turned-race-car blistered the paint of yet another car that didn't get out of their way fast enough.

"Good call! Get on the radio and tell dispatch we need an ambulance to meet us at the location forthwith with Haldol on board!" Das-Groot yelled above the roaring engine and siren as he continued to drive like a maniac.

Raphael made a grab for the mic, and on his second try he managed to pull it loose from its moorings and key it, "Yeah, this is, uh, Delta ... uh, Twenty-Three. We need an abulance to meet us on scene ...!" Somehow he managed to keep his voice relatively steady (he thought).

"10-4, Delta Twenty-Three, ambulance already on the way," the calm voice of dispatch returned.

Raphael looked over at his partner and saw him grinning like he was chasing the devil and winning. Raphael suddenly felt the adrenalin surging through his veins, and although he didn't realize it, he too was grinning ... the need for speed and another adrenalin junkie had just been born into the wonderful world of policing.

With a screech of tires, they came to stop in front on the address and both jumped out of the vehicle. Raphael saw the ambulance already there and waiting for them. Once the paramedics saw the police officer, they climbed out of the ambulance and joined them at the bottom of the stairs leading up to the front door.

"Gawd, I hate these old concrete stairs," one of the paramedics muttered as he looked up to the broken front door.

They could all hear the screaming coming from inside the rickety crack house, and then something crashed against the front door. They looked at each other, and Das-Groot shrugged.

"Fuck, it's 'Itchy.' I recognize the voice. 'Itchy' doesn't have an inch of fat on him, he's well muscled and he loves his drugs, although on the plus side he and I know each other fairly well and at times we get along in a kinda police versus druggies way, so I'll try talking to him first, although he sounds pretty stoned.

"Nothing pretty about it. I know how 'Itchy' gets," the other paramedic said sardonically as he looked casually in Raphael's direction, then nodded and added, "See you have a rookie with ya, Wilmer."

Before Das-Groot could respond, another police vehicle pulled up and a police officer got out. They filled him in on what was going on.

"Ok, here's the plan, as in plan 'A.' I go in first and start talking to him, and you guys slowly ease in behind me. I may be able to talk him down ... maybe. If he starts to get antsy and aggressive, we do the scrum, that being we rush him and leap on him, knock him down and, as my partner has said so succinctly, 'drop and drool' him. I take it that one of you paramedics has a syringe loaded with Haldol to stick him with ... and please let's make sure the drugs go in the right arm, ok?" Das-Groot said in a acerbic voice with a slight smile that took some of the acid out of his voice.

That statement brought on a general smile and small chuckle as a paramedic had done that very thing not that long ago.

They started to climb up the stairs, Das-Groot first, Raphael next, with the other police officer behind him and the paramedics bringing up the rear. Raphael had taken a deep breath and tried to focus on the inner stillness, calling it to him, feeling the calm at its centre, and with that all his senses seemed to sharpen as he climbed the stairs.

It had fallen silent in the house, an ominous quiet, and Das-Groot drew out his night stick. Raphael followed suit. They reached the landing before the front door and spread out so the paramedics were on the upper stairs. Wilmer Das-Groot slowly pushed the broken door open with his night stick; still no sound except the scraping of the door along the rug inside the house.

"Itchy,' it's me, Wilmer," Das-Groot said in a quiet voice.

They all heard the groan from inside the house, and they all tensed.

"Can I come in, 'Itchy'? I have some good drugs that will help you kill the bad things."

Another groan that sounded like a jumbled "yes." Slowly Das-Groot pushed the door further open and stepped softly inside, with Raphael two steps behind. It was dark inside after the bright sunshine outside and it took a few moments for Raphael's eyes to adjust before he took another side step so he was out of the way but ready to fight. He could feel the other police officer take up a position a few steps behind him and to his side.

"Where are you, 'Itchy'?" Wilmer asked in the same friendly, quiet voice.

There was a roar. "HERE! HERE! You thought to trick me with the spiders but I am really the SPIDER KING!! There was movement on the floor as "Itchy" started to rise from a pile of debris on the floor.

"SCRUM! SCRUM!" Das-Groot yelled as he leaped at "Itchy," driving his nightstick into his chest and driving him back down. Raphael drove his nightstick across "Itchy's" groin area and landed on top of his legs so he couldn't kick while the other police officer landed on his lower legs.

"We've got him down! Spike him NOW!! Das-Groot hollered at the paramedics.

They rushed in and with much cursing and struggling from everyone, the paramedics managed to plunge the syringe into the right arm while the police held him down.

Finally ... finally, after what seemed like an eternity of lying in the dark across the body that had not seen water or soap in years, "Itchy" finally settled into a drug-induced unconciousness and went limp. The paramedics, who had rushed back to their ambulance and grabbed a stretcher, with the help of the three officers, loaded 'Itchy' onto the stretcher and moved him out of the house and into the ambulance in order to give him an extra dose of Haldol to make sure he stayed unconcious for his trip to the hospital.

Wilmer Das-Groot looked around at his partner and the other officer and asked, "Is everybody ok? Nobody bleeding or got struck by that idiot? 'Itchy' is a walking vessel of viruses including AIDS. Let's go out on the landing and check."

They all checked each other and, other than sweating and dirty, they all seemed ok.

"Alright, before we all make up our notes, we gotta check this place for whatever female made the call. Take a breather first. Raphael, call dispatch on your portable and let her know we are all ok."

"Yes, sir ... uh ... Wilmer," Raphael said with a grin.

"You both did great, and welcome to the delightful world of police work, Raphael," Das-Groot said with an all-encompassing smile.

After taking a few moments to get their breath back, the three police officers went back into the crack house with its smells of rotting humanity, desolate and acidic. There wasn't a piece of furniture in the place that wasn't broken. There were plastic baggies everywhere and syringes—spikes, as the druggies liked to call them—were everywhere. Some still had blood and other substances in them.

"Don't touch anything with your hands. If you have to look closer, gently kick it over," Wilmer advised.

Raphael was checking what looked to have been a bedroom with a stained mattress on the ground, and beside it a pile of dirty rags and clothes, when he saw what appeared to be a hand of a large doll poking out of the pile. He stepped in to take a closer look and realized it was not a doll's hand. There was the top of a bloody head with what looked like bits of long, blood-stained blonde hair. The rags—clothes—had large patches of blood on them, and it seemed to him that the flies had found it before he had and were looking for landing zones. He stepped back carefully, trying to backstep on the path he had taken in to get a closer look. When he was far enough away so the smell and look of what he had found wouldn't make him throw up, he sighed before he called out, "Uh, Wilmer ... Wilmer, could you come in here, please?"

"What's wrong, Raphael?

"Uh, you better come in here."

"Ya want us both in there?"

"Nope, just Wilmer. The less the better."

"Awe, shit!" Wilmer muttered as he walked towards the room Raphael was in.

Wilmer walked carefully in and only up to where Raphael was standing. He took one look at Raphael's grey-green face and knew. "Are you sure it's dead?"

"Oh yeah, I've seen enough bodies in my time. If you take two steps directly in front of me, you will stay on my path and you can see for yourself," Raphael whispered not wanting to wake the dead.

Wilmer Das-Groot followed his directions and took a good look. He now understood why Raphael knew she was dead. He could see how her throat had been sliced from ear to ear and it was such a deep slice that she was near decapitated and had bled out. He forgot how many pints of blood the human body held but he figured that all her blood was on the floor or had been sopped up by the piles of clothes and rags that surrounded and partially covered the rest of her body. And of course the corpse flies were gathering in order to wage a full-on assault on the recently dead.

"FUCK!" he said as he cautiously backstepped in the same path that he took in.

"Well, partner, you certainly are having the full gambit of police work and all on your first day on the street. Good catch. Ya done good!" Wilmer said with grim smile. Raphael valiantly tried to return it without much luck.

"You ok here? I gotta get things rolling?"

Raphael nodded.

Das-Groot called the other officer just to the door of the room and told him to catch up to the ambulance as he was going to have to do continuity on "Itchy" as he was now a homicide suspect. He then, on his cell phone, called dispatch and advised her that this was now a homicide scene and to get ahold of Delta One—the district sergeant, the duty inspector and, last but not least, homicide staff-Sergeant and tell them what they had here. Then another car, a two-man crew, needed to be sent to help clear the rest of this crack house properly. He could hear dispatch typing his words into the police city-wide computer system.

After he finished on his cell, he stood at the door of the homicide scene and was about to tell Raphael he might as well start his notes, but when he looked in, he saw that he had already started writing. *Good kid, has potential*, he thought as he stood just outside the room and started his own notes while he waited for another car crew to arrive so they could do a proper house clearing.

CHAPTER FIFTEEN

He began putting the key in the front door of the Keep. His hand had a slight shake and he had trouble fitting the key in the keyhole, his nerves still rippling from the backwash of hours-old adrenalin.

What a fuckin' day, he thought. He couldn't wait to tell his father about everything that had happened on his first day on the job. Just as he got the door open, it occurred to him that his father and mother weren't here—they were on a plane or train on their way to Afghanistan. He felt his stomach drop and that bit of his soul and his deepest thoughts that retained the sentiments of a small child felt a bitter disappointment for the briefest moment before the adult in him took over and all he felt was lonely ... needing to talk to somebody as he gazed around the dark interior of the Keep. He wanted ... no ... needed to share what had happened today with someone. Then the corners of his mouth turned up as he walked through the great hall to the phone. But just as he reached for it, the phone rang. He knew who it was even as he picked it up.

"I hear you had quite a day," the throaty voice on the other end of the line said.

"Yes, it was beyond anything ..." He didn't seem able or capable of saying anything more over the phone.

She sensed how overwhelmed he felt, how alone, and it suddenly occurred to her that his parents had left yesterday for the Middle East.

""I'll be there. Are you hungry? What can I bring?"

"Just yourself. My parents left me with a full pantry," he said.

He felt his spirits rise as he shrugged out of his jean jacket, hung it up and gazed around. He felt the slight chill of emptiness and turned on a multi-coloured Tiffiny lamp. He went to the huge fireplace with the thought of getting some firewood together to light a fire and found that someone had all ready set up the kindling and logs so all he had to do was light it. He mentally blessed his mother and father for doing that for him as he lit the kindling and watched the wood catch. Then he closed the firescreen and went to the kitchen to pull together some type of snack. They had thought of everything. The larder and pantry were full and within a few minutes he had a large plate of various cheeses, fruit, crackers and had discovered a chilled bottle of white wine in the wine cooler. He had just set everything out in front of the fireplace when the large sound of the doorbell alerted him to her arrival.

He tried not to run, tried to walk in a circumspect way, but he had so much to tell her ... couldn't wait to see her. He ended up actually running the last few steps, and then stopped and tried to pull himself together.

He swung the huge oak door open and there she stood, wrapped in a soft, pinkish woolen shawl, her auburn hair loose and tumbling around her face, a faint smile on those lips of hers. She walked past him, leaving the scent of her earthy perfume for him to follow as he swung the outside door shut.

"I'm glad you built a fire. It's getting chilly out there, and I think it's going to rain," she said inanely and then, for the thousandth time wondered why, at times, she chattered like a school girl when she was around him. If she were honest with herself, she thought, it was because of his almost animal grace, his smile, his eyes of liquid mercury that held a certain light when he looked at her, his humour

... his everything, and then there was the unspoken bond, the push-pull between them.

Those thoughts coursed through her mind, and she was glad of the warm dark, lit only by a small lamp to one side. The fire hid the flush on her cheeks as she settled into the massive, overstuffed couch that was covered in the softest of leather. She gazed at the feast that Raphael had laid out on an ancient, tiled, low table in front of the couch; before her eyes travelled to the fireplace to watch the flames flicker and dance.

"Wine for my lady?" Raphael asked as he watched her staring into the fire and knew his words had pulled her back from the hypnotic gyrations of the flames.

"Why, yes, kind sir, I will indeed," Lula said, playing along with his word game.

After pouring his own glass of wine, he settled onto the couch and they both helped themselves to the food that Raphael had laid out. After a time and as they were working on their second glasses of wine, Raphael leaned back, his head resting on the back of the couch, his eyes half closed as he watched the fire.

"Tell me," she said as she turned partially towards him, one shoulder leaning into the back of the couch as she watched his face.

The day and what had happened poured out of him. Everything from the mad vehicle ride to the call, the heat, the yelling, to finding the body ... every detail right down to the short briefing with the homicide detectives at the end of the day, and when the shift was over, how he had torn off his uniform and had two showers just to get the worst of the day off of him.

Lula sat facing him, her eyes closed, and listened and saw what he had seen ... she felt the rush of adrenalin, the shock of finding the body and finally the boredom seeping in as he had had to await the arrival of the homicide detectives before he and his partner could be released from the scene. Then there was quiet in the room except for the low crackling of the fire.

Lula took another sip of her wine as she considered everything that had happened to him that day. She felt a small stab of envy. She would have liked to have had such a wild first day, although on consideration she knew there would be many such days ahead for both of them. She looked over to ask him a question and saw that he was asleep, a slight, almost relieved smile on his face. She knew he had needed to tell someone about his first day and she was glad she was the one who had been there for him. She leaned towards him and studied the pure lines of his face in repose and then, before she could stop herself, she leaned further in and kissed him lightly on the lips. Now why had she done that? she thought. He groaned in his sleep and whispered a name ... her name. She smiled softly to herself as she felt the bond strengthen even more.

She got up slowly from the couch and briefly touched his cheek with her hand, then looked around. She didn't want to wake him. She saw the throw at the far end of the couch and managed to move his legs so he was stretched out on the couch. She got the throw and covered him with it. He rolled over on his side but did not wake. She cleaned up the food and put it away. She knew he had an early shift in the morning, as did she, so she would simply phone him to wake him.

Lula left him sleeping in front of the glowing embers.

CHAPTER SIXTEEN

The annoying sound of ringing kept intruding into the pleasant dream he had been having, and finally the dream faded away as he realized that the noise was the phone ... his phone ... as the last wisps of sleep drifted away. He opened his eyes and at first couldn't think where he was, and then memories of last night crept in and he attemped to get up to get the phone and found that his legs were bound up in something. He looked down to find he was tangled in a damn blanket. By the time he had got loose of it the phone had stopped ringing, but he had a fairly good idea who had been calling him. He walked to the phone and just as he reached it, it began to ring again.

"Alright, alright, I'm up already," he said into the phone in a light voice. He listened to the light laughter coming from the other end and had to grin.

"I knew you were working the same shift as me so I thought I would just phone you this morning instead of searching through the house for your alarm clock last night," she returned.

"You know, you could have just stayed. There are plenty of beds in this mausoleum," he said with a laugh.

"Such a tempting offer but the thought of wandering around that massive place like a lost ghost was just not that appealing ... maybe some day or night ..." Her voice had faded off to a husky whisper.

Raphael suddenly felt the need for a cool shower. "Thanks for coming over last night. I gotta go shower and get going. I guess there is a big debriefing about yesterday's events, so I better be early. I'll call you later," he said and hung up, although his thoughts of her stayed with him until the cold water from the shower hit his body and he was able pull his mind back to police work.

On the other end of the phone line, Lula held the phone to her cheek for a short time as she thought of last night ... it would have been so easy ... not yet, the time was not right, but there was a part of her that hungered ... Stop it ...! She shook her head in an attempt to fling out those thoughts as she too sought succour in a cold shower.

CHAPTER SEVENTEEN

Raphael made it into work early, but Wilmer Das-Groot had made it in even earlier, and when Raphael walked into the zone office, there was his officer-coach going over their notes from yesterday's events. He had wordlessly handed Raphael a double-double as he continued to read. Raphael took a sip and found the coffee still hot, so Das-Groot had not beat him into the office by much. Raphael took a seat by the desk where his partner was reading and sipped in silence as he waited for him to finish.

After five or maybe ten minutes had past, with Raphael trying not to look at his partner's face, Das-Groot grunted as he finished reading both his and Raphael's notes and took a long swig of his coffee, then sighed before he turned to Raphael.

"Not bad ... Not bad at all," Das-Groot said as a slow smile crept across his face.

Raphael suddenly realized this was the first time he had actually seen his officer-coach really smile. Oh, there had been the perfunctory smiles when the plans had worked out and the specialty units had arrived, but mostly his face had worn a look of concentration as he went around organizing all that was needed when a homicide was involved, almost like the police version of a funeral director.

"Just before the crowd shows up to dissect and debrief everything that went on, I wanted to let you know that, in my opinion, you did a very good job yesterday. In fact, you were a good partner, and I had to remind myself you were a rookie on his first day of officer-coach training.

Also your notes were detailed, succinct and you recorded times of arrival; all that was needed, you had in your notes. On top of everything else, you managed not to hurl when you discovered the homicide," Das-Groot said with a short bark of a laugh.

Raphael felt his face redden at the praise. He had sensed from their very first day that Das-Groot was thrifty when giving out compliments.

"Do you have any questions for me? I know yesterday got really busy and we didn't have too much time to talk, so ask me now," Das-Groot added.

"I'm just wondering what's going to happen to 'Itchy.' I know he's the prime suspect, but there were lots of indications that there were others using that crack house," Raphael asked.

"Well, for the time being, 'Itchy' or Ross Cameron Jackson—his real name—is up in unit 21, at the hospital, detained on a mental health warrant until it can be determined if he is capable of ever being able to give us any kind of comprehensive statement about what went on yesterday morning. As you know, he was flying high yesterday and as I recall, he had declared himself 'Spider King' as he arose from beneath the debris. His over consumption of drugs has turned his brain into mush, but who knows, maybe if he is completely dried out there may be something left of the original conscious thought, but I doubt it. You're right though. That particular house is only a way station in the travels of many crackheads, and some who hang around there are very capable of killing if someone even looks at them wrong, or just for the sick thrill of the kill. I think the detectives will be taking a long, hard look at it and who knows, they may actually come up with some answers, although I doubt it," Das-Groot responded with a shrug.

"Who will be taking a long look at it?" Detective Jeff Davies asked as he and his partner, George Phillips of the Homicide Unit, walked into the office.

"Oh, we were just talking about the crack house from yesterday," Das-Groot returned.

"Yes, lots of evidence from possible suspects and our prime suspect has nothing left above the brainpan. I'm thinking, once we finish our investigation, the police department along with the health department will be putting in a request to the city to have that building razed because it is a health risk," George Phillips said as he shook his head in disgust.

"They are going to be doing the autopsy on the victim this morning and we will be attending. The Ident [Identification unit] has still not found the weapon used to kill the victim, although they have found a plethora of evidence that could fit any of the many crimes that are in the investigation stage. Having said all that, we just wanted to say that you both did a great job at the scene and you made our job easier. We heard it was your first day out on the street, Constable Campbell? Good job, and you can look forward to your first 'Atta-boy,'" Jeff Davis said as both he and George Phillips shook hands with a flushed Raphael.

The detective had stayed a while longer in order to talk to Raphael's and Das-Groot's zone sergeant about the zone and then had left.

Both Raphael and Wilmer Das-Groot gathered up what they needed for the day and hit the street. Both had gone over what had happened the day before for a short time before dispatch had called and given them the first of the day's calls, and Raphael set into what would be his new normal of answering calls, listening to complaints of the citizens of the area and on occasion dealing with some crisis, or some mayhem or some chaos created by some other citizen.

Raphael sensed and was grateful for his very first call on the street. It was that call ... that crazy, adrenalin-infused call that had assured him within his very core that this was his calling. Just like a priest who saw God bound up in everything, he saw the "job" for the good it could do.

CHAPTER EIGHTEEN

The zone or area within the large city where Raphael and his officer-coach worked was an area in transition, not upwardly alas, but sliding down, in an almost imperceptible way, towards and joining the slums on its eastern border. The zone boundary on the south-western side teetered precariously on the bustling downtown business and shopping area. The trouble with that was the downtown emptied out at the end of the day, leaving some to party at trendy bars and eateries. But even those closed around the witching hour, leaving only the creatures of the night who plied their malicious trades amongst the darkest shadows, like an ugly stain spreading into the zone ... through it ... and into the rougher, beaten down, east end.

Houses within the zone had their doors and windows shuttered and locked during the deep, dark of night, and those within shuddered at the muffled sounds of drunken laughter, the odd gunshots, screams and shouts from without their secured homes. There was no relief to the north either, for the boundary there was the river, grown huge as it flowed into the ocean with the multitude of wharfs and docks which had sprung up along its mighty banks over countless decades. It too was, for the most part, emptied out at the end of the day, leaving only a few seaman off some of the docked ships looking for illegal pleasures. There were also a few security officers guarding some of the large warehouses, but they stayed within the cavernous warehouses and minded their own business.

The zone was a combination of recent immigrants and refugees who mixed with the elderly who had become anchored to the area by the past glories and memories of when it was new and filled with shining hope and endless possiblities. One could pick out those homes of the aged, for they were relatively neat and tidy, but each year saw fewer and fewer of those orderly homes as their owners either died or ended up in nursing homes. Once they were swept into the "sweet by-and-by," their homes started to look like they were dying as well—rundown, with grass overgrown and brown, the odd broken window, and an indifferent, vacant look took hold of the exterior of the house. There was an additional tragedy to those old and dying houses, for some became crack houses as drug dealers bought them from families, eager to be rid of the old memories that they represented, or simply druggies and drunks squatted in them to get out of inclement weather while they carried on their deadly habits. As for the immigrants and refugees, they too would move on to better places within the great city as they became more acclimated to their new homeland, Canada.

Most of the immigrants and refugees were happy, grateful and thankful to be in a new land which was safe and settled, away from the almost constant war that was the greater part of the Middle East. Here the only worry they had was learning a new language and finding jobs. But unknown to most of them, there were serpents in their midst who had taken on their shape and demeanour. These traitors had no intention of staying in the new country. They would either return from whence they came or more likely would be screaming "Allahu Akbar" as they set off a bomb attached to their body or inside a bus or in a shoot-out with the police after they had shot many unbelievers. They thought of themselves as warriors of the jihad; however, in the language of the unbelievers, they were called terrorists and they were relentless.

Once in the selected city within the chosen country, "sleeper cells" or small groups of three to six affiliated terrorists were set up, and in some cases, one sleeper cell wouldn't know anything of another cell and each cell would set up plans on how to best cause panic, horror and dread within the city. In country after country they had committed acts of such shocking abomination that created paroxysms of fear. Now it was this city's turn, and they had found the perfect area to blend in and begin to plan.

CHAPTER NINETEEN

As the days and weeks flew by, at least that was how it felt to Raphael, he began to notice and then come to know some of the residents of zone Delta 23. Firstly were the elderly, those who had been in the area for many years, who called the police with complaints of theft or break and enter and other minor complaints. They were delighted when the police showed up, and some were reluctant to see them go, plying them with tea, cookies and gossip about their more recent neighbours. Raphael understood for some of the elderly they, the police, were the only ones they may have talked to in weeks, so when they had time Raphael and Wilmer would linger a bit longer than need be. The added plus was that the elderly saw everything while they were out working in their front or back yards or even just sitting out in an old armchair on their front porch. That was how they had met Mr. Joseph Longbotham. He had fought in both the Second World War and in Korea. In fact, not only had he seen action in both wars, but he had been an intelligence officer, so he looked at the things that were occuring in the zone with the eyes and brain more akin to those of a police officer.

He had told them that his new neighbours did not really see the long-time residents, perhaps because they were not of their own culture, or simply because they were old. But the elderly did see and saw much, especially him. For the most part he had seen families out with small children talking and laughing amongst themselves as they went to an old house that had been converted into a mosque to pray. Then there were the others ... angry, watchful, wary young men ... or so they had seemed, who never went to mosque but always to an old house that somehow seemed closed in and secretive with the blinds closed. Those young men seemed suspicious of and always wary of their neighbours even though they were all immigrants from the same area of the Middle East. Joseph had further told them the young men had walked and looked around like soldiers in enemy territory, like Germans going through a town they had just captured. They made him feel edgy, and his friends who lived in the area agreed and they too felt uneasy, for as he told Raphael and Das-Groot, they watched the T.V. news about what was happening and wondered.

A sudden blaze of an idea flashed in Raphael's eyes as a surge of adrenalin rushed up his spine. Das-Groot's eyes narrowed as he noted Raphael's sudden interest in what Joseph was saying.

Joseph Longbotham, who had been watching them closely, especially Raphael, gave a short bark of laughter before saying, "I thought as much! You boys are down here doing your regular police duties, but I sensed something deeper was going on ... I wasn't in intelligence for nothing."

Raphael flushed as he looked into the sharp blue eyes beneath the bushy, white eyebrows of the older man.

"You're going to have to learn how to control that blush young man, for it just answered my question without you saying a word," Joseph continued with a hint of a smile.

Raphael looked over and saw Das-Groot, his partner, looking at him with a certain, intense inquisitiveness written on his face. *Oh shit!* he thought to himself.

"Now, here's the thing boys. I think you have been here long enough, and that house I've been telling ya 'bout is across the street and down a few houses—it's 1413 Victor Street. They always have a watcher around. They are used to seeing marked police cars in the area and almost treat them as part of the background. I get the feeling they think the police here are as corrupt and inept as the ones back in their home country. But still, we don't want them to get curious, do we? Once you get a plan together we can talk further, and of course you can use my house ... if you need to ," Joseph said with a slight smile on his weathered face.

Raphael bid Joseph an enthusiastic farewell while Das-Groot simply nodded his head as he went past Joseph Longbotham. Raphael bounded out to their police car as Das-Groot followed slowly behind him, his face still, his walk slow and measured as if he was considering or thinking about something. He could almost feel Raphael's excitement radiating from the interior of the vehicle.

Time to find out what the hell is going on, he thought as he reached for the driver's side door.

CHAPTER TWENTY

Initially Raphael was almost babbling, he was so excited about a possible "cell" and terrorists and having some place to watch from, but gradually his voice faded off as he realized that Das-Groot was not saying anything, just simply driving. His face reflected nothing about what he was thinking; in fact, it looked like a death mask it was so motionless.

Raphael could almost feel a chill in the air as he suddenly realized the mistakes he had just made. He sat back, his back stiff, and stared out the front window as he thought about all he had just said to his officer-coach, and the repeated warnings he and his classmates had received about talking about what they were really doing rang in his ears. His mind started racing as he tried to figure out how to get out of this situation. The stupid things he had just said, like some overgrown kid, how was he going to dig himself out of the mess he had just dug himself into with his officer-coach? He suddenly looked out the window ... really looked out the window ... instead of staring fixedly while he thought of his own idiocy and realized they were headed to the isolated parking lot in the old park where they went that first morning.

Das-Groot pulled into their usual spot. For a long moment they both sat motionless ... silent.

"Joseph Longbotham is right. You really have to learn to control that blush that spreads over your face when you are excited or when you have a plan. And you really have to watch yourself when you speak, especially when your mouth starts running ahead of what you are thinking. There's an old adage you might want to think about before you open your mouth, 'Don't write a cheque with your mouth that your body can't cash.' You don't know who's around, you don't know me very well yet, and you certainly don't know Joseph Longbotham. I say these things because I'm your officer-coach and it's my job to continue your training on the street. Here's the thing. I like you, I think you have great potential, and I also have had my suspicions about the so-called special class you graduated from," Das-Groot said as he watched Raphael abruptly turn towards him and saw his face go pale.

"Yes, you have very nearly given yourself and your class-mates away. However, having said that, it's a good thing it was only to me, and I support what I think you ... your class and instructors are setting up. Now though, you must talk to your instructors, find out if they wish to discuss this with me. There is an opportunity here to act on some 'possibly' creditable information. However, it needs some senior, trustworthy constables to set it up. I take it you have a phone number or some way of contacting them should just this kind of situation come up?" Das-Groot asked.

Raphael nodded his head slowly, still visibly shaken by what he had very nearly done.

"Good, I'm going to go for a short walk while you call them, let them know what is going on and the probable potential for some type of operational plan. You need to point out to them that your officer-coach has figured out, at least partially, what is going on. Tell them that they should 'vet' me, and if they want to meet with you and me later, it should be in plain clothes at some agreed-to spot where we can talk ... it is not wise for me to be seen around the police college at this time. I think you will find they agree with me," Das-Groot said as he looked up at Raphael's face and saw the pale dismay written there and felt a rush of empathy for his young partner as he thought to himself, *This is a heavy load for those young shoulders, and yet I remember my first really good bust and how excited I was.*

"Stop worrying, Raphael, this may turn out to be a really good thing," Das-Groot said before he climbed out of the vehicle and walked a short distance away, then stopped and stood, ostensibly admiring the scenery.

It seemed like a long few minutes before Raphael called him back to the vehicle. Das-Groot strolled back and got back into the driver's seat before he turned and looked at Raphael and noted that he seemed more relaxed. His face had lost that excited flush, and he gave him a weak smile.

"Well, how'd it go?"

"I told them what had happened and what you said. They actually told me they expected something like this might happen, so they had 'vetted' all the officer-coaches before we were assigned to them," Raphael replied.

When Das-Groot heard that, he burst out laughing. It took him a few moments before he could say, "Well, they certainly thought of pretty much everything. What else did they say?"

"They do want to talk to us about what was said by Joseph Longbotham and agreed we should meet after work tonight in plain clothes at one of the picnic tables in this park and to bring our own hamburgers. Oh yeah, I was to say hello to you from Jim Bilidou and Trey Carstairs."

Das-Groot grinned before saying, "I might have known my first two rookies would be mixed up in this."

Raphael eyes widened at that revelation.

"There's a lot you don't know about me, Raphael."

CHAPTER TWENTY-ONE

The four of them had each parked in different lots around the park and walked in to where there were a couple of picnic tables. Each carried bags from different fast-food places. They all sat at the one picnic table furthest from the rest, in the middle of a large clearing. Although it was a beautiful late afternoon, there appeared to be no one else in the park. They all were wearing jeans and workboots and had on the brilliant orange vests of city workers, so anybody wandering by would think they were just city workers stopping for a break.

"Hail, hail, the gangs all here," Das-Groot muttered in a low voice as he sat on the wooden bench beside Raphael while Bilidou and Carstairs sat on the bench across the table from them.

After a brief greeting they all set about eating as they all casually glanced around to make sure that no one else had wandered into the area. After they had finished their food, they sat with only coffee or pop containers in front of them. Bilidou, after surreptitiously checking under the picnic table to make sure there were no listening devices attached anywhere, was the first to talk.

"Well, I guess we shouldn't be surprised it was you and Raphael who have inadvertently come across what could be our first hint of a terrorist. Although I must admit, we did stick you in the middle of an area where many of the refugees from Afghanistan and parts of Pakistan have been placed." Bilidou saw Das-Groot was about to interject and held up his hand before he continued. "I know ... I know, Wilmer, you have been posted down there for a couple of years working as a zone constable. But we all knew from our sources in the Immigration and Refugee Ministry that your particular zone was going to be set up as sort of a staging area for strictly refugees because it was ... is so well defined, and we anticipated that amongst the refugees who, for the most part, have very little in the way of paperwork identifying who they really are, there would be terrorists lurking within their midst. We've also known the zone was in the midst of a downward flux, so marked police cars would be constantly in the area dealing with the criminal element taking up residence there. Really you couldn't ask for a better scenario for the refugees to see the police as part of the background and start to ignore them. It would seem our plans have worked, in fact, rather faster than anticipated."

"What about our possible informant and the observation post he has offered us?" Das-Groot asked in a low voice.

"Ah, yes, Joseph Longbotham. I have already contacted our sources within Veterans Affairs and their records with regard to the Second World War and Korea. Mr. Longbotham was indeed an intelligence officer in both those wars and decorated on several occasions, including the Victoria Cross. From what I was told, he seemed to always be in the thick of things. He could be a real asset to the team," Trey Carstairs added as Das-Groot nodded, a small smile of relief crossing his face.

"Of course we have been in contact with our sources within the Ministry of Defence, the Ministry of Immigration and Interpol, and they have sent us some photos of certain terroists that they believe came into Canada with the latest group of refugees. Some may very well be within your area, including a terrorist who uses the name 'Haqqanis.' We do not know his real name yet. He uses that particular name because it's the name of a Pakistani network that carried out terrorist attacks along with the Taliban across the Afghan-Pakistan Hindu Kush area. We believe he has been trying to stir up certain groups within the Hindu Kush to start committing atrocities again. Take a good, long look at the photos and then destroy them or bring them back to us," Bilidou said as he casually tossed a newspaper on the table where it lay for a few minutes before Das-Groot picked it up and loosely folded it over.

"So I take it that we are going to move on the information in slow stages?" Das-Groot asked.

"Yes, for the time being. Number one, we want to see just how far we can go with Mr. Longbotham—we don't want him hurt. Also, we may bring in a team to set up wire in the place, and we have to get a sealed warrant for that. This is our first test of a new undercover team that works strictly for and at the behest the Ministries of Defence and Immigration, and they have gritted their teeth and swallowed their nervousness. But what is unspoken is 'Failure is not an option.' Everything must be planned and executed perfectly. Although we have a judge on the team, he will not sign the warrants for wire unless there is the appropriate evidence to believe, beyond reasonable doubt, there are individuals within the aforesaid residence who are planning acts of terrorism, including but not restricted to bombings, shootings and other mayhem and chaos in order to incite terror within the community," Bilidou returned.

"I see you have the wording for the warrants memorized, Jim," Das-Groot said.

"Yes, it's been a long time in the planning ... a long time," Bilidou said as he stared off in the distance for a moment, thinking of everything that had gone into the planning and excution of this team, before his gaze turned back to Das-Groot and Campbell. "You need a second notebook strictly for the operation ... nobody but myself and Trey will see those notebooks ... understand?"

Both Das-Groot and Campbell nodded.

Raphael had listened to everything that was said and struggled to keep his face impassive, while his brain was whirling with all the information he had just heard. The realization had hit him once again that this was no mickey-mouse operation ... this was a well-organized intelligence operation with, from the sounds of it, latitude and support from the highest government ministries, and nowhere was the Canadian Intelligence Agency brought up or spoken about at all, kind of agency non grata. He looked around at the three men and his eyes met with Jim Bilidou's. Bilidou smiled.

"I'm thinking that Raphael, having heard all that has been said here, is having a few sobering moments of thought, and given his abilities we will not be seeing too much extraneous excitement in the future. Although to give him his due, he is the one who got Joseph Longbotham involved. Plus he now understands completely what is at stake here."

Raphael simply nodded.

"For now, we go slow, as you've heard there are certain things that must be done and set into motion. The rest of the operational team must be brought in and brought up to date. Your job at this point is absolutely crucial. You must continue as always ... a police officer, who, along with your partner, is on regular patrol in your zone. Wilmer, once we have double-checked Longbotham, we will have him call you in about a week, and then you can explain what is required ... and no more," Bilidou said, and then added, "If anything untoward happens in the meantime, Raphael has the cell number to call. We will be in touch."

With that, Bilidou and Carstairs rose and left the park the way they came in. Wilmer smiled at Raphael before he gathered up the newspaper, told Raphael they would talk tomorrow and left. Raphael was last to leave, his mind whirling with all that he had heard.

CHAPTER TWENTY-TWO

Das-Groot and Raphael continued on as was usual within zone Delta 23, answering calls, writing reports while sitting in their police vehicle ... doing zone policing. But under the placid exterior, both were watching, studying the faces around them. They only drove by the suspect house at 1413 Victor Street when absolutely required in the normal execution of their duty, and on the second time they had done that, they got lucky ... very lucky.

It had been a sunny day and both had been their wearing sunglasses when they saw him. An unremarkable looking Middle Eastern male, wearing the traditional garb of an Afghani, with a short beard and heavy moustache, striding up the sidewalk and then turning into the front-yard walk for 1413 Victor Street. Just then, he turned his head to look at them. Neither of them gave him any untoward attention and kept driving up the street to the call they were headed to.

"Did you see the scar? Did you see it ... it's him!" Raphael said in a harsh whisper without even turning his head.

"I saw him! We just carry on to the next call. He's still watching—I can see him in the rear-view mirror. Raphael, we have to act naturally or we could fuck up the whole operation. We'll talk about him later," Das-Groot said as he pulled the police car over and parked in front of their complainant's house. Raphael pulled out his clipboard with the required paperwork on it, stepped out of the vehicle and joined Das-Groot as he walked up to the front of the house where the complainant was waiting to tell them about how someone had stolen her garden hose overnight.

Raphael had somehow made it through the call, smiling politely at the elderly woman and even going with her to see where the hose had been stolen from. He had felt like he was on auto-pilot while his mind had raced with the thought of who they had just seen in front of the suspect house. Finally, after eating a few cookies but refusing tea offered by the elderly woman, they were walking slowly back out to the car, getting in, pulling away from the curb and driving away. Raphael said nothing although he felt like he was going to burst. Das-Groot drove to a small park that was just outside of the zone and parked. Raphael continued to look down at the clipboard and said nothing while Das-Groot went into his briefcase and pulled out a file which had been hidden beneath all the paperwork and opened it.

Raphael saw the Interpol photo of "Haqqanis" was on the top of the file, both frontal and right-side view of the face, and there it was, the scar, a very unique, angry-looking scar, ropey in texture that started high on the cheekbone then worked its way down past the beard line in the shape of a question mark without the ending dot.

"That's him, I fuckin' know it's him ... even without seeing the scar I would know it's him, those fierce eyes, the mouth ...," Raphael sputtered in restrained excitement.

"I agree, the scar is a dead giveaway and he's cautious— he watched us until we walked into the house. Raphael, I think the ante has just been upped ...'Haqqanis,' whose real name is Adnan Mir, is a bomb maker," Das-Groot replied.

"What the hell is he doing here!"

"My guess is making bombs."

Raphael turned and looked at him, his face gone pale, almost as pale as Das-Groot.

CHAPTER TWENTY-THREE

"I see from the computer we are going to a B&E at Joseph Longbotham's house. We haven't seen or heard from him since we talked with him about his neighbours across the street," Raphael said as he studied the call that had popped up on the computer.

"Yeah, its been a couple of weeks. Mind you, it's only a couple of days since we saw and identified 'Haqqanis.' Shit, I've never seen that kind of reaction from Bilidou; usually he's pretty calm no matter what the situation. I thought he was gonna choke or stroke out. I think the slow-stages plan has gone out the fuckin' window. Nothing like the thought of a bomb maker in our city to expedite or grease the wheels of an operational plan," Das-Groot grunted then added, "From this point on, don't be surprised by anything you see."

They pulled in and parked by the curb in front of the house, and Raphael saw a bright, copper-coloured SUV parked ahead of them and wondered who else was here. As they walked up the sidewalk to the house, they saw Joseph opening the screen door. He had his arm around a young woman who looked familiar. And then Raphael almost jerked to a stop, before remembering where he was and who might be watching, and continued his casual stroll up to the porch. His eyes, thankfully, hidden behind the sunglasses he was wearing.

"Come in, come in, boys. I had a little trouble last night. Oh, have I introduced you to my granddaughter? Sandy, these are the two police officers I was telling you about ... constables Das-Groot and Campbell," Joseph said as "Sandy" shook hands with them.

Joseph urged them to come into the house. Once they were well inside and away from any windows, Raphael asked in a low murmur, "Ok, I give up ... what the hell are you doing here, Lula?"

"You two kids know each other?" Joseph asked as he looked between them.

"Ah, yes, we were classmates," Lula returned.

"More than that, I would say," Joseph said with a sparkle in his eye.

"Anyway ... what's up and why are you here?" Das-Groot asked in a gruff, low voice.

"I'm here so the bad guys get used to me and my car being in the neigbourhood. Also other members of the team will be around in casual roles such as gas readers and electricians, so we also blend into the neighbourhood. There is a plan afoot, but first we need some confirmation before it can be put into action," Lula said.

"Ok, makes sense. While we are doing the report, why don't you give us the short version of the plan," Das-Groot said with a slight shrug.

"That's pretty much it for right now. We have to get into that house to see what's in there. Once we know, then we can set everything in motion," Lula said.

Joseph, who was sitting across the kitchen table from Raphael, recounted that the night before someone had broken into his garage, and although he didn't think anything had been taken, he had gotten an uneasy feeling about it. Plus, whoever had done the deed, had broken the lock on the side door of the garage and while he had been checking the damage in the morning, he had gotten the feeling that someone was watching him. As he had looked up, he had seen the curtains move on a side window in the house next to him.

"I may be old, but I still got lots working above the old brainpan. I think someone is getting paranoid and suspicious about little old me," he rumbled in his gravelly voice.

Raphael looked up from the report he was writing when he heard those words. His eyes met Joseph's and he thought he saw a shadow of worry in them. And then it was gone and Joseph was smiling at him.

"Say, did Sandy tell ya? I got a look at some of those photos ... Sandy showed me them yesterday. I recognized three of them, the one with the scar on his face—he's in and out all the time. Always looking around then goes out ... comes back carrying parcels from the hardware store. I know because the bags are marked on the outside 'Bill's Hardware.' I just happen to be out in the front yard gardening or sitting on the porch when I see him. 'Course, I never look up, 'just carry on' like the Brits used to say during the war. Oh, and I marked down times and dates as best I could."

Raphael listened to Joseph as he spoke and thought he caught something in the tone of his voice. He looked up to where Lula was standing behind Joseph, one slim hand on his shoulder, and watched as Joseph reached up with a hand and patted her hand with his, which was shaking slightly with age's palsy. Raphael, as his gaze caught hers, saw the miniscule shake of her head. He understood.

Time to move the plan forward. Their asset, given his training and experience, knew that he had stepped into something very dangerous, which he would have revelled in had he been younger. But alas, with old age came the hard ropes and confines of caution.

Raphael finished the report and looked up at Das-Groot and Lula. He was grasped by a sudden feeling that time was running out ... running out on what?

CHAPTER TWENTY-FOUR

The man, wearing a bright orange vest with a large, fluorescent X across the back, got out of the gas company truck. He turned, got his bright orange-coloured hard hat and slapped it on his head, tipping the front brim down slightly so it shaded the sunglasses he was wearing, stuck a couple of sticks of gum in his mouth and started chewing. Those three items when put together in such a way were a very effective disguise, and any idividual asked to describe him would, at best, be able to say he was a white male, six foot and well built. Added to that was the voice, obscured by him chewing a wad of gum, and single syllable responses to most questions. He pulled out an aged leather tool belt with various tools attached or stored in large tool pouches on it. He belted it around his waist and finally grasped a clipboard and some type of electronic device with assorted buttons and toggle mechanisms on the square box with a long, yellow plastic snout.

While he retrieved the various tools of his trade, another man, dressed in Afghani apparel, stepped out of the passenger side and waited for the "gasman" to finish gearing up. Once that was completed, the one nodded to the other before each looked at some papers on the clipboard.

The "gas company" man spoke quickly to the other then pointed up the street with one hand, nodded, and they started walking up the street. As the so-called "gasman" strode up the street, he felt his stomach rolling with nervousness. He could feel hidden eyes watching him discreetly from behind curtains in homes on both sides of the street. The man beside him ... maybe an interpreter ... had to almost run to keep up with him. They stopped in front of 1425 Victor Street and turned and walked to the front door of the house where the gasman knocked firmly on the door while the alledged Middle Eastern man, discreetly and unseen, sprayed something from a plastic bottle he had hidden under his loose clothes. An elderly woman came to the door of the house. The gasman spoke to her briefly, and those who watched from behind blinds or curtains in other houses saw her put her hand to her mouth in alarm and then usher him into the house while the other man stood outside, his skills obviously not needed. Within a short time the gasman exited the house and the two continued their walk up the street to the next house—1421 Victor Street— and once again the gasman knocked on the door, only this time a heavily veiled woman came to the door, at which time the Middle Eastern man, after again secretly spraying something from the plastic bottle, stepped forward, and those who warily watched from behind blinds in other houses along the street saw him speak to the woman. The woman stepped outside and seemed to smell the air and then gestured for the men to come in.

The watchers saw the two men exit the residence after a few moments. Within a matter of seconds, the phone lines began to sing as those refugees who lived in houses along the block began to phone each other about what was going on.

Soon everyone on the block learned that there was a possible gas leak—very dangerous if true. Somewhere along the block, some said they had already noticed the rotten eggs smell. The man from the gas company was very polite and had brought an interpreter with him. He had a special machine that could smell the gas, and they only checked with the machine then left after just a few minutes. The gasman even left a card with a phone number if they smelled gas again.

And so the two made their way up the block until they reached 1413 Victor Street. Both men could feel their insides fluttering and rolling. Both were reviewing in their minds the photos they had been shown, the instructions they had been given. It took all their concentration to keep their outward actions indifferent ... just another job ... placid, even bored, as they made their way to the front door of the house. The man playing at being the interpreter was making sure that he discreetly sprayed more of the contents of the bottle around the front of the house.

Oh shit, I hope no one lights a match around us ... Jeff is going wild with that damn bottle! the gasman thought to himself as they reached the front door and he knocked, perhaps a little harder than he should have, he thought.

A hard-faced Afghani came to the screened front door. "What you want?" he asked harshly in broken English.

"I'm from the gas company and we got a report of a gas leak somewhere in this block, and we gotta check to make sure the houses are is ok," the "gasman" said around the wad of gum.

"Eh," the man behind the screen said and jerked his head towards the interpreter, whereupon the interpreter burst into singsong, perfect Farsi, about the gas-leak situation and the need to get into the house but only to ensure that the gas leak was not inside. Of course, the gasman understood every word that was being said, but he maintained his bored expression as he continued to chew on his wad of gum that was now tasting something like wet cement.

"Brother, what are you doing interpreting for this stupid bull. There are other things you could be doing?"

"I have a family to feed and this job is not too onerous. This one may be stupid for the most part, but he knows his job and he is too dumb to do harm. He even leaves a card with the gas company phone number on it if you wish to phone. For myself, I would let him check, and in a few moments he is gone and no one questions further," the interpreter said with a shrug.

The man stared at them for what seemed like a long, agonizing moment more before abruptly motioning them in. They stepped in and the gasman moved to where the livingroom was and raised his machine up and started waving it gently in the direction of the ceiling as he moved down the hallway to a room with the door almost closed. The green light on the machine had been shining, but when it came to the room it, started flashing red. The gasman went to open the door and one word escaped from their guide—

"No!"

"But it shows there might be a leak!"

"Brother, he must check or he will come back with more people!" the interpreter said in Farsi.

"Let me warn, ah ... tell him that is working in the room."

Both the gasman and the interpreter heard as the other man spoke urgently to someone in the room and told him to come out quickly and turn away while the oaf checked the room ... "There is nothing in there that this stupid oaf will recognize." There was a rustling and then a man stepped quickly out of the room and turned away from them, but not before both had seen the scar on the right side of his face.

"Let this fool of a man use his machine in there while you stay out here."

The interpreter shrugged indifferently and motioned for the gasman to go in but told him to be quick as they had many more addresses to check. The gasman nodded, went in and was back out in a couple minutes, the same bored expression on his face as he continued to chew on the gum.

"Nothing in there. The leak must be outside. Just tell him we're going to check the outside of the house by this room and then we're gone."

The interpreter complied and they walked out and around the side of the house. They could both feel eyes on them as they checked outside of the house by the room. The gasman nodded his head and they moved off.

The gasman and the interpreter continued up the block, doing three more houses before they made their way back to the gas company truck, got in and left.

Nothing was said by either of them until they pulled into an old garage where the exterior had been newly painted and now had new signs indicating that it was a gas company sub-station. There was also a new, tall chain-link fence around the "substation," topped with razor-wire. Everything was alarmed including the fence, although it still looked innoculous at least until the large sign that read "NO ENTRY UNLESS PROPER IDENTIFICATION SHOWN."

They both practically fell out of the truck, they were laughing so hard. Their laughter was a large part stress relief and one part the interpreter reliving and saying all the names his partner, the gasman, Jacob, had been called while they had done the gasman and interpreter scam and how well it had gone.

They walked around a large black van with dark windows that was parked next to a wall on which a huge cabinet was attached, and stepped into the office area of the garage. They stopped talking as soon as they saw their "boss," Jim Bilidou, talking on the phone, and they could hear from the one-sided conversation that he was reassuring someone that they could not find a gas leak and everything should be fine but if there should be anymore reports, they would be back.

The call at last terminated, Bilidou turned to them, "Jaysus, you guys were just a little bit too convincing. I've talked to three worried residents."

"Any of them our refugee friends?"

"Only one, and guess who that was?"

"Not 1413!"

"The very same. They must be very paranoid. I think they've got something planned and it's goin down soon. What did you guys see?"

"You're right. The other houses were just for show, but when we got inside 1413 Victor Street, I could smell diesel fuel almost instantly," Jacob, who had played the gasman said and Jeff, who had been the interpreter, nodded in agreement.

"And, Jim, the room they didn't want me goin' into was set up kind of like an office, only they had a table that extended around three walls of the room. It looked like the guy who had just left the room had thrown a bed sheet over the table so I couldn't see what he had been working on. I could see there was stuff underneath the sheet, so I took a little peek and I started sweatin' bricks when I lifted the cover up ... man, oh man! There were at least parts of three cell phones with the innards and little circuit boards exposed ... kinda looked like somebody had been doing some work on them 'cause they were scattered on the top of the desk with small pieces of thin wire which had the ends stripped off and were all over the place. Plus there were some small wire strippers and a small soldering tool with a tiny, tiny tip on it, and there was a definite scent you get when ya solder stuff. Oh ... I got a faint whiff of plastique or C-4 ... ya know that smell ... kinda like the stuff kids play with, with undertones of explosion. And, Jim, I saw a pressure-cooker pot under the desk! Hell, I covered it all up just like I found it and got the fuck outta there. Jim, I think they're planning something soon. They got two bomb makers that we've identified plus a couple of other terrorists that are on the top-ten hit list of Interpol."

"Fuck! Do we have confirmation that they've planted anything yet?" Bilidou asked.

"Naw, the asset has only seen our Acc #1, scarface, carrying shit in."

"I worry 'bout them taking stuff out at night."

"Jim, we got 'eyes' on that place 24-7. They haven't taken anything out ... yet."

"'Kay, we figure they got four livin' there, right? And all have been identified as terrorists by Interpol, right?"

Jacob nodded.

I'm gonna go to the judge for the warrants. Fuck the wiretaps—we don't have time."

"Judge gonna be cool?"

"Yeah, it's called exigent circumstances. We can kick 'em in now but better to cover ourselves with the proper paperwork, and our judge was selected by the Minister of Public Safety, a.k.a. Minister of Defence, our team's boss. Time to see if this judge has the stones everybody says he does. I shouldn't be long. Jacob make the calls to the team ... code word "pressure cooker." In this instance Das-Groot is part of the team. The list is in my folder in the desk drawer ... this is night work. They know what to do when they get the call.

CHAPTER TWENTY-FIVE

It was an hour past what some would call the witching hour or 0100 hrs, and the darkness was almost complete. It was cloudy, so the moonlight could not cast its light upon what went on. There were very few overhead lights working along Victor Street, most having been shot out by drug dealers long ago, not that it mattered. For they were the darkest shades amongst black shadows moving smoothly, quietly with only hand signals and night vision binoculars attached to their helmets to guide them. Each of them were completely clothed in black with bullet-proof vests with pouches that held extra ammo and stun and smoke grenades. Their belts held holsters bearing semi-automatic glocks with silencers and more ammo. Each one of them held a specially modified AK-47 with silencer attached. They all had a small earphone bud in one ear, with a small microphone on a wire that ended just at the side of the mouth, the wires for which ran down and attached to the portable radio on their belts. The team members maintained radio silence, for even a whisper on a quiet night like this would reverberate and break the silence.

Raphael, whose target-mark was the south-west corner, front of the residence, could feel the adrenalin starting to surge, and he forced himself to feel the stillness within, to focus the surge as they moved closer to their target. He could feel the others around him as they moved in on their marks. His breathing was smooth, inaudible, his eyesight sharpened by the inner stillness, the calmness, and then he was up against the front south-west corner of the house. He could feel the others moving into position ... then abruptly the night was shattered by fevered talking within the target house. They must have had windows open ... an argument in what! Farsi, no Urdu! Violent voices speaking loudly about jihad and their iman [cleric]. Then, of a sudden, without warning he could hear that infamous cry from within ... Allahu Akbar! Allahu Akbar! One of the voices appeared to come from the room with the bomb-making equipment. An argument ... he caught enough of the words ... something about where and when bombs should be placed ... the heated words seemed to be reaching the precipice of verbal violence ... the edge of the abyss ... and could go no further except for the inevitable ... an argument he knew could cause shakey hands and false moves—stupid moves—and he sensed what was about to happen and he shouted into his mic, "EVERY-BODY BACK OFF! BACK OFF!! "

He could sense the startled, hesitate pause within those around him, and then they understood and started moving backwards, then turned and ran ... faster! Then he heard a final scream ... Allahu Akbar ... a millisecond frozen pause, and the ground was suddenly lifting below his feet ... a roaring sound growing larger and larger, and then the block ... the sky was lit up with a hot light! He could feel bullets? Shrapnel buzzing by him like a thousand angry wasps had gotten together to attack the neighbourhood, and he kept running even as he was lifted up and then pushed out by the pulsing, searing air. He was lying on the ground. He could hear voices but they seemed muted ... WHAT THE FUCK!

A black figure was bending over him and seemed to be talking, but his voice seemed so far away. "You ok?" He felt his vest being pulled. He was being pulled up, and he stood up gave a thumbs up with his hand as he heard the hooded figure say, "Meet at the designated meeting place! "Leave now!"

He retreated the way he came in. He saw other figures moving back ... clearing the area.

His mind started to clear and he knew they had a minute ... maybe two ... before people in the homes around the explosion would start to recover from the shock of the light, sound and shaking. Then they'd start calling the police as they stepped out of their homes to see what was going on.

He looked around as he started to move and saw a dark form crumpled on the ground close to him. He bent, grabbed the figure by the back of the vest and dragged him a short way before he stopped, picked him up and slung him over his shoulder and started to run in a graceful, gliding movement. He didn't know who he had, just that it was one of the team.

Within mere moments, he was a block away and running up the stairs and into the abandoned building that had been quietly cleaned out and locked up 'til the time it might be used as a designated "safe house."

He stumbled into the house and someone immediately helped him with the figure he had carried back, and then he slumped into a chair and watched as a few other figures came in, some stumbling, some limping, some walking, and all still breathless from what had happened.

"Alright ... alright, that seems to be it as far as those returning ... let's do a count to make sure everybody got away from the explosion," Jim Bilidou said as he stood in the middle of the room and pulled off the black hood he was wearing. He looked decidedly odd with the black camo-paint around his eyes.

They did the count, and one seemed to be missing ... did the count again, still missing one.

Raphael looked up suddenly. They kept missing one name ... one name he knew so well. He came out of the chair and someone grabbed him by the shoulder as he went for the door. He tried to shake off the hands that held him back. He had to go back! Find her! The hands were like quicksand holding him back ... pulling him down into desolation!

CHAPTER TWENTY-SIX

He was still struggling, fighting the hands holding him when a voice in his ear yelled , "She's ok! She managed to make it to Joseph's place! She's ok!"

He slumped in relief, and then forced himself to stand up straight. His hearing was still fucked up from the blast, and the words the other shouted at him seemed to come from down some long, dark tunnel. But they had practiced for just this kind of eventuality, and he knew what to do until his ears cleared.

Once everybody was accounted for, they all made their way through the old house and exited it via an old, lower door hidden in the shadows. The large black van was parked on the street right beside the exit door, and they were gone in a matter of two minutes, leaving the night to the confused neighbours, the police and fire department.

The debriefing would have to wait 'til the next day when things had quieted down. The team had changed back into civi clothes and were gone from the "substation," all that is except for Bilidou and Carstairs who, acting as gas company employees, were answering anxious phone calls from panicky neightbours that surrounded the blast site. It was a good thing that they had left cards and they actually had an agent, of sorts, within the real gas company who had been pre-warned about just such a situation.

Raphael, whose hearing had just started to return to normal, was the last one left and was about to leave the "substation," when he heard Jim talking on his cell to one of the Ident members assigned to do the forensic investigation of the explosion at 1413 Victor Street. He heard Bilidou call him by his name, and knew he had come from their team. "Christ, they had thought of everything," he thought.

Bilidou saw Raphael and waved him over to where he was talking on the cell.

"Raphael, I need the short version of what you heard ... saw ... that caused you to tell us to back off. I've got our Ident member on the phone, and he needs some details so that they can discount the theory that the explosion was caused by a gas leak."

Raphael, who had been lingering in case Lula came back to the "substation," walked in to the office and said, "Tell him I got right up to the south-west corner of the house. They must have had some windows open because I could hear them arguing about placement of the IED and pressure-cooker bombs where their iman had suggested they place the explosive devices ... fuck, I still can't get past a religious, supposed holy man telling them where to place bombs ... and yet I know down through the centuries it has not been unusual to see so-called holy men, popes, priests and their ilk who've led so-called religious wars that have killed far more innocent civilians than soldiers. Anyway, sorry." Raphael gave his head a shake. "Back to the topic at hand ... I heard someone inside the room where the bomb-making equipment was, joining in the argument. As luck would have it, the window in that room was also open, and I was only a few feet away from it. Abruptly, he yelled ... almost a scream ... for others to be quiet. Then all of a sudden, I heard him swear in Urdu and scream Allahu Akbar and I sensed ... knew ... he'd done something wrong. That's when I yelled for everybody to back off. Also the Ident guy should look for shards from pressure cookers because, from what I understand, some pressure cookers were seen in that room, and since they were on the floor, some may not have been totally destroyed. I don't know ... I'm just guessing. Jim, you have told him there should be four bodies?"

Jim nodded at him before he spoke into the cell again.

"They certainly seem to have thought of everything before we started to do this raid tonight. Even though it kinda exploded in our faces, both figuratively and literally, they seemed to have everything covered, even the team getting split up, which is comforting. I hope we ... they ... haven't missed anything," Raphael thought as he studied Bilidou. And yet he felt a small niggling worry that somehow they had missed something within the grand plan, somehow this night was going to come back and bite them in the ass.

With that thought orbiting at the back of his mind, he left the substation and headed home to, hopefully, a phone call from Lula.

CHAPTER TWENTY-SEVEN

Jim Bilidou hung up the phone one last time, praying with wane hope that there would be no more urgent ringing, and it seemed his prayers were answered—quiet, almost still, except for the old furnace knocking slightly in protest as warm air was forced through it. He called out to Trey. There was no response. Trey must have gone to get Lula.

He was alone. The first time in many, many months it seemed like. What an odd thought, he reflected. There had been other times when he had been alone, and yet not alone, for this mission ... this team had been all-consuming, and since this had started, he had had little ... actually no ... genuine time for introspection.

The idea had started over drinks between friends. Odd friends, to be sure, given that he had been a major in an intelligence unit in Afghanistan. The general had just returned from the genocide in the Congo, and the Minister of Defence had only just finished dealing with the debacle of a civilian flight that had been blown out of the sky by a terrorist bomb. The three of them had grown up together, even gone to university together, before life had sent them in different directions. Yet somehow, perhaps it had been fate or karma, or the reality of a funeral for another old friend who had been suffering from P.T.S.D. and had just commited suicide. The three of them had attended the required death ritual where they had met after years apart. There had been a wake after, but somehow the three of them had ended up going to the general's house house instead.

The idea, which somehow had turned into a plan, not because of an overabundance of alcohol but rather an overabundance of revulsion-repulsion, trauma that had seared their very souls, there came an idea so outrageous, so extraordinary and unconventional when it had been proposed by the general, who had been so burned out and disgusted by what he had seen done by terrorists in their own home land and how easily the terrorists had moved through Europe, creating fear and horror wherever they went. Then, using Canada as a base and border crossing, they had created such a gruesome, malicious maelstrom in the United States and they had done so with impunity because they, like those few other refugees-immigrants who committed criminal acts within Canada or even within their countries of their origin before arriving in Canada, knew even if they were caught, in all likelihood would be released on bail so they could disappear again. Hell! Even a terrorist who had killed a medic who had been trying to save a life was returned from jail in the U.S. to jail in Canada, then immediately released and given a large sum of money by the government. Even though during the war in Afghanistan, over three hundred Canadian soldiers had lost their lives.

Yet the idea that had turned into a plan, in a weird way, sounded almost feasible, and given what they had in the way of an intelligence agency here in Canada, which was an inside joke to many other countries, there was certain validity to the plan. All three of them had looked at each other, then there was a rush of excitement between them … maybe … it could be done? The three of them had high-placed contacts throughout the government, contacts just as fed up as they were.

The rest of the night and the following day they sat there, after the general had pulled out pads of lined paper, and worked out the plan—who would be involved … had to be involved … who could be trusted, who couldn't and those who were on a need-to-know-only basis ... where to start and what they would need. It had been the most exhilarating, terrifying time of his life.

"Can we really do this?" he remembered asking as he looked back and forth between the faces of his two friends. The living room was lit only by a couple of table lamps casting shadows on their faces and partially concealing the crumpled papers, glasses and coffee cups scattered on the side tables and the floor.

"Fuck, ya know, I think we can. But you know, with our luck, the Intelligence Agency that we got right now, who as we all know wouldn't know a terrorist if they fell over one, just might stumble over what we're doin'," The general had said with a grin,' and suddenly they had all been laughing.

Since then it had been a white-knuckled roller-coaster ride, but they had pulled it together with the help of certain friends within the government. Amongst those friends the Minister of Defence had and had insisted on notifying in a very basic way was the P.M. That was all he ever called him ... the P.M ... and the other two had nodded, their faces pale. Within hours of the minister talking to him, the P.M. had reluctantly agreed to the plan although he would not put his signature to any paperwork. The minister had told them that the P.M. was still reeling intellectually from the gunman who had gotten into parliament and the firefight that had erupted just feet from the door behind which the P.M. had been holding a caucas meeting. So the P.M. was onboard and was to be kept informed in a very discreet way.

Tonight had been their first operation, and Jim Bilidou sat there wondering if this night could be considered a success or a failure. On the success side, the terrorists were gone, not shipped out of the country, true, but certainly blown into the next life. And most important, none of the team was discovered, or more importantly, killed. Also they had used the intelligence they had gathered to identify the terrorist and they, the team, had strengthened their ties with international intelligence agencies such as Interpol, Homeland Security, MI-5, Israeli Intelligence and others. He knew and understood the contempt some of the agencies felt towards the original Canadian Intelligence Agency because their fumbling of intelligence and warnings given to them.

It had always been part of the triumvirate's plan to quietly supersede the Canadian agency, using them as a shield or cover while they, the team, did their due diligence, acting on their own and other agencies' information. Basically, they would plug the leaks and develop leads that led to the lawful arrest of those about to or having committed a heinous act that would bring the laws of Canada into disrepute, and in cases where they, the accused, were not Canadian, send them back to their country of origin. That had been the creed of the original agency, but their seeming inability to act appropriately with regards to terrorists, bike gangs, international drug smugglers, mob racketeers and other major criminals, had resulted, in some cases, in terrible loss of life.

He also knew their team was the prototype, the test team as it were, so they had been careful about which city and area of the country they selected. Since he had been born and raised in this particular city, was aware of both its positive and negative aspects and most importantly was good friends with the current police chief of the particular city, was the reason it was chosen.

Richard "Rick" Wardner, Chief of Police, was a stand-up guy who had worked his way up through the ranks and was respected and well liked by his men. There was one thing that was every bit as crucial as the rest of the requirements and that was he wasn't a "brown-noser" with the Police

Commision ... didn't play politics with the mayor or any of his ilk and only told them as little as possible to keep them happy. He had specifically invited Rick over to his house for dinner, and over a couple of beers before dinner, then throughout dinner, he had sounded him out about certain things.

Midway through an after-dinner brandy with their coffee, Rick had sighed and shook his head before saying, "Jim, you're a typical intelligence officer. Now quit fuckin' dancing 'round the tulips and tell me what you've got going, and tell me how I can help."

All he could do was give Rick a sheepish grin before laying out the entire plan and what they needed. Rick listened intently and every once in a while nodded his head in understanding. When he finally finished, Rick sat for a few minutes without saying anything, obviously deep in thought as he took a sip of brandy.

Finally, after another sip, he spoke. "Well, Jim, it sounds like you've thought of everything. Now let me get this straight. I get twenty or so highly trained rookies who, for the most part, are retired military and horseman (RCMP) types who have all served overseas and in the Middle East, speak several different languages, who will be legitimately doing actual police work while also gathering 'intel,' getting and serving search warrants on the really bad guys, including terrorists, drug cartels, etcetera, and on top of that will be working with immigration officers to get these ruthless criminals back to their country of origin on the next plane out, more or less. And I get to keep these police officers?" Rick asked and watched as his friend gave him a nod and weak smile.

"Man, oh, man, Jim, you must truly trust me 'cause right now I could blow you and this wild plan right out of the water. Secondly, and this hinges on if I agree to this plan, I'm thinking you plan on being one of the sergeants who will train out these recruits?" (he watched as Jim nodded). "Well, you have to be recognized as a real police officer and sergeant by all the other sergeants-teachers up at the police college, and I'm thinking, aside from me, you can't, and have to make sure no one, outside of me and of course those in the class, know how much extra knowledge is being taught in that particular class." Rick watched as his friend's face took on a stricken, ashen look as he picked up his glass, and then took a large drink of brandy and immediately began to choke. Rick had actually had to pound him on the back a couple of times before the stiff drink went down the right way.

"Hey, it's ok, Jim! I just wanted to point out some things to ya. Other than that, I think it's an excellent plan. Jaysus, I don't want ya choking to death in your own house! How the hell would I explain that? Don't worry, I know how to get around the sergeant-teacher situation, but you will be joining my police force, and let me be the first to congratulate you on joining our fine police department!"

They had both looked at each other and burst out laughing and that had been how he had joined the police force while still serving as a major in an intelligence unit in the army.

His thoughts drifted back to that night's events and the smile of remembrance remained on his face as he went over the explosion which had very nearly ... but hadn't ... ended the team just as they were getting off to a good start.

On the negative side ... sorta negative ... it would have been nice to scoop the bad guys, whisk them to the judge, then ship them out of the country and into the waiting arms of their own governments, some of which would ensure they

had a speedy trial on the way to the firing squad or decapi-
tation. But, he thought, you can't have everything the first
time out.

"What are you grinning about?" Trey Carstairs asked as
he strolled into the office.

"Oh, I was just thinkin' it's been a long fuckin' road to
tonight. Lula ok?" Jim Bilidou returned.

"Yeah, she's ok. More excited than anything. Joseph was
almost as excited—he's a good asset. We lucked out there. As
to the other, you're right; it has been a long road and a long
road yet to go. I keep thinking of that poem and the phrase
'A road less travelled.' That's the road we are on,' I think."

CHAPTER TWENTY-EIGHT

He had been in such a sound, warm, REM sleep. He and his wife had been on a picnic along a beautiful beach with the ocean, with a slight heat haze over it before them, while at their back were the mountains that reached up and touched the blue sky. He had thought of the phrase from a song "The purple mountain majesty plunging down to meet the deep blue of the mighty ocean," so grand, so apt on such a perfect day. He looked at his young wife, so lovely as she laughed, her face slightly sun-seared, her blonde hair a shining cap that danced and curled in the slight breeze off the ocean. Such a wonderful day ... wait ... why was it fading away into the darkness as he felt a sudden bodily urge pulling, yanking him out of Morpheus' arms. He tried to hang onto the sleep, but it was no good—he had to take a piss. With a sigh, he let go of the lovely place he had just been in as he spiralled down and out of the dream, thumping down into the grim reality of being an old man whose bladder had shrivelled in the opposite direction as he had gained in age.

He flipped the covers back and groaned slightly as he pulled himself out of his warm bed and made his way to the bathroom. He didn't bother turning on lights—he'd lived here so long he could've found his way blindfolded. He got to the toilet, assumed the position as he thought to himself, *That's the only good thing about living alone—'the toilet seat is always up.'* He felt the warm rush of relief as his bladder emptied.

He had been staring out the bathroom window, which happened to face the front of 1413 Victor Street, as he relieved himself and thought he saw movement, someone leaving by the front door. A light was on inside the house and there was a brief silhouette, seconds really, and then it—he—was gone. But Joseph's eyes were used to the dark, and he saw the slight motion of someone carrying a large bag and staying in the shadows as he moved quickly away from the house. The one thing that had never failed him as he grew older was his eyesight, and he thought to himself, *I hope whoever's got the 'eye' on that house tonight saw that person leaving.* He watched the surreptitious movements until it seemed the person disappeared around a house further down the street. He suddenly realized that he was still standing over the toilet with the crown jewels hanging out. He chuckled to himself as he thought, *Well, I certainly emptied the old bladder out tonight,* as he tucked everything back into his pajamas and made his way back to bed. But there was a part of him, the soldier part, that checked the clock to see the time before he climbed back into bed.

It had only been 2300 hours when he had seen certain things from his bathroom window.

Within two hours Joseph Longbotham was literally blown out of his bed by the explosion from across the street, and within a minute of the blast, Lula, all dressed in black, carrying an AK-47, was tapping at his door. In all the excitement, he had forgotten about what he had seen earlier ... forgot, that is, until he had been having his tea in the morning as he sat on his porch looking at the bits of debris that were all that remained of 1413 Victor Street, while the fire department boys and the police picked through them like vultures worrying a carcass.

CHAPTER TWENTY-NINE

"Jim, I think we've got a problem. Maybe a huge fuckin' problem," Trey said as he walked through the door of the substation, worry and strain clearly written on his face.

Jim Bilidou took one look at Trey's face and felt his guts knot up. The singular thought, *Oh, shit!* stood at attention in his brain and saluted.

"It can't have really been a fuckin' gas leak, or did someone see our guys last night? What ...?" Jim Bilidou asked in a calm voice that belied the sudden disastrous news he felt was coming his way.

Trey shook his head as he said, "I only wish it was that simple."

"Well, fuckin' spill it. It's not gonna get any better with you standing there looking like you're expecting a bomb to go off at any time," Bilidou replied.

"You're real close to what might happen."

"What the hell ... no wait ... you're kidding," Bilidou said, his face suddenly leeching of all colour, leaving it a pasty white tinged with pale grey.

"Jim, they only found three bodies, and believe me they have torn what was left of the house apart."

"Did they check the roofs of the houses all around the explosion? 'Cause ya know, as a result of the power of the blast, bodies end up in the oddest places. I know that from working around explosions in Afghanistan ..." Bilidou voice faded even as he said it when he looked at Trey's face.

"They've checked, I've checked, and then we all rechecked. Then I got a call to go see Joseph Longbotham. He told me an interesting and, in the end, an alarming story of taking a piss 'round eleven o'clock last night.

"What the fuck does the old guy takin' a piss have anything to do with the price of rice in China?! In other words get to the fuckin' point!"

"I'm trying to! Apparently his bathroom window faces the front of 1413 Victor Street, and he just happened to look out and see someone leave by the front door of the address, carrying a large bag. He never thought anything about it, 'cause he figured we had the 'eye' [surveillance] on the house, so he went back to bed only to be roused out of bed—more like blown out—by the explosion, and then Lula tapping at his door only seconds later. So Joseph never thought anything more of what he'd seen 'til this morning when he saw everybody digging through what was left of the house. Joseph may be old, but he hasn't lost any of his smarts."

Bilidou started to ask a question, but Trey held up his hand and stopped him.

"I know what you're gonna ask. I checked with our surveillance guys, and they don't think anybody left around the time that Joseph saw what he did. But let me tell ya, Jim, I gotta funny feeling they were kinda hedging around the topic, so I took a look at where they had their 'eye' set up, and given how dark it was out last night, they could very well have missed someone coming or going."

"Shit! Why didn't they move their surveillance! And maybe Joseph's eyes aren't as good anymore. He's an old guy after all."

"Jim, those guys couldn't move their position without getting spotted. As for Joseph, I thought about his sight as well, and ya know what, he proved to me that his eyesight is still excellent. Thing is, he saw the guy leaving at eleven and maybe the guy came back, but what really worries me is ...

what the fuck was that guy carrying out of 1413 in a large bag, and where the hell is the fourth body?!"

They both stood there staring at each other across the huge steaming mass of 'Oh shit,' and for a few brief nano-seconds, neither of them could say anything, never mind think of what they were going to do.

CHAPTER THIRTY

Jim Bilidou sat back down on the chair with a sigh that dribbled into a low groan. Trey Carstairs sat down on the old wooden desk chair, kitty-corner across the battered, old steel desk from Jim and watched as he leaned forward with his elbows on the desk, his hands supporting his head, his eyes closed.

Trey watched his friend—really his partner—and could almost see the wheels turning in that head of his as Jim figured a way out of this unexpected mess. Trey thought back to how they had met in Afghanistan when he had been posted to an intelligence unit that Jim ran. They had become friends almost immediately. Jim had been fascinated by the fact that Trey, who was in the reserves, and was a police officer in a large western Canadian city where he worked as a team leader of a TAC Team unit, had volunteered for Afghanistan. They had shared many a "war story" and laughter over beers. Trey, as a result of his training in both the reserves and as a TAC officer, including a month down in Ottawa on a specialized bomb course, was assigned to the Intelligence unit because of his knowledge about IED's and other weapons that caused massive destruction and death. His had taught military bomb squad members how to recognize those weapons and disarm them. Trey thought of the odd times when maybe after a beer or two too many their talks had been edged in bitterness at what they both had seen on the battlefield and in the villages. Bombs, so indiscriminate, so unnecessary, sparing no one, from babes-in-arms, their mothers, children, all the innocents, and how there were some who took pleasure in the deaths.

Yes, they had bonded over what they both had seen, and had kept in touch when Trey's tour of duty was over. Then one night when Trey was just getting off his shift, Jim had been waiting for him in the TAC team office. They had gone out for dinner and that was when Jim told him the plan. Funny, he thought, but it had seemed like the idea ... the plan had been what he had been waiting for ever since he had joined the police department and gradually seen what had been going on. For with certain officers, the longer they-he-she was on the job, the more they had learned about a government that had lofty ideals that were wonderful on paper or tripping out of the mouths of certain politicians, but alas, in reality, did not take into consideration the truly evil creatures that sat back and laughed at those they considered to be the witless and the foolish, then had taken advantage of certain laws and how they were interpreted. Yes, there were many who had taken advantage of the laws on immigration-refugees and the Mental Health Act and as a result, there were more than a few of those creatures who had killed and yet had been released to kill again.

He was still deep within those thoughts when he looked up and saw that Jim was looking at him. Jim had a slight ascerbic smile on his face as he looked at him.

"I don't know where you were, but it didn't look to be a particularly happy place."

Trey reddened then responded, "Just thinking about how we met and all that has gone on since ... most good, some bad. So have you thought of how we are going to get out of this mess?"

"I don't know if 'mess' is the word I would use but, yes, I think I've got an idea or way to resolve this possible problem."

Jim Bilidou knew just how bad the problem was, and it could very well exceed the "mess" that Trey had thought about and said, but there was no sense in using words that might lead to panic 'cause if they started to panic, then the brain would start to shut down and only focus on the mess rather than looking at the bigger picture where the possible solution was.

"Alright, we are reasonably certain that someone, probably one of our terrorists, survived the explosion because he left early, and if we go by what Joseph saw, may very well have removed some IED's. Now, my guess is if he has heard about the explosion, he may very well think it may have been as a result of a possible gas leak. I'm thinking he has no clue we are onto them or in this case him. He may have gone out to place some of those IED's. The first thing we have to do is identify the remaining terrorist and that may—will—give us an idea where those bombs are placed. Because if it was one of our bomb makers, then we might be able to assume that he has set them to his specifications so he can be in the vicinity in order to set them off by remote control. If ... and I say IF ... it is one of the two bomb makers we identified in that particular cell, we know that bomb makers are very visceral. Their egos thrive and grow when they set them off in crowded areas for maximum destruction, maximum horror, maximum terror. But most importantly, they want to watch, to see, to smell, to hear, not only to set them off but to watch from close by, that is their 'Tell.' Do you understand when I say 'Tell'?" Bilidou said as he looked at Trey watching as Trey started to visibly relax, and his mind moved away from the panic that had started to grip it and turned instead to possible solutions.

Trey gave him a grim smile before adding, "Before this I always thought a 'Tell' was a gambling thing. Now I understand it can be used with other kinds of behavior. So there is a chance we can find the missing terrorist and whatever he was carrying?"

"Yes, I think so, but we have to be quick in case he stashed the IED's somewhere until he can set them. He probably has heard about the explosion but may very likely think it might be as a result of a gas leak. But he certainly doesn't know about us. I think he may have stashed the IED's somewhere until he can set them off. Today is Wednesday; in two days we have the Pacific Edge Fair starting, and as usual it will be packed with people. I'm thinking, and this is only an educated guess, I think ... maybe ... the fair is his target. I say that because it fits all the requirements, all the maximums come into play and satisfy his needs ... his thirst for slaughter on a grand scale," Jim said as he looked at Trey.

Trey returned his look before he said, "We've gotta get the ME's [Medical Examiner] office and get a look at the three bodies."

"Yes, I've got the photos and descriptions of the four in that cell. How badly damaged are the bodies?"

"I didn't see them myself, but I heard they were pretty bad."

"On the way over to the ME's office, I need you to call Campbell and Das-Groot and tell them to meet us over there ... in fact, notify the rest of the team that they are now on emergency standby," Jim Bilidou said as he pulled out a file and grabbed the keys to an unmarked car that was parked just outside the garage. They both strode to the car as Trey thought it was a good thing they were both wearing street clothes.

"When you get ahold of Campbell and Das-Groot, tell them to wear ratty old jeans and whatever."

"They are both off today," Trey returned.

"Good, tell them not to shave, especially Campbell."

Trey nodded as he started calling. The corners of his mouth turned up slightly in relief—*Jim has a plan*, he thought.

Trey had just finished making all the required calls as Jim pulled the unmarked into the parking lot for the ME's office and parked.

"Trey, head into the office and make sure the coroner hasn't started the autopsies yet. I have to make a few phone calls before I come in. Here, take the file with you."

Once Trey was gone, he made three calls—one to Rick the police chief, one to the defence minister and one to the general. He explained what had happened and the fact that three terrorists were dead by their own perfidious actions and that his team was on the trail of the fourth terrorist. His conversations with the minister and the general were brief and to the point with assurances that he would get back to them with further updates as they became available. His conversation with Rick was longer, with more detail, and he explained the plan that was being put in place as they spoke. Rick listened in silence until Jim was finished and then had asked several questions about the identification of the bomb makers. Jim had responded that they were going into the ME's office to make identifications right now. Rick indicated that he would make sure they had full cooperation from the ME's office and that he was going to add two more bomb squads to the one that would be on duty at the Pacific Edge Fair. Jim thanked him and assured him that he would be updated as soon as they knew.

He finished with the phone calls and was just stepping out of the car when Raphael pulled into the parking lot followed closely by Das-Groot. He waited for them and as they walked into the office, he filled them in on what was happening.

Trey was waiting for them in the outer office waiting room area with a puzzled look on his face.

"Hey, Trey, what's up?" Jim asked as he looked at Trey.

"Well, strangest thing. So I'm out here having what you might call a negative discussion with one of the ME's about us going into the morgue to ID the guys that got blown into the next life. The ME informs me that I don't have the right identification for that and she's not letting me in. And let me tell ya, the words are getting kinda heated when all of a sudden she gets a phone call and after she finishes the call, she comes back all nice as pie and invites me and you guys into the 'sanctum sanctorum' to view the bodies. I gotta tell ya though, her face is all flushed and she looks like she's chewing nails at having her power taken away."

Jim felt a slow grin starting to break out on his face, and he had to look away from the ME so she wouldn't see it as he thought, *Sometimes having the power on side does feel kinda good and having the P.C. on side is a definite plus.*

The four of them followed the ME down a long, steel-clad hallway. The further down they, went the cooler it got. There was a certain odour that in the outer office had barely been noticed, but back here it had gone from a minor tickle to a strong redolence ... a reminder that the dead lay near, too cold to decompose but balanced on the very edge as the coroner worked over them, trying to unlock the reason for their untimely demise.

The ME pushed open a door and the tempature dropped several more degrees as they looked around at the white-sheet covered corpses resting on their beds of steel in neatly ordered rows. Three of the steel trollies had been pulled out, each with their cargo covered in white sheets. There was a faint stench of burnt meat seemingly emanating from the three hidden under the sheets. The rest of the large room was hidden in semi-darkness while these three were positioned under a pow-erful surgeon's light, the white of the sheets reflecting under the light almost like they were waiting to take their final bow.

CHAPTER THIRTY-ONE

The ME who had led them to the morgue now rolled back the sheets so they could see what was left of the three who had been caught in the explosion of their own IED's. Suddenly, the smell of burnt meat strengthened, and although none of them made any comment or stepped back, they all felt the skin of their faces tighten around the nose area, and each began to breathe through their mouths while the bright light showed their faces had gone somewhat paler and if possible even harsher at the sight of what an explosive device could do to the human body.

"Let's get this done so we can get the fuck outta out of here. I swear I saw a sheet move on one of those corpses back there," Trey said in a stage whisper that caused them all to give him a tight-lipped smile as they stepped in to get a closer look.

The ME gave them a smirk and said, "Call me when you're finished so I can put them in line for the autopsies." With that she turned and left.

"Man, she's colder than this room," Trey said after she left.

Jim pulled out the photos of the four terrorists who were supposed to be in the residence at 1413 Victor Street, and they all studied them before they looked at what was left of the faces of the three corpses.

The three corpses had sustained massive damage— some had had limbs torn off by the force of the explosion. It looked like someone had done some very preliminary work of matching limbs to bodies. The bodies had sustained extensive burn damage as a result of being in such close proximity to the heat energy of the blast. The three had had most of their hair burned off. In fact, they looked like triplets that had been through some type of nuclear attack.

"Shit, they all look the same," Das-Groot muttered as he looked from the photos to the corpses' faces.

"Exactly, look for the scar ... the scar on the right cheek. They all kinda looked the same even before they managed to blow themselves up except Haqqanis—you know, Adnan Mir. He had that real thick, ropey scar on his right cheek. There should be some sign of the scar even after all the damage done by the explosion," Raphael said in an excited voice.

They all studied the right side of the burnt faces ... nothing ... no scar, just burnt, torn skin and bone.

"Ok, before we get real excited and real worried, let's get the coroner, the doctor, in here just to confirm the thing about the scar," Jim said as he continued to stare at the faces of the three dead terrorists.

"I saw his office on the way down here. I'll go back and see if he's there."

"Yeah, see if you can grab him, Wilmer."

Das-Groot strode out of the morgue and within a few minutes returned with the coroner.

Once they explained about the scar, with a detailed description of it and a very abbreviated version of why they needed to identify who was who, the coroner, double-gloved and went to work. First he felt the right cheek area of the corpses, and then he went back to one and felt it again.

"One way to be sure, if any of you are squeamish now would be the time to leave. I don't want anyone puking in my morgue."

None of them moved. The coroner shrugged and went to one of the steel shelving units and selected a towel-wrapped container, brought it over to the steel trolly, opened it, removed a scalpel and stepped to the right side of the one corpse, by the face.

As he bent over, he began to talk almost as if to himself, "As you can see on this badly damaged face, there is a swelling that is hard when I try to manipulate it ... this could be a large hematona ... bleeding under the skin, or possibly the remains of a scar. Just to make sure I will open it up." The entire time that he was talking, his fingers were working with the scalpel as he opened the section of the face only to have a slow oozing mass of partially dried blood escape the fresh incision.

"Well, there you have it. This individual clearly had no scar on that side of the face. If he had had a scar, the texture would be ropey all the way down to the bone and I would have felt it. So now it is confirmed that this or any of these other two are not your man ... dare I say happy hunting," the coroner said with a slight smile as he looked at the four police officers in front of him.

CHAPTER THIRTY-TWO

The four had left the ME's office in silence, each lost in their own thoughts. Once outside they had all slowed so they could take in large gulps of fresh air as each headed to their own vehicles.

"We'll meet you up at the garage," was all Jim Bilidou said to Raphael and Das-Groot before he and Trey climbed into their vehicle and left.

Trey pulled out of the parking lot and blended into the heavy afternoon traffic as he started the drive back to the office-garage while Bilidou made brief phone calls to the three people he had called prior to going into the office-morgue. As each had picked up the phone, he had identified himself and simply said, "Haqqanis Mir is in the wind."

"Trey, can you pull over and stop? I have one more call to make."

"Sure, Jim," Trey returned as he glanced over at Bilidou with a worried expression.

Trey pulled off the main road onto a treed side street and stopped, "You want some privacy? I can step out?"

"No, I'll explain as soon as I make this call," Jim said as he punched buttons on his cell phone.

Trey knew just from the number of buttons being pushed that it was an overseas call.

"Issac, the Master's in the wind ... send Master Catcher," Bilidou said into the cell phone, listened for a moment, then hung up. "Ok, let's get up to the garage."

Trey pulled back out onto the busy street and drove in silence for a few minutes. He felt the small hairs on the back of his neck stir as adrenalin started to trickle in and start working its way up his spine. He knew he was only one of the cogs in this mission. He also knew there were others high up within the government who were also involved. But having thought that, he also understood what Jim had said on the overseas call was a code phrase that released an operative from outside of Canada into their fray—their mission—and he wasn't entirely comfortable with that. As those thoughts flashed through his mind, he heard Jim clear his throat.

"Trey, I can sense your discomfort and I understand it. The call I just made was, as you probably guessed, an overseas call. It was to Interpol, who have an operative who has worked with Haqqanis before both in the Middle East, Syria to be specific, and the States. This operative has been 'turned' by Interpol and has given them a large amount of intelligence on how Haqqanis works and where he is likely to be." Jim, seeing the look of apprehension mixed with outrage on Trey's face, nodded his head before adding, "Yes, he has been in Canada with him ... I know ... I know what you are thinking ... how can we trust this asshole? Well, what I'm saying is we don't!

He's going to have a new buddy with him on this trip, and that's going to be Raphael, and Raphael is going to have very specific instructions about how to deal with him, with both of them, and of course Raphael is going to have backup ... lots of backup."

"Look, Jim, I understand, but shit! This is our first fuckin' gig, and Raphael is just out of police college! Man, oh man, this could go sideways so fuckin' quick."

"Don't you think I know that? But we've got less than two fuckin' days, forty some odd hours, to catch or terminate this so-called Master Bomb Maker and hopefully find his IED's. And if we accidently 'terminate with extreme prejudice' this so-called operative ... hey, shit happens! I don't think Interpol will be too unhappy 'cause they've squeezed him for all his info and now he's just a tool to make an intro for us. And don't ever think they and other intelligence agencies aren't watching to see how we do with what we've got. Hey! If ya got another plan, speak now, brother!"

There was a stone cold silence within the car.

Each man stared out at the cars flashing by. Each was wrapped in desperate thoughts, each in their own way slammed by the realization that they were at the edge of the big leagues now, and how the game was played in the next two days would either confirm that Canada was turning into a country capable of dealing with high-level terrorist threats, other major criminals and racketeering mobsters, or should be sent back down to the farm team to languish with the so-called Canadian Intelligence Agency.

CHAPTER THIRTY-THREE

The rest of the drive up to the garage was spent in a taciturn harshness as both driver and passenger were lost in calculation and rationalization of everything that could go right or terribly wrong with the scheme.

Just before they reached the garage, Trey pulled over and stopped, then turned and faced Jim and asked, "Why Raphael? We have plenty of others on the team who are far more experienced in this type of thing ... what is it about Raphael that makes you think he can carry this operation off?"

Bilidou stared at him for a moment, the lines of his face hard, his eyes flashing stone cold, and Trey felt a sudden chill as the thought flashed through his mind. *I wouldn't want to be the terrorist Jim was going to interrogate. He would be absolutely relentless in finding out the truth no matter the cost*, and he abruptly remembered Jim's credo when they were in Afghanistan together: "The end justifies the means." And then Jim spoke to him in a low, grating voice.

"There are many things you don't know about Raphael that I found out personally when I spoke to his father before we allowed him into the class. First off, he, his father and mother had to fight their way out of Kabul when the Taliban and al Qaeda took over. He was only eleven at the time, yet he carried and shot a gun in the retreat. Secondly, they ended up finding succour amongst the Falash Tribe in the high mountains of the Hindu Kush, and while there his parents allowed him to be schooled along with the Falash children. At a certain age, the warriors took over his schooling, and as a result, he became a warrior at twelve and was out actively hunting and killing the Taliban. Those experiences have stayed with him. I discreetly watched him throughout class, and not only is he one of the best shots but he has a certain quietness ... a calm within him when the shit hits the fan, that allows him to react quicker than anyone I have ever seen. Do you remember when Jacob challenged Lula's right to be in the class?" Trey nodded. "I saw Raphael and Lula whisper to each other before she fought with Jacob, and I believe that if Lula hadn't won but got injured, Raphael would have dealt with Jacob, and it would have been very nasty. Also, when he speaks Farsi or Urdu and some of the other dialects of the region, he is always idiomatically correct to the point where you can't tell the difference between him and another tribesman of the area. And finally, under all that veneer of polite society beats the heart of a Scot with the training of a tribesman of the Hindu Kush. He is a man who is not only highly intelligent but also has a savage heart. In other words, he will do what is required to win out, and I for one would not want to get in his way when he has a goal, be it to protect, or conversely, destroy that which threatens those he holds dear, be they persons or his ideals. There is an added plus in that he bears a remarkable resemblance to the Afghani, with those grey eyes, dark, curly hair and fair skin. So, yes, Raphael is the man for this job."

Jim's words had forced Trey to think back to the class and the look in Raphael's eyes when they had intimated that he and Lula had done something dishonourable. And then his thoughts harkened back to other instances when Raphael had stood out, not intentionally, but just because of how he had reacted to certain situations and how his solutions had always been right, if unique, in the end. He nodded his head in understanding and gave Jim a grim little smile.

"Now that you mention it, I can see your point." Trey turned and gripped the steering wheel and completed the drive to the garage.

CHAPTER THIRTY-FOUR

They arrived back at the garage within a matter of min-utes and could see both Das-Groot's and Raphael's civilian vehicles parked out front. Trey drove the unmarked he had been using around back and stopped while Jim got out, went to and entered the code in the automatic lock for the rear gate. The gate slid open and Trey drove the vehicle in, backed into a parking stall by the large garage door and parked. Jim had punched in the code to open the garage door and it slid up, revealing the large, black van they had used the other night. Now parked next to it was a medium blue sub-compact car with touches of rust around some of the wheel wells; it had out-of-province plates on it. Jim walked around the car and looked inside and smiled thinly as he thought, *Rick has outdone himself in finding a vehicle that was so unremarkable that it was remarkable.* He looked up and saw Raphael and Das-Groot standing in the door of the office watching him. He waved them back into the office as Trey stepped through the garage door as it began to close.

"Hey, we got another vehicle? Kinda a beater, eh?"

"Yes, but as with all things, sometimes how things look on the outside hide the jewel that exists beneath," Jim returned as he leaned into the car, reached down and popped the hood.

Trey lifted the hood up and gasped. "Holy shit! A tricked out police special!" he said as he gazed at the engine. He took a closer look at the tires and whistled in awe, "Man, those wheels are high-preformance ones that cost a grand or so each." He looked up at a smiling Jim with new respect.

"All I ask is, can I drive this beast just once before it goes back, and I swear I'll die a happy man."

"Trey, you're too easy to please ... all car whores are."

Trey just shrugged and grinned before saying, "I is what I is."

"'Kay, time to go have our meeting with the other two. We've got maybe seven hours before the plane comes in from Europe."

Trey's smile dropped off like it had been pasted on with cheap glue.

CHAPTER THIRTY-FIVE

They walked into the office from the garage and saw that Raphael and Wilmer Das-Groot were sitting on some rickety folding chairs by the glazed window. Trey took a seat on the old wooden chair while Jim took the chair by the desk and pull out a file from one of the drawers. Bilidou saw Raphael pull out his notebook.

"Constable Campbell, or rather Raphael, you won't be using a notebook. I want you to listen and absorb everything I'm about to say here. Wilmer, take notes as you think advisable. You are going to be Raphael's main backup. First off, did either of you see who brought the car in?"

They both shook their heads before Wilmer added in a dry, slightly acerbic voice, "Funny thing though, I did see our glorious leader, the police chief. He was a passenger in a car being driven by one of the guys from his escort team, just down the road from here. Kinda odd really, and I had ta wonder what he was doing out here?"

"Don't wonder, don't think. I'm sure it was just an illusion. I know everybody has been tired what with everything that has been going on," Bilidou said pointedly as he looked directly at Das-Groot, and Das-Groot simply shrugged his understanding.

"What I'm about to tell you goes no further than this room. Other members of the team will be getting other directions, but essentially Raphael is the key of this operation and, at the risk of sounding overly dramatic, this is definitely a Black-Ops, meaning if you have to terminate a bad guy, you do it, and we will figure out an explanation for it later. There may be thousands of lives at stake.

Those dark words were the introduction to the scheme … the plan that Jim Bilidou had hammered together. An operative, probably a reluctant one, that was being brought in from overseas, the equipment and most importantly Raphael's role right in the middle of it that, hinged on his ability, his believability, with both the operative and Haqqanis. Could he do it?

Raphael felt his stomach twist and turn as he listened. He felt a surge of adrenalin climbing up his spine, sending out crackles of electricity as it surged up towards his brain where the excitement could cloud his thoughts. As he sat there, he began to think of Tirich Mir, topped with the diamond sparkle of snows that never melted, the highest peak looming above the rest of the mountain range at the top of the Hindu Kush. He sent his thoughts there and let them cool upon the very tip of Tirich Mir as he searched for the inner stillness. He felt it on the top of the peak and drew it deep within himself. The calm, the serenity was within him, and he felt renewed … refreshed. He heard Sergeant Bilidou's words with a pinpoint clarity, and he looked up and met his gaze.

Bilidou eyes widened as he looked into those steady, quick-silver-coloured eyes, eyes that seemed to hold an ancient understanding, and was unexpectedly reassured.

CHAPTER THIRTY-SIX

The next few hours roared by with what Raphael thought of as mixed anticipation given that they were after a bomb maker who planned to create chaos and destruction in their city.

Bilidou, who appeared to have thought of everything, had provided him with a dirty, overlarge hoodie and an unbleached, long-sleeved cotton shirt with no collar that buttoned to the neck. It reminded him of the shirts that some Afghani males wore. He was also given a dark baseball cap and advised to pull it down as far as possible so the bill of the cap shaded the upper part of his face. Raphael wore a pair of old, worn jeans and old sneakers that completed the exterior image. What could not be seen was a glock semi-automatic handgun with suppressor [silencer] actually built into the barrel. Raphael had taken a few minutes to admire the deadly weapon; the regular glocks that he had dealt with had a silencer that you had to attach and were awkward to handle, and the detachable silencer reduced their accuracy by several feet. This new one was light, easy to handle and, according to Bilidou, had excellent accuracy. But as Bilidou had warned him, like all handguns it was only good for close-in work of up to nine feet. It tucked nicely into the small canvas holster hooked onto the top inside of his jeans at the small of the back where someone doing a quick, cursory search would never find it.

There was one more piece of equipment that Raphael had never seen before, and it was so tiny that when Bilidou had shown it to him, he had been afraid to pick it up. It was an earpiece that was not only a receiver but a transmitter as well. It was just past the experimental phase and eliminated the necessity of wearing a wire, which was dangerous especially if a thorough search was done and the wire was found taped to the undercover's body. This tiny device could actually not only transmit but also receive. In other words the undercover's conversations with bad guys could be heard by "control," and his or her "controller" could transmit or give the undercover operative information and warnings. Not only that, it was also a GPS—a homing device so the surveillance team following him could stay back and not be "heat-burned" by the bad guys he was with, even if the bad guys did "heat-checks." They actually had to have the Ident member, with the aid of the physician who had developed the device, come in and, with small forceps, delicately and precisely place it deep within his right ear. Once in his ear, he had been shown how to turn it off and on with a certain twist of the cartilage of the ear. The first time his "controller," Bilidou, had tried to transmit or speak to him, he had nearly blown Raphael's eardrum out. A slight whisper seemed to work best. At first the device in his ear had been uncomfortable, but he had soon gotten use to it.

Bilidou had gone into great detail about the individual being brought over from Europe, the intro he was expected to do between Raphael and Haqqanis and Raphael's undercover background as a disaffected refugee who felt his family were becoming unbelievers, doubters turning away from the old ways. Bilidou had advised him the name he would be using was Musa Mullah, and for the next couple of hours that's what they would be calling him, so he could get used to the name. Raphael had listened with an intensity, knowing his life and the operation depended on him absorbing all the intel on this character he was about to become ... *Enter stage right*, he thought sardonically. He also wondered about the so-called operative that an Interpol agent was bringing over. Bilidou had described him as a friend of Haqqanis who, unknown to Haqqanis, had "rolled or been turned" by Interpol and had been squeezed 'til he had spewed out all sorts of information. Raphael guessed from Bilidou's words and tone that this operative, by the name of Zarak Afridi, was, in a "worse case scenario," expendable, and Raphael suspected the only reason Afridi was still breathing was because he could make the intro to an even bigger, more vicious terrorist. Raphael understood and accepted that particular cold-blooded suspicion in the name of expediency, namely because he had, in his life, seen what had happened when someone had hesitated to act, and the results had been disasterous.

"Musa, I'm sorry this got dumped on you so suddenly. It would have been lovely if we had had weeks, months, to set this up. It just wasn't in the cards. It's going down within a matter of less than forty-eight hours, so we are flying by the seat of our pants," Jim Bilidou said with a regretful shrug.

Raphael looked up at Jim Bilidou and laughed before saying, "You know the funny thing is my mother has always said that my father and I seem to share the same temperament when it comes to crazy, dangerous ideas. She calls it our 'damn the torpedoes, full speed ahead, swashbuckler attitude.' But she has always added it has been that very frame of mind that has pulled us out of some very tight, precarious positions. So, quite frankly, as far as I can see, this is an excellent plan given the time you've had to pull it together. Let's get to it.

They had been in the garage for hours while Bilidou filled Raphael in and made numerous phone calls to set up the rest of the team and their positions within the next day. Even Trey and Das-Groot had left to meet up with the team.

Jim Bilidou had looked around as he heard Raphael's words, and he had felt a sudden loosening in his shoulders and the harshness had left his face as he realized he had done everything he could. He returned Musa né Raphael's grin as he said, "You're right! Damn the torpedoes! Full speed ahead!"

CHAPTER THIRTY-SEVEN

Bilidou had the keys for the new unmarked. He and Raphael locked up and left the garage. They stopped briefly at a drive-through, grabbed burgers and shakes, devouring them while the burgers were still hot. Neither realized how hungry they were. Bilidou looked at his watch.

"Jeez, we've got a few minutes before we have to be up at the airport. Let's take this beast out on the freeway and see what it can do."

Raphael merely grinned as Bilidou took the roundabout that sent them on their way out onto the freeway, and he opened it up. They could feel the power surging beneath them as Bilidou pressed on the gas pedal, and soon they were blowing past the other vehicles. Raphael reached down and turned on a rock 'n' roll station on the radio. For a few short minutes they both felt the years roll away, and they were riding with a buddy in a muscle car as more pressure was put on the gas pedal. Of a sudden there were blue and red lights behind them and both heard the siren.

"Fuck! And that is exactly what happened the last time I was in a car like this! I'll tin 'em. You say nothing, Musa ... it's a good thing ya know how to turn that earpiece down."

Raphael simply nodded as Bilidou pulled to the side of the freeway and showed his badge to the traffic cop, and the traffic cop reluctantly let them go with a warning to slow down.

"Oh, if only he knew. Say, that reminds me. You got your badge on you?"

Raphael nodded and handed over his badge.

"Time to get out to the airport. You ready?"

Bilidou glaced over and saw the hooded head nod. The rest of the way was driven in a kind of quiet introspection as each thought of what lay before them.

They pulled into the airport parking lot and spotted Trey sitting in the other unmarked.

Bilidou got out of the car, and as Raphael stepped out of the car, he threw him the keys. They walked into the international arrival area. They both knew Trey was a short distance away, making his way into the same area.

Inside they checked the large overhead screens and saw that the flight they were expecting had just arrived and knew they had a bit of a wait as those on the flight still had to go through customs. Bilidou had notified his contact in Airport Police about the two they were waiting for were Interpol and just to let them go smoothly through customs as neither had luggage.

Within fifteen minutes Bilidou saw the two he was waiting for and simply nodded at the well-dressed man escorting the other coming through the doors from customs. The other male dressed in typical Afghani wear, including the baggie cotton pants and a vest over a shirt similar to the one Raphael was wearing.

The well-dressed man came up to Bilidou and briefly shook his hand as he asked, "Jim Bilidou from college?" with a slight French accent.

"Yes, indeed. And I see you brought a friend?" Bilidou responded.

The man merely nodded.

"Let's go out to the car."

Raphael had gotten a fairly good look at the Afghani male, the one called Zarak Afridi, as they walked out of the customs. He had spotted the Frenchman immediately and discounted him as Bilidou's problem. His interest was the other, and he studied him from beneath the bill of his baseball cap. He could see he was short, shorter even than the Frenchman, and even under his baggy clothes, he was thin, too thin. When he looked up and towards where they were standing, Raphael could see the dark bruise-like circles under his eyes, and those eyes shifted here and there quickly like he was looking for something or someone ... rescue or escape. He didn't know but he felt immediately wary, instinctively knowing this was a man not to be trusted. The rest of the face was a skeleton with skin stretched over it, aged well beyond its purported years. His hair was ragged curls with some falling over his forehead. He was unshaven but Raphael suspected any attempt to grow a beard, even in good times, would meet with little success as the skin on his face seemed incapable of supporting much more than a few scraggly hairs here and there. He saw that Zarak Afridi was attempting to size him as well, and he was glad that the clothes he was wearing prevented Afridi from forming any accurate idea of what he looked like aside from the fact that he was tall. He wondered how this small rat-like creature had ever become friends with Haqqanis. When he had read Haqqanis' profile, the man had been touted not only as a master bomb maker but also as a leader of men and highly educated. His photos had shown a tall, slender man with the burning, fervent eyes of a fanatic. He gave a mental shrug as he thought perhaps, like certain other occupations, terrorists made strange, unlikely friendships.

Raphael could see Trey off to the side standing by the luggage carousel as if he was waiting for someone.

Bilidou had ushered them out of the airport and over to Trey's vehicle. There was a moment of uncomfortable silence before Bilidou cleared his throat and then looked towards the Frenchman and made a short introduction.

"This is Musa, your man Zarak Afridi will be with him. You and I can talk in the car."

Raphael, with a final look at Bilidou, signalled to Afridi to follow him and walked to where the blue sub-compact was parked. He unlocked the passenger door and indicated that Afridi get in while he walked around to the driver's side and climbed in. Out of the corner of his eye, he saw Bilidou, Trey and the Frenchman drive by. He was on his own now. He was no longer Raphael. He was Musa Mullah.

CHAPTER THIRTY-EIGHT

Musa got in the driver's side of the car as Afridi climbed in the passenger side. Afridi's eyes were wide as he stared around the interior of the car. One hand tentatively reached out and touched the dashboard.

Almost as if he had never been inside a car before, Musa thought, as he said in the Urdu vernacular, "Thou must do up thy seatbelt."

Zarak Afridi jerked at the sound of Musa's voice, almost like he was about to be struck, and then hesitantly looked at Musa as he searched for a belt.

With a sigh, Musa reached across Afridi and grabbed the belt above Afridi's head, pulled it across his body and clicked the end in so Afridi was belted in. As he had leaned across him, he could smell the fetid stench of almost primordial fear emanating from the scrawny form. For a moment he felt a flash of what ... sympathy ... pity? Then it was gone as quickly as it came.

He pulled out of the parking lot and got onto the freeway. As he was driving, he sensed Afridi trying to get a look at his face, but he remained silent and focused on his driving. The last thing he needed was to get stopped by the police now. He had a specific place in mind where he could pull off, park and then talk to this emaciated little creature.

For his part the man, who Raphael had thought of as a creature, was looking around watching cars flashing by, the freedom of feeling the car moving, knowing he was outside even though it was night. He had been in a dark, dank, stagnant room for what had seemed like an eternity, his only company were those who came in to talk to him every once

in a while about who and what he knew. Only that was not
entirely true. He had had his own memories for company,
but gradually those had died off just as they had in real
life and madness had gained hold of his mind. Before he
had been captured, he had lived a lifetime amongst family
and friends, loved and loving until the Russians had come.
That had been when the killing had started, and he like
many others in Afghanistan had joined the Moudjahidine.
He had left the learning of the university to take up the
learning of bomb making, shooting, killing. At first revenge
had tasted so sweet, and in the end the Russians had fled
the country that only the true born could love. Then had
come the terrorists. First al Qaeda, then even more poison-
ous, the Taliban. Both groups of terrorists, after attacks on
other countries, had used Afghanistan as their base. The
soldiers of the countries attacked were like a nest of wasps
stirred up, and they had fallen upon Afghanistan hunting
for those who had caused those heinous attacks. Soon there
nothing left but the camaraderie of other terrorists who
had banded together to free Afghanistan of the interlopers.
He had known Adnan Mir since university, best friends.
Adnan was tall and serious while he short, the jokester of
the crowd. Both had lost many of their family, but it was
when he lost his beloved, she of light and laughter, all his
happiness had expired with her, drowned in sorrow. Both
he and Adnan had been caught up in the so-called jihad,
and once involved it had been impossible to pull away from
the dark maelstrom. They had travelled much together he
and Adnan, or rather Haqqanis, as he perferred to be called
after the famous liberator. They had been to Canada, the
States and Europe, and both had been bitter over what they
had seen. All those complacent countries that sent their
soldiers to make war on Afghanistan and yet none of their

countries suffered the agonies of war, that is 'til the terrorists brought the war to them. At first he had felt a certain joy in giving those countries a taste of what he and others had endured, but soon those feelings had paled and he simpy went through the motions. He and Adnan had been separated and worked in different cells in different countries and had lost contact with one another, had not seen each other in a year ... two years?

Then had come that distant night when he had been walking back to his lodgings in a French town. He had been swooped up by French intelligence agents, and so his long darkness had started, to be left alone in the inky-coloured murk with nothing ... no light, no sound, not even the voice of an inquisitor ... nothing. Time slipped away and was lost, memories reviewed until they faded became tattered, fragile, confused and had finally been lost, sucked into the vortex of nothingness. Then there was nought but madness in the constant midnight of that space where he only existed, deprived of even his senses. He threw open his arms to insanity and welcomed it in. Then and only then when he was very nearly a gibbering idiot did they come, and he was so grateful in his lunacy that he told them everything just to hold them there, other human beings, when he thought he had lost all.

Sensory deprivation had been a cruel but effective tool, and in the end, all his knowledge had been extracted. It had been easy to control him by simply allowing him the use of his simplest senses and should he show signs of balking at what they wanted, they would simply take him back towards the door, behind which lay nothingness and insanity. Instantly, he would begin to struggle and in absolute fear beseech them to ask him anything and he would answer.

When it had been explained to him, this last thing they needed him to do, he had agreed with alacrity. Of course he would introduce his friend Adnan to a friend of theirs; it would be his honour. Such eagerness, and they had studied him with steely gazes ... wondering.

The plane ride had almost been sensory overload for him ... so much noise ... colour ... people. He had finally had to lay back in his chair and, with the permission of the Frenchman, one of them who was travelling with him, closed his eyes. What his tormentors had not realized was the Afghani were a race hardened by centuries of invasions, murders, genocide and breeding, and although Zarak Afridi was a man defeated and balancing precariously on the very edge of total lunacy, there was a tiny, hard seed of survival, of honour, within him. That seed, which retained and held the core of the man, was showing signs of a secret blossoming.

CHAPTER THIRTY-NINE

Musa pulled into the park where he had first gone with Das-Groot just weeks before, although with everything that had happened since, it seemed like decades ago. He had been rolling around in his mind how he would start the all-important first conversation with Afridi. He could almost feel the pounding heart of the fearful little creature beside him. Of a sudden it struck him ... Gollum! From *The Lord of the Rings* by J.R.R. Tolkein! Of course! That was it! The wretched little being who tried to kill or betray Frodo Baggins, the hobbit, at every turn during their long quest.

Raphael wondered to himself what Zarak Afridi's "Precious" was? He almost smiled to himself at that odd, wayward thought 'til he remember a saying ... your first gut instinct is, in almost all cases, right ... and his senses, his gut instinct were vibrating with forewarning.

He turned into the empty parking lot and stopped. At night the green grass of the park took on shades of light grey that darken to inky black shadows cast by shrubs and trees in the moonlight. He looked around checking to make sure there were no pedestrians in the area ... nothing ... nobody.

He partially turned towards Afridi, so his voice was not muffled, although his face was still hidden in the shadows created by the baseball cap and hoodie. He had felt that the less Afridi saw of his face the better, the safer. Also, not being able to see his face created a certain ominous aspect to it.

"Do you prefer to talk in Urdu, Pashto, or Farsi?"

"Either ... any," Afridi said nervously as he tried to look into the shadows that hid Musa's face.

"Dost thou understand what is required of you?" Musa said in the venacular of Pashto.

"What is your name?" Afridi asked.

"Musa, although that is unimportant. What is important is that thou understand." Musa heard a whisper from his earpiece and added before Afridi could respond, "Thou knows what lies behind the door?"

Zarak Afridi's reaction to the last statement was startling. He gasped, his eyes widened in terror, he jerked and his back, slammed into the interior side of the passenger door. His hands went up in a beseeching manner. "Please, please, hizhoner not behind the door. I beg you! I understand the request!" Afridi almost hissed as his throat seemed to be squeezing closed.

Raphael was grateful that his face was in the shadows so Afridi could not see the shocked dismay written there. He let Afridi calm down for a few minutes while he contemplated what he had seen since he had been with Afridi. If Zarak Afridi acted like this in front of Haqqanis, Haqqanis would know something was amiss, which could be far worse for then the only option would be to kill both Haqqanis and Afridi then try to find the IED's before they exploded! It was an end-game option where many things could go wrong, number one being if the meeting was in a crowded area, there was the potential for collateral damage amongst innocent bystanders if there was a shootout, and secondly, a bystander being taken hostage. In the ensuing mayhem, he could lose both amongst a panicked crowd.

He felt himself stiffening up with worry as he thought of what could happen if he, or more likely Afridi, made a mistake while dealing with Haqqanis. Think of a solution, he reasoned to himself, not what could go wrong. In his mind he could feel the cool breeze off the Tirich Mir and his inner eye saw the glistening peak, and he felt a calmness that washed away the the stiffness. And then the idea came to him—he was taking a chance, and he hoped that those who were listening would understand his idea.

CHAPTER FORTY

"Dost thou know what is expected?" Raphael asked in Urdu from the shadows of the hoodie and baseball cap, although he had let the hoodie slip back a bit so some of his unshaven chin could be seen.

"Yes ... to introduce thee to Adnan or Haqqanis, as he is known now. Are thee from the hills brother?" Zarak Afridi returned in Pashto.

It's now or never. I have to let myself become totally Musa, Raphael thought as he answered in Urdu, "Yes, in the shadow of Tirich Mir." Musa let his voice soften with longing. "But that matters not. I simply need to know if thou can do what is expected of you? Then I'm expected to say something about a door to you, but I grow tired of the games they play here," Musa added in a low voice tinged with frustration.

Musa felt Afridi trying to get a better look at his face as he replied, "Nay, nay, brother. I can take you to a place he will be at. It is a place he goes to when he works alone. Why dost thou hide thy face beneath that hood and cap?" Afridi asked.

"Because the signal for trouble is me pulling back the hood," Musa returned with a shrug.

"Then what would happen?" Afridi asked.

"I lose my job and you get dragged back behind some door," Musa answered in a soft voice. He could hear a whisper within the earpiece deep within his ear ... one word.

"Understood."

"Ah, so that is how they play this game,"Afridi said in a voice that had lost some of its fear and there was just a slight touch of anger in it.

"So it has always seemed to me," Musa said as he thought to himself, *So much for the broken creature that Interpol brought over here.*

"Would thou be interested in going back to the hills and mountains you so long for?" Afridi asked in a whisper which seemed full of promise.

"Yes, without a doubt, but neither you nor I will ever gaze upon them again, I think."

"Ah, but there is a certain phrase that I can whisper to Adnan. He has always had a plan should either of us be captured to get us away and back to where we belong."

"But he didn't help thou escape from them this last time you were captured," Mursa pointed out.

"Because he didn't know. He was in a different part of the world when I was captured. Nobody knew, or assuredly I would have been rescued," Afridi said with confidence.

Musa looked at him and wondered at his confidence.

"But they hunt him and the 'things' he makes. How can we get away ... any of us?" Musa asked, letting a note of despair enter his voice.

"We help him with the 'things' he makes, and in the distraction when they explode we disappear. We've done it before," Afridi said with a grin and Musa felt a chill go through him at the casual way Zarak Afridi spoke about explosions and death.

Somehow those listening felt his anger, or perhaps it was a kind of rapport or empathy that had developed between him and those listening in on the other end of the "receiver/transmitter," but he heard the whisper in his ear to hold onto his anger; he was doing great as Musa and they were with him.

"Come, let us go. I am looking forward to seeing Adnan again and introducing him to you, the lone wolf we will bring into our pack," Afridi said with a cackling laugh.

CHAPTER FORTY-ONE

"Sweet Jaysus H. Christ, thank gawd the kid is quick on the pickup or the plan would've been fuckin' blown as high as an explosion of an IED. I thought you guys in Interpol had broken Zarak Afridi ... what the fuck happened!?" Jim Bilidou asked in a harsh tone as he looked towards the Frenchman. They were sitting in the back of a dark blue van with the windows darkened so no one could see in, and the van had magnetic signs on either side that said "City Gas. Troubleshooting. You Gotta Leak, We Plug It Fast!" in brilliant yellow.

The Frenchman studied Bilidou for a moment before he answered with a Gallic shrug and said in a heavily accented English, "Trust me, mon ami, Afridi is broken. That he has gained some confidence is only because he thinks Musa trusts him. But there will come a time, probably when the stress becomes too great for him, the cracks will begin to show, and then he will snap and perhaps betray everyone. You must listen very carefully to what he says and does so you can maybe warn Musa in time."

Bilidou studied the Frenchman for a brief time, wondering if they were being led down a murky path from which there was no return.

The Frenchman gave him a thin smile before he added, "Trust me, James ... uh ... Jim. We want to see you succeed with this noble experiment. We understand that Zarak Afridi will probably not survive, but that may be to the greater good. And from what I have seen of your team, I'm very, how you say ... ah ... it is très bon, très bon, especially young Musa. If there ever comes a time when he might want to broaden his ... ah ... experience as a policia or agent, we would welcome him at Interpol."

"I will pass that on to 'Musa' and I thank you for the compliment. I suspect though Musa is rather involved with what is and will be going on for the next little while," Bilidou said in a low voice as they both listened in on the receiver. Any conversations in the car driven by Musa were being sent through the transmitter to the van and recorded. Trey Carstairs was driving, Das-Groot rode shotgun while Bilidou and the Frenchman sat in the back of the van, and they could all hear Afridi talking, almost babbling to Musa in Pashto and occasionally Urdu. Every once in a while Musa would ask a brief question, but for the most part, Musa let Afridi talk, with only grunts to indicate his interest.

"Holy shit! You do speak Urdu or Pashto, right," Bilidou asked the Frenchman, who merely shook his head.

"I don't know just how much information ya got outta this guy, but he's really spilling the beans to Musa about planned terrorist attacks, who is invoved, what is being used and even gas attacks that are, were, in the planning stage and where the toxic gasses were stored. You guys got all that did you?

"The Frenchman had suddenly paled before reaching in and grabbing his cell phone from his coat and making a phone call. Whoever he called answered, and the French-man spoke quickly, quietly and urgently into the phone, and then hung up.

"You are making recordings of everything Afridi says?" Bilidou nodded.

"May we have copies? It would seem that our interpreter may not be as good as we thought."

"We will be delighted to hand over everything we get on these guys," Bilidou said before adding, "Didn't ... Don't you have your own people, talking with and interpreting for you?"

"Ah, sometimes, but sometimes not and that may be a problem, n'est pas?"

"Yes, it could be a problem. All our team is fluent in Pashto, Farsi, Urdu and many other languages and dialects. Any time you need some help, all you need to do is call."

Bilidou and Carstairs continued to listen in on the conversation as they drove in the general direction. Das-Groot was monitoring the surveillance teams as they switched off with each other in different cars so they weren't "burned" by Musa or Afridi.

"Holy shit, Pat, you're gettin' too close! Back off before they spot you!"

"Fuck! I think we're being followed!" Musa muttered to Afridi.

Afridi stopped talking and started monitoring the sideview mirror, and after only a few moments of watching said in a tense voice, "You are right, brother! Can we lose them? If we cannot, I daren't take you to the place I spoke of!"

"Yes! Yes, hold on while I lose those cursed corpse flies!" With that Musa made several quick turns and then slipped into an alley and parked behind a large garbage bin, turned off the lights and slouched down in the driver's seat as Afridi did the same. They watched as the car that had been following them drive slowly up the cross street like it was looking for them.

Afridi looked towards the shadowed face with admiration. "Very good, my friend. You have confounded them for now."

"Yes, for now, but they will be looking for us, and now I have stepped into the enemy camp and I fear my next meeting with them will be very unpleasant and possibly painful while you will probably be killed in a very ugly way," Musa muttered.

"So what should we do?"

"I say you should tell me where we are to meet with this Adnan. If I know of the meeting place, I can go a certain way, and they will never know," Musa murmured as he looked to Afridi, wondering if he would take the "leap of faith."

Those listening in the van gasped at the audacity of Musa's plan.

There was a tense hush in both vehicles ... like dangling by one hand over the edge of a precipice, and to take a breath would surely cause a slip.

CHAPTER FORTY-TWO

Zarak Afridi stared at the shadowed, shrouded face. His eyes narrowed, and suddenly Musa saw not the pitiful creature he had become but the intelligent, calculating terrorist he had been, and perhaps underneath all the pain and torment still was, and he thought, *Have I pushed him too far ... too fast?*

"What you say is perhaps the truth. You are asking for my trust and yet you have not given me yours," Afridi reflected.

Musa heard the words and knew what Afridi meant, and yet he had to play the game, to be obtuse because beside him was not the little creature that he had picked up at the airport but one who was starting to salvage what had been lost.

"But I have lost them! Those that followed, I warned you and then I lost them! I have committed myself to serve your interests so I may go back to the hills where I belong!" Musa said in the voice of a young, trusting boy.

"There is one more thing I need in order to trust you."

"But you know that they said if I took off the hoodie, they would know I was in trouble and attack," Musa returned.

"They are not here. We are hidden away here. Once we start driving again, the hoodie will be back in place. I must see your face. What is it you hide? Trust must go both ways, brother."

With a sigh and a shrug, Musa lifted his hand and grabbed the edge of the hood and pulled it back enough to reveal his face, and looked towards Afridi.

Afridi smiled a little before he said, "See that was not so bad. You have a good face and definitely one from the hills with those grey eyes and so young for this type of work. Why, your beard is barely there. Thou must wait a few years for it to fill in." Afridi chuckled as he had said it, and Musa dropped his head as if in embarrassment. "Now, now pull your hood back on and we will go all these back roads thou knows so well. We go to a small café that is hidden back in amongst some old apartments down by the docks along View Road by Pacific Highway, although there is no view, at least not anymore, and the highway is long gone and covered over.

There had been a collective sigh of relief by those listening in the van.

"That boy has got fuckin' stones of steel! That was close ... almost too close!" Trey gasped.

"That's our man! I know the place! He has just given us the time to get everybody set up in the area and nobody had better get burned. Wilmer, you know the place, don't you?" Bilidou asked, and Das-Groot simply nodded as he was already on the phone calling other team members and telling them where to set up.

"Shit, we only got one problem."

"What's that, Jim?" Trey asked.

"We can't send anyone into that little café to cover Musa 'cause we've got no one that can blend in there. Musa is on his own, inside with two terrorists we know and how many unknowns."

CHAPTER FORTY-THREE

Because of the address that Musa had gotten for them, Bilidou and Das-Groot had managed to get team members into the area quickly. They had even had time to set up a member of the team with camera equipment, including a zoom lens, as well as a sniper rifle with scope, in a vacant building directly across from the entrance of the café in order to get photos of those entering and leaving the café. The sniper rifle was in case the-kak-hit-the-fan, and they had to shoot bullets instead of photos. It was the closest thing to backup they had for Musa.

A whisper in his right ear had informed Musa when the area was covered and he could move in for the meet.

Musa had listened to Afridi talk about Afghanistan, the jihad, setting IED's in both his own country and other countries and his friendship with Adnan né Haqqanis, all jumbled together. He thought of a phrase he had read or heard somewhere, "the ravings of a madman," as he drove down side streets, through alleys and even parked behind a few other garbage bins with the headlights off, all in a very dramatic fashion that seemed to convince Afridi he was dodging surveillance by the police and other agents. As he drove, he waited for the sign ... the whisper that all was clear so he could head to the café for the intro.

When he had finally heard the whisper he was waiting for, he drove in a zigzag fashion to the meet, all the while thinking on what he could say to Haqqanis to persuade him that he was the disgruntled youth that wished to join the jihad. He knew it would be far more difficult to convince him than it had been to convince the crazed Afridi.

He had carefully driven past the café with Afridi almost jumping up and down on the passenger seat like a small child and had found a dark alcove to park the car halfway up the block. They had gotten out of the car, he had locked it and they slowly made their way back to the single splotch of light in the sea of dark, battered old warehouses. Musa could feel eyes upon him in the dark, and he wasn't sure if all of them were friendly, while Afridi continued to babble excitedly. He had finally turned to Afridi and told him to hush so he could make sure no one was following them.

Those words had had an almost magical effect on Afridi and he had shut up although he had grabbed Musa by the sleeve of his hoodie and tried to pull him forward. Musa had jerked his arm free, so at least if he had to go for his gun, he wouldn't be impeded by Afridi clinging to him.

Then they were at the door of the café and Afridi reached down, grabbed the handle and swung the door open before he could stop him. It would have been better if they had made a more circumspect entrance so at least Musa could see who was in the café and where they were positioned, but Afridi had burst through the door, and then with quick steps was working his way to the back of the brightly lit but smokey place. He greeted this and that sitting figure as he continued his headlong rush towards the back where Musa could barely make out someone sitting alone at a small table, smoking. The clouds of smoke partially hid his face although Afridi seemed to know him, and his thin face was lit by a grin.

"Adnan! Is it you, my old friend? How I have missed you!" Afridi said in a loud voice as he moved rapidly towards the sitting figure.

Suddenly there was movement. Two who had been sitting at a table midway through the room, leaped to their feet and grabbed Musa by the arms, effectively pinning his arms to his body while one had produced a wicked-looking knife and was now holding it to his throat. Nothing had been said, but Musa knew he was mere seconds from death. While Afridi, oblivious to what was happening behind him, kept rushing forward, only to be stopped when the figure he had be rushing to had, in one graceful motion, stood up, taken two steps forward and had driven Afridi back and down with one thrust of his hand. He produced a small handgun with the other and was now pointing it at Afridi's head as he lay upon the floor stunned.

For an instant it was a scene frozen in the seconds of time. Nothing was said, no one moved. Only clouds of cigarette smoke swirled and curled about the still figures.

CHAPTER FORTY-FOUR

"What the hell ...?!" Bilidou muttered before he spoke into his portable radio.

"Barry, you have the eye. What the fuck is going on inside the café? We heard a couple of thumps and now nothing."

"Don't know, Jim. I saw a sudden flash of movement then nothing except hookah and cigarette smoke plus the windows also seem to be steamed up, even with the 'scope, I can't penetrate it. Can't you hear anything?"

"Naw, that's the trouble. It sounded like someone falling and then nothing, like the fuckin' silence of a tomb," Bilidou returned.

"Shit, I hope not!" Barry added.

"What?"

"Like a tomb ...! Want me to get in closer? Might be able to see more," Barry asked.

"Just an expression, Barry. We give it a few minutes, then we move," Bilidou said into the portable, his voice harsh with worry.

CHAPTER FORTY-FIVE

Of a sudden, over the receiver, those in the van heard a voice scream out in Pashto, "NNOO!!" They recognized the voice. It was Zarak Afridi and adrenalin mixed with the tension already rushing through the men in the van created a high-test mixture of fuel as they readied to rush the café in case that was the dying word of Afridi. Then they heard another voice, a tense, low voice, and they relaxed sightly.

"Adnan, do you not recognize your old friend Zarak Afridi?" Musa urged, in a low voice, as he kept absolutely still because of the blade pressed against his throat. In fact, the pressure of the knife blade had cut into his neck just enough for him to feel his own warm blood trickling down beneath where the blade was held.

Musa heard a whisper from his earpiece say, "Give the word and we'll rush the place," but he knew if they rushed it now, he would be dead before they hit the door. He had to talk himself and Afridi out of this mess.

"Adnan, Zarak was so excited to see you that he forgot all his training and rushed in just to see you, his friend. You maybe do not recognize him as he has been through a terrible time and his mind is not as it was last time you saw him." Musa heard a whisper from the earpiece, "Understood," as he observed Adnan with narrowed eyes, and if he could have, he would have given a sigh of relief when he saw Adnan relax his grasp on the handgun. After another moment of studying Afridi's face, the harsh, hawk-like look had gentled, and he had smiled tentatively as he lowered the gun and offered his other hand to Afridi in order to help him up.

Afridi had grasped the offered hand with a quick smile and was pulled to his feet. Adnan né Haqqanis gave him a slight smile in return and suddenly, spontaneously threw his arm around the smaller man's shoulder.

"Come, sit. Tell me what has happened to you that has left you in such a state. But first tell me who is this that you brought to us and why I shouldn't kill him and throw his body into the ocean as shark bait," Haqqanis asked in a low hard voice as he squeezed Afridi's shoulder to the point where Afridi gave a grimace of pain.

Haqqanis released his hold on Afridi and guided him to a chair at the table where he had been sitting and then sat down himself. It was only then that those who had be holding him loosened their grip ever so slightly and Musa was able to move his head just enough to see Haqqanis' face. There ... there it was! The scar, the ropey scar on the right side of his face, it was there! He was facing Haqqanis, the master bomb maker! *Now I'm halfway out of the pit that Afridi got us into when he ran through the door,* he thought to himself.

"Now, my old friend, tell me how you got in such trouble and how it came to pass that this one helped you? Abed, pull that hood back so we can get a better look at this man," Haqqanis ordered.

Abed was about to yank the hood back when Afridi gasped and almost shouted, "Nay, nay! Do not do so, for if those who followed us see him with the hood off, they will know there is trouble and perhaps attack!"

"What are you babbling about, Zarak?" Haqqanis asked as suspicion started to refill his voice.

It was then that Afridi told Haqqanis all that had happened since they had last met. It was a strange tale which had gotten twisted with fantasy, hell and hope as the months of sensory deprivation had tangled his thought processes to such an extent that, although much of what he said was the truth as he saw it, it was out of sequence in some cases. And what he said of Musa and their meeting was so confusing even Musa's eyes widened as he wondered where he had been during the times of his alleged exploits of derring-do.

Adnan né Haqqanis had listened without interruption and his eyes had widened in wonder, then in understanding and pity as he had stared at Zarak or rather the wasted shadow of what was left of his old friend.

It was only after Afridi had finished his tale did Haqqanis turn to where Musa was being held and asked him if perhaps he could fill in some of the spots where Zarak seemed somewhat confused.

Musa knew this was his chance, his one and only chance, to gain Haqqanis' confidence and trust. He also knew it was better to stick as closely to the truth as possible for it was easier to remember, and if there was even a slim chance that Afridi might regain some of his real memories, he wouldn't be caught in a lie.

Haqqanis called out to Abed and Yesal, who had been holding him, to release him and for him to sit down. Both Abed, who had been holding his one arm, and Yesal, who had held the knife to his throat, sat down on either side of him. Yesal still clutched the knife in his hand, but his knife hand was in his lap, no doubt as a reminder of just how quick he could stab him if Haqqanis so ordered it.

As Musa sat he gave a low cough to clear his throat, his mind working at what seemed like the speed of light to put a plausible story together.

CHAPTER FORTY-SIX

As Musa had settled himself into the chair, he pulled back the hood and tilted the baseball cap back enough so all in the room could see his face. He looked up and met Haqqanis' raptor gaze and did not flinch. His face was calm, his demeanour dispassionate as he met Haqqanis' look, and then he began to speak in Pashto.

"I work for the police."

He could hear a small gasp in his earpiece and see the sudden tautness in those within the café ... he could almost feel Yesal's grip on his knife tighten.

"I thought you should hear those words from me. It's true. I do work for the police but it is as what is known as an apprentice rookie. I do all the menial jobs such as driving others around, and since I speak several different languages, I was ordered to drive Zarak Afridi around while the real police officers followed. I think they were seeing who he would meet and then arrest them.

I despise this country and want to return to the Hindu Kush. My heart, my soul belongs there among the high hills and mountains. When my parents immigrated here, they forced me to come with them, and then when I was old enough, my uncle got me into the apprentice program with the police. My uncle, my parents said this would bring honour to our family. But I do not see this as honour ... only betrayal of our people. Tonight, when I was ordered to drive Zarak Afridi around, he spoke to me of Afghanistan and the high hills and offered to get me back to my real home. I could not refuse. As part of my training, I have had courses in driving, even advanced driving courses to avoid those chasing me. Tonight I used those skills to lose the ones who followed, and because of this training we arrived here without being followed. I stake my life on this. If you do not believe me, I offer myself up for you to slay! At least then my spririt can return to Tirich Mir in the Hindu Kush," Musa said passionately as a single tear trickled down his face from the outer corner of his left eye as he looked with such longing at Haqqanis.

For a brief moment, Musa could see the countenance of the master bomb maker change to one of a university student, full of hope and happiness for the future, but only for a nanosecond before it seemed to ripple as it changed back into the intensely fervent, cynical face of a terrorist who took joy in the death of those he thought of as unbelievers.

All Musa could do was sit there and await his fate.

CHAPTER FORTY-SEVEN

"Jaysus fuckin' Christ! What a fuckin' performance! The kid deserves an Oscar! He almost had me in tears," Trey Carstairs said in a stage whisper and shook his head.

Jim Bilidou had been touched and even moved by the story as well, although he remembered a classroom conversation about sticking as close to the truth as possible to avoid being caught in a lie. It was hard to fight your way back when caught in a deception and complete trust may be gone forever. Raphael's father had told him about the year he, his wife and Raphael had spent amongst the Falash tribe and how Raphael had initially refused to leave. It would seem that Raphael had used that time and his feelings about the tribe to good use, even his telling Haqqanis that he worked for the police, a statement which had near taken Bilidou's breath away. The kid, or rather the man, definitely had the stones.

Even the Frenchman had commented and then reiterated that anytime Raphael wanted to come work with Interpol, he would be more than welcomed.

Bilidou had leaned forward and told Das-Groot to tell the team to stand by to move, for he sensed that a decision was going to made sooner than later. If Haqqanis decided to do away with Musa né Raphael, they would have to move really quickly to try to save him and dispose of the terrorist. But Bilidou thought to himself that hopefully Haqqanis would buy into the story Musa was telling and then maybe ... maybe they would get a line on where the bombs were planted.

Bilidou pulled out his own cell and called Lula's number. She picked up after one ring.

"Yes."

"He has talked himself in, be ready."

"10-4. Still want me at the main entrance?"

"Yes. At least until we find out which vehicles they're going to use."

"You have the package with you ... easy access ... loaded ... easy to sight?"

"10-4. It can be together in under twenty seconds."

"10-4."

Bilidou disconnected and he thought to himself, *Best sniper I have ever seen. If anybody can do it, this sniper can.* Then another odd thought crossed his mind, *Women are far more ruthless than men, especially when a loved one is threatened.*

"Ok, let's be ready to move when we hear the words from Musa."

CHAPTER FORTY-EIGHT

The stillness in the room grew chill, and he felt a shiver of anticipation dance along his spine. The quietude grew louder and restless thoughts raced through his mind as he stood on the edge of the blade between life and death. He knew he could take at least two with him if it was his karma to pass through death's door. He felt the comfort of the small glock handgun resting against the small of his back. Lucky thing they had only done a shoddy pat down, looking more for a wire, when they searched him. His gaze had not left Haqqanis' since he had told his story.

The seconds seemed to stretched into an eternity of waiting.

Haqqanis sighed, leaned back in his chair and rubbed his eyes with one of his slender hands before he spoke.

"Only an insane or very brilliant man would tell me about working for the police. However, having said that, someone very young and ingenuous who has been forced into something he did not want to do and torn from the country he loves, might tell the truth in the hopes of returning to that country. I think I can help you with your wish, but in return you must help me with something I must finish doing. Do you think you can help me?" Haqqanis asked as he watched Musa.

"Yes, anything! Name it!" Musa said with all the eagerness of thoughtless youth.

"It may be bloody and if you are caught, you may be killed."

"I don't care. It is a slow death living here!" Musa returned with all the drama of the untested.

"Alright. I need a driver, a good driver, and it seems from everything Zarak has said tonight you might be just such a one," Haqqanis said as he looked at Musa with speculation.

"I am such a driver. When I took all the driver's courses, my instructors had nothing but praise for my abilities," Musa said with all the overweening pride of an unsophisticated young man.

Haqqanis burst into a bitter bark of laughter before saying, "How perfectly ironic that one who works for the police is helping me with my explosive task. It is time we leave. I still have some IED's to set, and Musa will be my driver and Zarak will come with us in the dark green car—it is the faster of the two. Abed, you and Yesal will take the black car and meet us at the prearranged spot in the park. Musa, where did you park that police vehicle?"

"It is but half a block away, hidden in a dark alcove," Musa replied as he got up.

"Fine, leave it there. It may not be found for a day, possibly two. We have the two cars parked in the shadows of this building in the alley," Haqqanis said.

They were all standing now. Haqqanis motioned them all out the back door of the café which led to a small hallway at the end of which was another door that opened onto a crowded alley.

As they stepped out into the alley, Musa looked up and could see a very faint lightening at the tips of the peaks to the east and thought, *Dawn is coming.* Then he looked around the alley for the two vehicles and spotted them tucked into the shadow of the building. When he looked to either end of the alley, it looked like both were deadends, and as he climbed into the driver's seat of the dark green vehicle, he looked at Haqqanis with questioning gaze.

"Abed and Yesal, you two leave first and remove the barricades that hide this alley. We will follow. We will not see this place again. Go now. We will wait but a few minutes 'til thee have gone. Musa, pull up thy hood and pull down thy ballcap so it all seems safe should some who search for thee come upon us. Then you will have to lure them up to the car so I may dispose of them."

Musa nodded before he said, "Understood," as a savage thought raced through his mind. *He means to kill any police officer who is foolish enough to stop us. I hope they understand.*

There was a whisper in his ear, "Understood, the way will be unimpeded. Hold in the rage 'til the time is right."

"Musa, in a few minutes pull out and turn to the right. Abed has gone on ahead to remove the barricade that has hidden the alley. Zarak, you must slouch low in the back seat so you are not seen. We go now to finish what I have started."

CHAPTER FORTY-NINE

"Everybody move! Move! Those at either end of the alley make sure you've got good cover— they're moving now. Confirm only when dark green vehicle is out and gone," Das-Groot said calmly into his portable.

There was a chorus of 10-4's in response.

"Everybody stay well back."

Within a matter of minutes, the four sitting in the dark blue command van heard a voice confirming that the green sedan, Musa at the wheel, had left the alley and turned left onto Ocean View Street and was now lost to sight by static undercover. Das-Groot, after consulting maps of the area between the lower docks to Pacific Edge Park, had set up follow-cover vehicles in a large rectangle where they were several blocks away from the green sedan that Musa was driving. They had let the black vehicle through the rectangle knowing they would pick him up at the meeting place in the park, but just in case they had an unmarked keeping way back and following them.

Bilidou had been in contact with the TAC bomb squad and two bomb squad units were hidden in garages within the park waiting for word from him. For now all they could do was follow at a leisurely pace, listen to the conversation within the green sedan and trust in Musa to give them ideas where explosives were planted.

"Wilmer, you've talked to our guys keeping a very long eye on the black car to make sure no marked vehicle decides to stop that black vehicle with Abed and Yesal in it?" Bilidou asked.

"10-4," Wilmer Das-Groot answered from the front seat as he thought to himself, *That's only the fourth time Jim has asked me that question. His nerves are starting to show.*

CHAPTER FIFTY

It was quiet inside the green sedan. Afridi had fallen into a restless sleep in the back seat. Haqqanis rode shotgun in the front and gazed out the front passenger window, seemingly in deep thought.

Musa, for all intents and purposes, was focussed on his supposedly superlative driving skills, at least, he hoped, where Haqqanis was concerned. In reality he was on autopilot, an instinct that had been highly honed when they were all in class. His mind was trying to sort through all thoughts and worries that were bouncing around in his brain. Keeping up the façade of a younger, unsophisticated man in front of Haqqanis, his body guards and Afridi had been and was draining. But Haqqanis had seemed to accept the persona and let his guard down, or so it seemed. Raphael had silently thanked the gods that resided on Tirich Mir for the memory and inspiration of his time amongst the Falash tribe. Now all he had to worry about was how to pass along IED positions in the park to those who followed and listened. Inwardly, he groped for and found his inner stillness, pulling it closer to him and let its calm flow through him.

Haqqanis straightened and turned to look towards Musa with speculation as they reached the front entrance to Pacific Edge Park. It was still dark although the eastern sky was starting to turn a lighter shade of lavender over the eastern mountains and Musa, who had his window partially open, could hear the high, clear notes of the early morning birds as they warmed up their voices ahead of the true dawn.

"Musa, turn left after you enter the park and slowly do a circuit of the interior of the park. If we see any sudden movement, be prepared to leave in a hurry. If all is quiet, then I will tell you where to go," Haqqanis said in a voice just above a whisper.

Musa merely nodded, as he felt his stomach quelch slightly then settle down into stillness.

A voice whispered in his right ear, "Understood ... park is clear."

As they drove the road that circled the interior edge of the park, there was nothing except a slight pre-dawn breeze that fingered through the old weeping willows, making the branches sway and sigh. Then, of a sudden, they heard a crash then a bang and the sound of hydraulics lifting, then a man cursing, but it wasn't in the park. Musa turned, looked and saw through the trees at the park boundary a garbage truck outside the park, picking up garbage. A large man was walking beside the back of the truck, cursing out the driver for apparently going too fast.

Musa turned to smile at Haqqanis and the smile froze and broke apart as he saw Haqqanis pointing a handgun directly at his head. The bore end of the gun looked to be the size of a cannon.

"Shit! It's naught but a garbage truck outside the park, picking up garbage! Put the gun away, Adnan! Garbage trucks are always out at this time of the morning!" Musa said in a slow, low, shocked voice and those listening knew he was not acting.

Haqqanis looked at him through the site on the top of the handgun for a few moments more before giving him an acerbic smile as he lowered the gun. Then he added words to the gesture, "If thee betray me and mine, thee may see the gun before I shoot you but it is just as likely thee will not." With those words hanging in the air between them, Haqqanis gestured for Musa to continue driving.

Musa turned back, took hold of the steering wheel, being careful not to grip it too hard, took his foot off the brake, and gently pressed on the gas pedal as he thought to himself, *It's a good thing you can't see my face, for the revulsion, loathing and abhorrence written there would surely have caused you to pull the trigger.*

They continued their slow drive around the park, and nothing more untoward happened, but the tension within the car actually woke Afridi up.

"What is wrong? Something has gone awry!" Afridi muttered in alarm.

"It is nothing, old friend. Go back to sleep, and I will awake thee when I have need of you," Haqqanis returned in a soft, low voice, and his tone was such that Afridi slumped back down onto the seat and fell back to sleep.

"Look there, see the big bandstand? Park the car beside it. You and I have some work to do underneath it," Haqqanis said as he pointed to the freshly painted bandstand that had bunting drapped around the outside of it.

And so it begins, Raphael thought.

CHAPTER FIFTY-ONE

Musa had parked close to the bandstand. One could see the park entrance way off to the west. The area around the bandstand was a huge meadow of perfectly mowed grass where a large amount of people could either sit on the ground or on lawn chairs while watching bands and other types of entertainment. The area in front of the bandstand was shaped in a shallow bowl so all had a good view of the bandstand no matter where they sat or stood; there were no trees to obstruct the view.

Haqqanis moved to the trunk of the vehicle and motioned for Musa to come and help him. Haqqanis opened the trunk of the sedan just as Musa reached the back of the vehicle and saw what was contained within the trunk. It took all of his inner control not to gasp in fury at what the interior trunk light revealed.

On top of a neatly arranged stack were four large, round, old-style, military steel mess kits, or at least that had been their original use. Now they were used as IED's, Improvised Exploding Devices. Musa né Raphael had, during classes, studied how the devices were made and how they were disarmed and just how deadly they were when they exploded ... collateral death and damage was on a horrific scale. And it would seem that Haqqanis was going to plant them around the bandstand, where in about nine hours a large music festival would be starting where hundereds or even thousands would be in attendance, getting ready to dance and party to the music. It took all of his inner stillness and training not to finish Haqqanis off right then, but he knew there were other IED's planted throughout the park already, and he had to find them first.

"Here, Musa, have you ever seen how one of these is made?" Haqqanis asked.

Musa shook his head and Haqqanis waved him in for a closer look. Musa stepped up to where Haqqanis stood by the trunk. Haqqanis picked up one of the devices and moved the steel arm that extended from the middle of the flat, round top to the edge then curved over and under the lower part of the mess kit. The arm was the locking mechanism, and he slid it to the open position and removed the top.

Musa moved in for a closer look and saw what he had been dreading. It looked like Haqqanis had used two sticks of C-4 [a military explosive that can be handled easily and needs a detonation device to explode] and had taken them out of their packaging and moulded them so they fit around the inner curve of the mess kit. There was a det-cap [detonation cap] pushed into the C-4 with a wire coming out it, then he had poured in several small ball bearings as added projectiles. Haqqanis had just finished adding a tiny digital clock which he had wired into the det-cap and set it for 1500 hours. Haqqanis had actually let him hold it and as he pretended to study the IED, his hands had run along the underside and he felt some type of steel reinforcing plate attached to the underside and tilted slightly.

"May I ask a question?" Musa asked.

"Of course. It is always good to learn," Haqqanis returned.

"What is this light grey moulded stuff? It looks like children's play dough."

"That is C-4. Do you know what that is?"

"Explosive, I think?" Musa asked as he appeared to study it.

"Very good," Haqqanis replied sardonically.

"And this plating on the backing, it appears to have a slight tilt to it. Why is that?" Musa asked, artlessly hiding his antipathy.

"That is to ensure the blast goes outward and into the crowd, while the slight tilt ensures the shrapnel hits the upper bodies and heads of those within the crowd, ensuring maximum damage amongst the infidels," Haqqanis said harshly.

"So this must be some type of blasting cap, and this must be the timer set to go off at three?"

"Yes and yes. Now come and help me put these up," Haqqanis said as he kneeled in front of the bandstand and lifted up the ribbon and bunting.

"Won't the banging alert park staff?" Musa asked with pretend alarm.

Haqqanis actually snickered before he replied, "We need not hammer anything in. North Americans are so clever with their inventions. I have found a glue that, once hardened, will not loosen its hold on anything even if a hammer should be used, and if these are discovered and if some police or military tried to loosen them, they will likely set them off."

Oh fuck! was all Raphael thought as he heard a whisper in his right ear, "We copy."

There was no more talk as Haqqanis, with Musa's help, set all four IED's on the upright border under the stage so they faced out towards the large empty meadow, and then they redraped the bunting over them.

The bandstand was now, for all intents and purposes, a bomb.

CHAPTER FIFTY-TWO

As soon as they knew Haqqanis was on the move again, Trey Carstairs called the TAC bomb units waiting in the utility garage. He gave them the information about the mess-kit IED's and how they were set up. Bilidou could only hear Carstairs's half of the converstion, but he gathered from when Trey told the bomb squad about the C-4, the plating and especially the glue, the conversation became very intense.

Trey ended the call after assuring them he would get right back to them. He shook his head before he turned so he faced Das-Groot and Bilidou, who, sitting in the back seat of the van monitoring the transmission from Musa, could hear him clearly.

"Shit! We've got some problems," Trey said.

"I gathered that from your side of the conversation. So tell me," Bilidou returned.

"Well, first we gotta get a couple of the bomb guys under the bandstand to do a rekki [reconnaissance]."

"Ok, you TAC guys are good at doing rekki, or so the bragging goes," Bilidou said with a slight smile to take the sting out of the words.

"We are the best. Trouble is, we have two vehicles with bad guys in them in the park circling around and at least the bad guys in one vehicle are setting bombs. So the worry is, as our guys are slithering around doing or trying to do the rekki on the bandstand, they're worried about becoming a silhouette in a bad guy's headlights and blowing the plan all to shit."

"I can see your point, but it's a chance we will have to take. Now, what else is troubling you, partner?"

"The fuckin' glue. Our guys are gonna hafta get some samples from the IED's without disturbing the bombs, so we can figure out what it is, and that sounds like it might be a problem. We don't wanna joggle the IED's 'cause quite frankly, given that they, that being the terrorists, managed to blow up their own house with most of them in it, I'm thinking the IED's are not that stable if ya follow my drift," Trey returned.

There was a sudden silence in the blue van as everyone digested that thought.

"Fingernail polish remover!" Das-Groot blurted out.

CHAPTER FIFTY-THREE

"Holy shit!" Tony Smitter muttered to himself as he checked his gear, including his AK-47 with the new sound suppressor on it. He was wearing black right down to his bulletproof vest instead of his usual cami gear—even the AK had blackening on it. Dawn was still an hour away, and it was blacker than the hubs of hell outside the utility garage where the two units of the bomb squad were set up. Sargeant Banks, "Sid," had called for two volunteers—one from Alpha 1 and one from Alpha 2 to do a rekki up to and under the bandstand to check the IED's planted there.

Everybody on both teams had volunteered ... anything to break the monotony of "hurry up and wait," especially with what was at stake on this set-up. Sid Bank had finally had to pick the two who would be going.

The very thought of terrorists setting bombs at the Pacific Edge Fair! This was Canada for fuck sake! Snitter's thought as he checked his night-vision glasses which were attached to the front of his helmet by a small, movable arm so he could raise them or pull them down so he was looking through them, hands free. As he pulled on his thin black gloves, a small smile crossed his face as another thought flashed through his mind. *Thank gawd I don't have to wear black paint on my face ... one of the bonuses of being Black, I guess.*

"Alpha 1 to Alpha 2, how do you read?" he whispered into his cheek mic that was wired in from the portable on his belt.

"You are 10-4, Alpha 1," Frank Parker whispered into his mic.

Just before they exited a small side door of the utility garage, Sid had looked over the equipment they were wearing to make sure they wore nothing shiny, and everything was tucked into pockets so there would be no inadvertent jingling. Then he had given them a thumbs up and they had stepped out of the partially opened door and into the tired night, which dawn was starting to push towards the ocean. They both knew they had an hour to do the rekki and get back to the safety of the garage. They had both studied the map of the park and then started working their way towards the bandstand by a route offering the best concealment.

They did not run, per se, but rather moved in a quick sliding walk that was less jerky, therefore harder to see, should anyone be watching. They also had their orders ... if caught by any of the suspects, they were to terminate with prejudice and try and hide the bodies.

Both had their night-vision goggles pulled down from their attachment on their helmets so they could see in the dark; the park took on a greyish-green colour. They could see clearly as long as they didn't look towards any light source. Luckily, the moon had set so they were in the darkness before dawn. They kept a certain distance between them and moved from bush to tree quietly and quickly until they came to the large, clear area around the bandstand.

Both were tucked well back into the shadows of a weeping willow when they saw a dark sedan moving slowly along the park road like a large shark looking for prey.

"Alpha 1 to base, we have just spotted a dark, four-door sedan on the park road."

"10-4. Can you tell if it's the one with our operative in it?"

"Can't be sure, but driver doesn't appear to be wearing a hoodie."

"Has he spotted you?"

"Negative. Just appears to be trolling."

"Will you be able to make it to bandstand?"

"10-4. He has driven past."

This was it, the final slide and slither to the bandstand ... the adrenalin was surging now. With hand signals they indicated to each other that Alpha 2 would go across the open ground while Alpha 1 covered. Both gave each other a thumbs up.

Alpha 2 was halfway across the open when he heard Alpha 1 whisper warning, "Drop and still. Vehicle coming!" Alpha 1 watched Alpha 2 drop and lay motionless, then he turned his attention to the vehicle and saw it was another sedan driving slowly—the driver wore a hoodie.

"Alpha 1 to base, operative driving sedan. Alpha 2 is down and motionless in the park. Tony watched the sedan move slowly ... looking. And then he saw the driver put his hand up to the hoodie and seemed to pull it further down over his face ... *Shit!* He spotted Alpha 2, he thought, but the sedan kept moving at the same slow pace 'til it was out of sight.

"'Kay, it's clear. Move now ... keep low, I think it was operative driving," Tony, Alpha 1, said and watched as Alpha 2 made it across and then dive under the bandstand.

"'Kay, your turn Alpha 1. I got ya covered ... stay low and slide man!" Alpha 2 whispered into his mic.

Alpha 1 did the slither and slide all the way across the field without having to drop, and dived under the bandstand.

"Shit, what a fuckin' rush!" Tony whispered as he lay under the bandstand looking up at Frank Parker grinning.

"It's a good thing you weren't smiling when you were making your way across the field 'cause those pearly whites of yours are like the bright light in a lighthouse," Frank said, and they both giggled.

"'Kay you two quit congratulating yourselves and get the job done. Ya still gotta make it back here," Sargeant Banks said into their earpieces.

"10-4, they both said at the same time. Ok, let's get that little bottle out and try it on the glue." The thought of the way back had drowned their exhilaration considerably.

CHAPTER FIFTY-FOUR

The light of first dawn was starting to win out over the blackness of night, and things that had been hidden in the dark were starting to take on the vague promise of what they might be once the dark grey light brightened to daylight.

"Soon it will be too light. We must leave," Musa said tightly as he continued his slow drive. They had stopped four more times after the bandstand, and Musa had helped Haqqanis place assorted IED's including two pressure-cooker bombs beside the doors of the main male and female washrooms, both nestled in a pile of rocks from the unfinished back walls. Haqqanis had removed the handles and Musa had seen him place small throwaway cell phones with the backs removed, exposing small wires attached to tiny circuits on the circuit boards of the cells. The wires led to det-caps pushed into C-4. Haqqanis had been holding a cell phone, and before he wired them in, he had done a test call and had seen the throwaway cells light up with the number and start to ring. He had smiled as he turned off the throwaways and completed wiring them to the det-cap and fit them in amongst the ball bearings, then closed and tightened the lids down on the pressure cookers.

Musa had been unable to read the phone number dialed. As much as he had tried to angle himself, Haqqanis had blocked his line of sight. Musa knew the next time that number was dialled, the connection within would ring, completing the circuit, and the det-cap would set off the bomb and the blast and shrapnel would rip apart whatever, whoever, was close by.

"Just one more, my young friend. Turn here and we go to the children's rides. You need not get out of the car for this one as I have merely to set the time, and then we have to head back to the bandstand. I have to check on one more thing." Musa merely nodded as he tried to watch where Haqqanis had set the bomb in the children's area. *Fuck, I should just shoot this guy now, but I can't 'cause he told me that he has already placed other IED's in the park the night the house blew up. That's why he didn't get blown into hell with the other three!* he thought as he watched him go close to the merry-go-round and kneel down and fiddle with something, then stand.

Musa muttered to himself, "I wonder what he is doing down by the east side of the merry-go-round? Looks like he's setting something in the ground."

"Eh ... Eh, what are you, who are you talking to, Musa?" asked Afridi from the back seat.

The sound of Afridi's voice gave Musa a start, for he had forgotten Afridi was with them, and now Haqqanis was walking back to the car. He had to think quick! "I was talking to none but myself which I do when I'm interested or watching." Afridi grunted his understanding and lay back down just as Haqqanis reached the car.

"Let's go back up to the bandstand. I have to check something," Haqqanis said as he got back into the car.

CHAPTER FIFTY-FIVE

"Alpha 1 and 2 get your asses out from under there right now! They're coming back!"

"No can do! We will never make it! We'll try to work our way up into the back struts!"

"Do it! Do it now!" Sid said urgently.

Both Tony and Frank could hear the soft grinding sounds of tires slowly moving over gravel as they had scambled to the back end of the bandstand, at the opposite end from where the IED's had been placed, and pushed themselves up into the crossed two-by-four struts, which supported the floor, at the back end of the bandstand. They had just managed to brace themselves by their backs, legs and arms against the underside of the stand and had tried to control their breathing as they heard a car door softly close and the small rustle of quiet footsteps walking around the bandstand. They could heard the sound of voices murmuring, low and at first incomprehensible, but as they drew closer they could hear what almost sounded like an argument of some sort going on. One voice had an almost hissing tone while the other sounded younger and wondered why they had come back here when it was almost dawn. Then both had started speaking in another language, and Tony and Frank could hear the bunting at the front of the bandstand rustling. They both held their breath, waiting for the sounds of detection, alarm and possible gunshots coming their way. They could hear a soft scraping on wood then the rustling sound of the cloth bunting, then nothing for but a moment before the soft rustle of footsteps walking away, a car door opening and closing softly, then the same sound of tires moving away from their position. They waited for what seemed an eternity more and then finally loosened their legs and arms from where they were braced and fell the short distance to the ground. They then lay there in the dark and the dirt trying to get their limbs to loosen and relax.

"Fuck! Oh fuck! That was too fuckin' close, and tell me again why we volunteered for this mission?" Tony Smitters, Alpha 1, gasped as soon as he had gotten his wind back enough to speak.

"No shit! I was sweating so much the sweat washed all the blackening off my face, and if the bad guys had actually looked under the bandstand, they would have seen my white face hanging upside down from the crossbeams like a fuckin' white bat!" Frank Parker, Alpha 2, returned.

"We've got what we need. Let's make like Bobby Orr and get the puck outta here!"

There was a crackling over their earpieces and then Sid's voice saying, "I concur. You boys have enough breath to swear, you've got enough to get your asses back here while both suspect vehicles are now heading to the other end of the park."

"That's a 10-4 from both of us."

They scrambled out from beneath the bandstand and tucked low, did a sliding run across the lawn 'til they found concealment in the trees as the grey of early dawn lightened. They made the rest of the journey to the garage, hunched over, dodging from tree to tree.

Tony and Frank arrived at the garage just as the small side door opened partially, and they stumbled through. The door closed as they stood inside bent over, hands on knees, grasping for breath. They were met with a bit of sarcastic applause by other members of the two squads as they handed the piece of wood with the supposed impervious glue on it over to their sergeant, along with the plastic bottle containing clear liquid as Tony said, "The info you were given is right, Sid—four IED's attached just like you said. That operative is good ... scary good."

CHAPTER FIFTY-SIX

Musa, at Haqqanis' direction, drove to the far end of the park on the park road. Every once in a while, Haqqanis would direct him to stop, then would get out of the car and walk a short ways and look at the ground, then return, get in the car and drive a short distance and repeat the procedure. Each time he did this, Musa would try and give a description of where they were although this was becoming extremely difficult and dangerous because Afridi was now awake.

After four such stops, Haqqanis directed him to go to the parking lot at the end of the park by the sea wall. Upon arrival at the parking lot, Musa saw the black sedan with Abed and Yesal in it parked by some tall cedars. Both stepped out of their car, and Musa got one of the worst shocks of his life. Both were dressed as park employees!

It was a good thing that Haqqanis couldn't see his face, but he had to get his voice under control in a hurry. It took him a moment to pull the calmness back to him.

"Are Abed and Yesal truly park employees, or is it a clever ploy?" Musa managed to ask in a voice filled only with a mild curiosity.

Haqqanis laughed sardonically before he replied, "Ah yes, that would have been truly better; however, they were denied jobs here. But two who did wear these uniforms have no use for them now. What is that saying? Ah, yes, the sea rarely gives up her dead ... although in this case, it would be the ocean."

Both heard Afridi snickering from the back seat.

Haqqanis turned and smiled at Afridi before saying, "It is good to see you awake, old friend. Do you feel more yourself now?"

"Yes ... much better," Afridi replied.

"Time to leave the park for now. Abed and Yesal will watch over what has been set while we go get some rest before the festivities start. They have the number to call me should anything go amiss while we are away, and they will also give the ok before we re-enter the park. I must say these new cell phones are quite the miracle of modern ingenuity. Just think, I can call one number and reach a friend, then dial another number and cause such fireworks. I think the fireworks will be beyond anything anybody has seen or heard before," Haqqanis said in a voice filled with sarcastic mirth as he patted the chest pocket of his jacket where Musa had seen him put the cell phone, while Afridi began snickering again.

All Musa could do was clench the steering wheel until his knuckles turned white and grit his teeth. Then he heard a whisper in his right ear from his tiny earpiece. "Copy and understood. Their time upon this earth is short, take heart."

"Drive out of the park by the same park gates you came in, Musa," Haqqanis said. "I know of a place where we can rest for awhile and even more importantly hide, for I suspect the authorities will be looking for all of us, and I certainly don't want to be picked up before the fun begins."

CHAPTER FIFTY-SEVEN

"Wilmer, do you have the number for the chief of operations for the Pacific Edge Park? And Trey, follow the GPS signal but stay way back. I just wanna know what hole Haqqanis has found to crawl into to rest. It's probably another safe house that is connected to the terrorist, so we will want to flag it," Bilidou said as he wearily rubbed his eyes. He thought to himself, *I'm tired but Raphael must be exhausted and running on shear adrenalin supported up by his youth,* as a thin, mordant smile twisted his lips for a brief spark of time.

"Jim, I've got that number. You want me to call it?" Wilmer Das-Groot asked.

"Hold off on that, Wilmer, 'til we put these guys to bed somewhere," Bilidou said as he saw they were driving into a tough part of town with old, shabby houses which were matched by a dilapidated, ancient hotel.

They all saw the green sedan parked between an off-centred house, from which the paint had been scrubbed off by weather and neglect over countless years of indifference and the old, exhausted hotel by what had been a park which had dissolved into an overgrown patch of weeds, now only a "fix stop" for junkies on their spiral down into the pits by the River Styx. *Gawd, I must be really tired to be coming up with descriptions like that,* Bilidou thought.

"Can you park us somewhere close but out of the way so we can see them leave, but they or the other denizens of this little corner of hell can't see us or make us out for what we are?"

"Yeah, I know just the place," Trey said.

Within a few minutes, Trey had driven down a block, turned south and then drove a block east and had driven them into an old YMCA parking garage. He followed the concrete road between stalls as it wound up to the third floor and parked by an old concrete partial retaining wall. He had parked in such a way that they could see over the concrete and directly onto the street with a unobstructed view of the green sedan and the surrounding area.

Bilidou simply smiled and nodded.

"Ok, this is what needs to be done. Trey, I need you to call Sid Banks and tell him the situation with Abed and Yesal. We have photos of them and will send them. And warn him that they are wearing park uniforms so the TAC guys need to be in plain clothes and wearing the fluorescent vests all the fair volunteers are wearing today as they disarm the IED's. One should be standing six while the other disarms, and since we know how they were armed, it should be a simple matter to leave them where they were planted once they are disarmed. That way if Abed and Yesal check, they can see they are still there and they won't sound the alarm. Having said that, if those two fuckers get in the way, terminate them. I don't want any of our guys going the way those two poor park employees went. Having said that, if one or both get terminated, our team gets notified ASAP. They will have to get the cell phones off the bodies. We know Haqqanis will call them to ensure all is clear in the park. At least all our team speak the same languages and may be able to bluff their way through the call.

The problem we have, as I see it, is there are at least four IED's that were placed when Raphael wasn't with Haqqanis. But we know they are cell phone detonated so Haqqanis will come back to the park not only to set off the IED's but to watch. We have a sniper, and perhaps TAC can get one of their snipers in. I just don't know where Haqqanis will be in the park when he dials in those numbers. I know Raphael will go for Haqqanis' cell phone, but we need the snipers just in case. And I know there is one big IED in the children's playground, and I'm willing to bet there might be another one. He's a sick bastard.

Wilmer, patrols of the park need to go on as usual, and just make sure they leave the park employees and voluteers alone. Make sure they do the usual patrols for the Pacific Edge Fair, kinda hide in plain sight. But here's the thing—don't give the uniforms any more info than you need to. They need to be doing their jobs as usual," Bilidou finished explaining what he wanted and both Trey and Das-Groot started phoning.

Bilidou sighed. He had one more phone call to make and that was to the chief of police on his private line. He dialed the number. It rang once before he answered.

"Jim, I've been waiting," the rich baritone voice on the other end of the line said.

"It's been quite a night, Rick."

"So I've gathered from the reports from TAC, the bomb squad and a couple of district sergeants. So tell me," Rick Wardner, Police Chief, said.

Sergeant Jim Bilidou then filled him in on everything that had happened during the long night and where everybody was placed at the moment.

There was quiet at the other end of the phone and Bilidou waited, letting Rick digest everything, every nuance of what had transpired in the last forty-eight hours. Finally, the voice on the other end of the cell phone call broke the dead air on the line.

"How's Raphael holding up?"

"I'm in constant contact with him, Rick, and I feel his rage at some of the things that the terrorists have done and are planning to do. Interesting though, and there were times when he was in class I saw him do the same thing, there are certain times when I think he's going to lose it, but he suddenly pauses, if only for a few seconds, then there is a calm, a stillness that seems to wash over him and he carries on with what he is doing. It's almost like he compartmentalizes whatever angers or outrages him, to be dealt with at another time. I get the feeling he is biding his time. Personally, I think he can be very dangerous but in a way that will surprise these terrorists. For now he is playing at being an unworldly, callow youth, and it seems to please Haqqanis especially when he told them he worked for the police. I thought the game was over when he said that, but he pulled it off. I think Haqqanis finds it ironic and enjoys the thought of one of our police officers turning against our perceived authority. I still can't quite believe Raphael pulled it off myself," Bilidou said.

"I know Raphael's father, and in a way it doesn't surprise me. Stuart Campbell is one of the most dangerous men I know, but it is hidden under the veneer of a diplomat. As to the operation at hand, it seems to be going well except for the IED's that we can't account for. Is it time to call off the Pacific Edge Fair? Is it worth the risk to continue? What I need from you Jim is that every, and I mean every, bomb has been disarmed. Can you do that?" the police chief asked.

"I believe we can, sir, between the TAC bomb squad and my team," Bilidou replied.

"They open the gates for The Pacific Edge Fair in less than seven hours," Rick returned, his expectations unspoken.

"I understand. There is one thing I would ask of you," Bilidou said.

"What do you need?"

"As you know there have already been two homicides—those two park employees. We need to know their identities and especially nothing be released about them 'til the end of the day. I was wondering if you could talk with the chief of the park employees. The last thing we need is for an alarm to go out about the murders. It would definitely warn our bad guys."

"I know the man, and I will deal with that situation. I'll be in touch," the police chief said, before he hung up.

Bilidou turned his phone off with a sigh of relief.

"Trey, I need you in constant contact with Sid Banks and his guys and our guys who are dressed as volunteers."

"Wilmer, ya need to monitor the uniforms who patrol the area. I don't want one of them walking in on something they know nothing about," Bilidou added. Both men nodded their understanding.

"Oh shit! I knew I forgot something!" Bilidou said as he picked up his cell and punched in a number.

"Yes," a female voice answered.

"Musa and our bad guys have settled in for a rest away from the park. We are watching from great heights. Have you selected a place and taken cover?"

"I saw them leave the park from my position and have settled in here to await their return. I'm on top of Pacific Point and can see the entire park from my position. You might want to consider it as the place where our number one terrorist might want to use as he would have an almost three hundred and sixty degree vantage point for the remote control," the female returned.

"Holy shit! You might be right. We will notify you when they are on the move again," Bilidou said with weary excitement.

"10-4."

"Trey, let the TAC sniper know our sniper has Pacific Point covered. The TAC sniper might want to consider a position between the bandstand meadow area and the children's playground area, and make sure he has those photos of Abed and Yesal. I suspect he may have to take them out," Bilidou said.

"Yeah, 10-4, Jim. The photos have already been sent to Sid, and his sniper will be moving out to the position you suggested within a few minutes."

"Ok ... we all good for the moment?"

Both Trey and Wilmer nodded. Even the Frenchman nodded before adding, "You are very detailed—a very good trait in an intelligence agency."

Bilidou settled more comfortably into the back seat in preparation for the wait and tried to relax although his mind kept racing, trying to think of anything he missed. In the end he closed his eyes although the inside of his eyelids were like a screen upon which all the possible scenarios ran on a continuous loop.

CHAPTER FIFTY-EIGHT

Musa né Raphael was, like Jim Bilidou, beyond weary and was, in fact, on not his second wind but was way past that marker and onto his third or fourth wind at least. The last few days had at first been exhilarating and even now the excitement, which always brought on surges of adrenalin, was still working. It was the constant tight rein he held on his emotions, which was what was draining and pulling him down. He had had to pull in more and more memories of his time with the Falash tribe in the Hindu Kush and his training as a Falash warrior. The thoughts of the massive peak, Tirich Mir, helped him draw the inner stillness to him, and he wore the calm, the quiet-like armour protecting him from the emotions at seeing what was happening around him. To hold the tranquillity close and, for now, to eat the rage, put it away, so he could see and hear clearly every bit of minutiae, every tiny detail or hint of the evil that was occurring around him.

He thought back on the drive from the park to this place. On the outside it looked like just another old, shabby house in a rundown part of town. He had parked the car and followed Haqqanis and Afridi into the house and been shocked at the difference between the outside of the house and the inside. The outside had looked like a strong wind would blow it down but inside ... what a difference. The walls were nicely painted with several paintings on them while the furniture looked comfortable and there was incense burning somewhere. A man dressed in an expensive suit greeted them and, from the way he talked to Haqqanis, they appeared to be old friends. They spoke in Pashto and Afridi joined in while Musa listened, saying nothing. After talking with Haqqanis and Afridi for a bit, the man turned to him and spoke in English.

"You will have to excuse my manners. I am Ahmed Khan, and you are?" he asked politely with a slight smile that did not reach his brown eyes, which were hard and lifeless as rocks.

"My name is Musa Mullah," Musa replied in Pashto.

"You are originally from Afghanistan I understand?" Khan asked.

"From the border up in the Hindu Kush," Musa returned in Urdu venacular.

"Ah, I see. You are helping my friends, so whatever you need, you have only to ask," Ahmed Khan said with all the high born breeding of a Prince of Persia, then with a small bow left the room.

Musa watched him go, his eyes narrowed slightly. He had heard of Ahmed Khan and seen photos of him. A deadly, dangerous man who was wanted in many places including Canada. He hoped Jim was listening when he heard a whisper in his ear, "Understood."

"I think you can take off that hoodie and ball cap, Musa. There is no one in here that will recognize you as a betrayer." Haqqanis looked at him with a small, acrid smile. "Time to rest, for we shall be busy later. There are beds in the rooms if you wish," Haqqanis said before lying down on the chaise lounge in the living room.

Musa shrugged and pulled back his hoodie and took off his cap, with what he hoped was a believable sigh of relief, and returned Haqqanis' smile.

It was the first time Haqqanis had really had the light and time to study his face as Musa looked at him. All Haqqanis could see was a tired young man with faint stubble on his face. The grey eyes were those of some who called the Hindu Kush area home and his dark hair was rumpled with crushed curls on his head from wearing the ball cap so long. There were dark circles under Musa's eyes, which added to the look of strain on his face, no doubt from thoughts of deceiving his family and the police he had worked for, he thought. Haqqanis was satisfied for now and urged Musa to get some sleep, then abruptly, perhaps out of some sense of sympathy, maybe even an odd empathy, told Musa he would see the valleys and peaks of his true homeland when this was over.

Haqqanis wondered why he had added that sentence because he had every intention of killing Musa when they were finished this job.

Musa indicated he would take a room and found a comfortable bed in one, and within a few moments was pretending he was asleep.

Musa had heard murmurs coming from the other room, but they were so low that he could not decipher them so he tried to relax as he kept his eyes closed. He was lying on his back, so if he moved a certain way he could feel the comforting lump his handgun made against the small of his back. Raphael had sensed Haqqanis had no intention of helping poor Musa get back to his own land but, he thought, it is what it is, because he had every intention of killing Haqqanis before this day was out.

CHAPTER FIFTY-NINE

"For fuck sake, Frank, what are ya doing, making love to those IED's?" Tony asked in a stage whisper as he pretended to rake the gravel around the bandstand. He was hot and sweaty already even though he was in plain clothes. He was wearing a bullet-proof vest under his shirt, his glock semi-automatic handgun with silencer was tucked in a shoulder holster over his shirt on the left side and a portable was hooked from his belt with wiring leading to his earpiece in his ear. A small mic was hooked close to his mouth on the front of the fluorescent vest of a volunteer, which covered his shirt and all the other accoutrements of an undercover police officer. The combination was worse than full TAC gear. At least when he was in full gear, he felt balanced.

"Sweet Jaysus, Tony, you're the one who keeps voluteering us for these things. Who was the one who said to Sid, 'Oh, we'll take the bandstand 'cause we already know where the IED's are?' Yep, Mister Volunteer, that's you, Mister Helpful ..." Frank had started into a soliloquy involving his many complaints when suddenly Tony was shushing him.

"Quiet, Frank, we got two park workers coming our way," Tony said in a stage whisper as he discreetly loosened the handgun in its holster with his right hand while he held the rake in his left hand. "Sid, you copy we got two guys dressed as park workers coming our way? Can't tell if they're our bad guys—they're 'bout the right size."

"Everybody else, stand by," Sid said through the earpiece. "Terry, you got line of sight from your position?" Sid asked the sniper.

"10-4, but only can see them from the back, so no ID."

"10-4, Tony. If they're the ones we're looking for and they look like they're suspicious and they don't move on, take 'em out ... try for a head shot ... we need the cell phones," Sid said.

There was quiet waiting amongst all those with earpieces ... waiting for the soft, hissing, thunking sound of a handgun or sniper fire. There was nothing, no sound except some birds in the background and then the crackle in the earpieces and a voice.

"'Kay, these two mo-mos are not our bad guys. I repeat, not our bad guys. They are two actual park employees, both clean shaven with light-coloured hair, wondering where we got the rakes from," Tony said in a whisper.

"10-4. Base copies," Sid replied.

"10-4," Terry said into his mic.

"'Kay, everybody stay sharp."

"Say, has anybody seen many park employees around? Those were the first I've seen all morning," Tony said softly into his mic.

There was a blank, almost thoughtful silence as everybody tried to think if they had seen any park employees.

"Sid, I'm thinking the silence means nobody has seen any this morning. Could someone have let something slip?" Tony asked upon reflection.

"Shit! You may be right. Everybody, keep acting natural, and get those damn things disarmed," Sid said as he picked up his cell and made a phone call.

Within ten minutes Sid was back on the radio. "'Kay, boys and girls, apparently there was a misunderstanding that has now been corrected. Go about your supposed volunteer duties. In other words, keep working, and once you have completed them let me know. Also Bilidou's team, we need to get an eye on the bad guys so start spreading out and finding those two bad guys so we know exactly where they are and what they are doing. We've got two snipers out there, and they are watching as well. People, we've only got a couple of hours left before we see a bunch of citizens crowding through the gates, and then we're in trouble."

Sid heard a bunch of acknowledgements over the radio, and he sat back and rubbed his neck, which was stiff from the strain of trying to be polite to some idiots who felt their positions in civilian life gave them the right to override the operation and do what they wanted. It had taken a call to Jim, who had contacted the police chief who then had to call the chief of park employees and read him the riot act about who exactly was in charge, to get things moving. Then the radio crackled again.

"Jacob to base."

"This is base. Go ahead, Jacob," Sid said as he felt his gut twist. He knew it was one of Bilidou's team.

"I'm down by the children's playground, a distance of about a hundred feet from the merry-go-round. Two of your guys are doing a good job of raking by the merry-go-round, and I got two park employees kinda edging their way towards them. The park guys match the description, beards and all. I'm working my way towards an area where I can get a positive ID and a get a good shot if I have to," Jacob said over the portable in a calm, quiet voice.

Sid looked at the map, which showed which bomb squad members were working by the merry-go-round. It was Ted Anderson and Rob McLean.

"Base to Anderson and McLean ... Copy."

"Anderson here."

"You got two possible suspects coming your way. Finished your work down there?"

"Just the one we already knew about. Still looking for the other one. We see the two. They are walking directly towards us. One has a broom in his hand."

"Terry, you copy?"

"10-4, got 'em in my sights."

Sid looked quickly at the map again and immediately saw the danger!

"Terry, we got a possible crossfire situation!"

"Jacob, cover only from the prone position ... Copy!"

"Jacob copies!"

"Ted, make the call."

Quiet ... everybody listening ... then the sound ... soft, hissing, thunk, times two!

* * * * *

Terry Myers, TAC sniper, was positioned nicely in the broad crook of an ancient elm tree. The three massive limbs of the tree joined in such a way that there was a broad area that was almost flat, like a natural platform that he could lay his six foot, lanky frame on comfortably. He was up approximately twenty-five feet in the tree and the leaved branches provided excellent cover, and thankfully it wasn't a windy day. In fact, it was still ... so still. He had positioned himself in such a way that there was a natural hole formed by two twisted branches so he could clearly cover the children's playground and all the way to and beyond the bandstand area. He had his AK-47 with the new, built-in sound suppressor set up, with scope attached. He had a map with the entire area on it and which bomb members were where. He also had photos of Abed and Yesal. He had a clear kill area, so he relaxed as he watched through his scope after he had checked each area where bomb-squad members were working. He enjoyed working by himself. He got the first possible sightings from Tony and Frank's area by the bandstand and was focussed in on the two possibilities within seconds and waiting for the sign. Like the ancient Romans, thumb-up or thumb-down, life or death reduced to the direction of the thumb ... they were thumb-up. Within a matter of ten minutes, he heard another possible, this time down by the children's playground. He focussed in—yeah, there they were approaching the plain-clothed bomb guys, and wait ... yep, there was one of Bilidou's team, and he just dropped for cover and to avoid a crossfire.

He focussed in on the bad guys ... Holy shit! That's them! ... Finger on trigger ... squeezing, ever so gently back. Shit! Fuck-wad's pulling out a handgun! ... Terry gently squeezed the trigger back all the way ... only need 6 ounces of pull pressure. He felt the slight thunk as the bullet left the nozzle and then moved his eye a mere nano millimetre, looking through the scope ... yep, other one had gone for a gun. He could see the stock ... sighting in and gently squeeze. There was a gentle thunk ... two down. He got them both in the occipital notch at the back of the head. He smiled to himself as he reset his scope before he got on his portable and called Ted, who he knew, and asked if the bad guy's eyes were crossed. There was silence on the portable and then Ted's voice.

"That's a 10-4, Terry."

"10-4," Terry responded. He had heard about that particular physical oddity from other snipers. Apparently if your bullet struck the bad guy in the occipital notch at the back of the head, the force of the bullet exploding in the brain caused the eyes of the bad guy to cross. Kinda interesting when he thought about it; not only was the bad guy going to hell with his eyes crossed, but it showed just how accurate his shooting was.

* * * * *

CHAPTER SIXTY

Jim Bilidou was still reviewing possible scenarios on the inside of his eyelids when he heard Trey's cell phone ring. He didn't move, didn't open his eyes, he just listened at first 'til he heard Trey's voice stiffen slightly. Something's happened, he thought, and opened his eyes.

"It's Sid from the park," Trey said as he handed the cell over to Bilidou's waiting hand.

"What's happened, Sid?" Bilidou asked, his voice soft.

"Jim, I've got two dead terrorists here. My guys had just finished disarming a big mother fuckin' IED from beside the merry-go-round in the children's playground, and were raking the ground over it so it looked undisturbed when I got a call from one of your team, uh ... Jacob, I think his name is. Anyway he, Jacob, had spotted the two terrorists we were looking for. To make a short story even shorter, the two were moving quickly towards my two guys who were trying to act natural. One of the terrorists started to pull a handgun out, and our sniper, who had been advised, saw the other actually pull his gun out. Terry, our sniper took them both out ... head shots ... nice and clean. Your guy, after making a full ID of the bad guys, has their cell phones. My guys have placed the two bodies in some large, wheeled plastic garbage bins that we had found in this garage. Those bins are now in a deep, dark corner of the garage, and the area where the incident happened has been cleaned up, and aside from our guys, there were no witnesses," Sid said in a tone usually reserved for court when in the witness box, and reading from a notebook.

Jim Bilidou recognized the tone immediately. It was the tone taken when a major incident had happened involving the police and probable death. There was no emotion in it. Sorta like the old detective show ... just the facts ... just the facts. It was easier at this point in time to stick to the facts and later deal with the gut reation, the passion, the feelings, the worry. Time now to be stoical, matter of fact and dispassionate.

"Are Terry, Rob and Ted and Jacob doing ok with this situation?" Bilidou asked.

"Yes, we all knew this would be a possible scenario," Sid returned.

"Terry ok with sniper duties still? Or does he want to assume a different role?"

"No, he's good and maintaining his position."

"Ok, could you have Jacob come in. I need to talk to him and probably call in Jeff from my team as well. They are going to be handling the two cell phones that were recovered from the terrorists' bodies."

"10-4. I'll get them in here forthwith. Just so you know, we have most of the identified IED's disarmed and are now looking for the others," Sid said.

"For what it's worth, everybody did a great job ... and doing a great job," Jim said.

"It's worth a lot, Jim, thanks. And I will pass it along to the guys," Sid replied.

Bilidou turned the cell phone off and looked at the other three in the van. He knew that at least Trey and Wilmer would have guessed what had happened but he wasn't sure about the Frenchman.

What was a distinct possiblity and possible fly in the ointment had, in fact, happened. The two terrorists left in the park were now dead and two of their team had, at least cell-wise, taken on their identity.

"I kinda guessed that from the tone of Sid's voice," Trey said and the other two nodded.

"I gotta make one quick call and then I'll have a conversation with Jacob and Jeff," Bilidou said and then punched in another number.

When Rick came on the line, he let him know what had happened and that all the police members involved were alright and most of the bombs had been disarmed.

"Time is beginning to slide quicker and quicker through your fingers, Jim."

"Yes, so it would seem. But we know Haqqanis, along with our operative, have to be back in the park before it opens, and we think we know where they will go to. We have a sniper set up in that location so if Raphael fails, the sniper will take Haqqanis out," Bilidou responded.

"Although you have a good plan, we all know that plans can disintegrate in a matter of moments. All it takes is one loose thread," Rick Wardner said softly before he shut his phone off.

CHAPTER SIXTY-ONE

Musa né Raphael was lying on the bed, his body completely relaxed. His eyes were closed but he was listening. He heard the murmur of voices in the other room and the sound of traffic that came through the partially opened window as he reviewed all that had transpired in the last two days, and he had independently come to the same conclusion Jim Bilidou had come to. The plan was a good plan, but it had one weak point. In fact, it could, if they let it, develop into a fatal flaw.

Abed and Yesal were the flaw, and perhaps it was why he had been so shocked when he had seen them in the park dressed as park employees. They were the two terrorists it was almost impossible to keep total track of. He suspected that at some point while they were disarming the IED's, those two would get in the way and they would have to put them down. His mind went in circles trying to figure another way out, but there was simply none. Although, perhaps, since the team had members who spoke fluent Pashto, Urdu, Farsi and Persian, they could get two to wing it and hope Haqqanis would buy it. If indeed that happened, he knew there might be something he could do to help ... some distraction.

As he pondered those thoughts, there was the faint whisper in his ear. The small, clear whisper of Jim Bilidou's voice telling him not to try to talk, just listen, and then told him the details of what he had suspected might happen. He heard what they planned to do when Haqqanis called to check that all was well. Bilidou also told him about Pacific Point, then the whisper was gone and he was alone.

He hadn't moved, his eyes had remained closed after the whisper was gone, and he remained still even though he had felt someone watching him for a time.

At last he heard Afridi's voice calling him and he opened his eyes, sat up and stretched.

"You seemed to have managed to get some sleep," Haqqanis said as he watched him from the doorway.

"Yes, I didn't think I would but thoughts of the hills and mountains of my homeland lulled me into sleep," Musa replied with an innocent smile.

"It is time. Mayhap after we are finished here, I will send you back there."

Musa looked up abruptly as a sudden thought flashed in his mind. *He plans to send my spirit back without my body to contain it.* He gave Haqqanis a brusque smile at the thought that they had both planned similar endings for each other.

They opened the front door and re-entered the rundown neighbourhood. The door closed behind them, closing off the genteel world Ahmed Khan had built in the interior.

Musa knew they were being watched as the three of them walked to the car, not by anything Bilidou had said, it was simply something he knew would be done.

Once they were in the car and had started to pull away from the curb, he saw Haqqanis pull out the cell and Musa said indifferently, "You going to call them now or wait 'til we get closer?"

"Why do you care?" Haqqanis returned.

"I don't, it's just that the traffic will start to get heavy from here on because people want to find parking close to the park."

Haqqanis merely nodded, but he did put the phone away.

They made their way through the thickening congestion 'til they were closer to the park. Haqqanis pulled out the phone again, but before he punched in the number he turned to Musa and said, "Find a spot to park this car close to the entrance of the park, then we will walk from there. I know a place where we can cut through some woods to get into the park without going through the front gates. We still have almost an hour before the gates open," Haqqanis said.

Musa merely nodded as he continued to drive. Out of the corner of his eye he watched Haqqanis punch in a number. He had the audio turned up on the phone and Musa could hear someone answer, but the background noise was so bad that they could barely make out the voice speaking in Pashto.

"Yesal ... Yesal! Is that you? Is all well?! The background noise sounded like the music from the merry-go-round, and loud crackling then broken words.

"All ... well ..."

Haqqanis turned to him and Afridi, "Could you make that out?"

"Sounded like Yesal ... maybe Abed? I don't think anybody else speaks Pashto," Musa replied.

Afridi nodded his head in agreement.

"Why would those stupid fools be down by the children's playground?"

"They could be anywhere in the park. I know they would be checking the speakers on the bandstand and in the playground, so sounds would be blasting ... loud," Musa returned with a shrug.

Afridi leaned over from the back seat and added, "If there was trouble, wouldn't they have called you before this?"

Musa could have kissed Afridi for adding that in. Haqqanis may not entirely trust him, but he certainly trusted Afridi.

"Alright, alright, we will go in, and those two better answer me or I will skin them alive for being such idiots! Musa, see that alley that backs into the hillside by the park?" Haqqanis said as he pointed to a short alleyway which was heavily treed on the west side. "Go in as far as you can, and we will walk up to the point from there."

Musa pulled in and managed to pull the car in so the one side was almost entirely covered with branches. The three of them climbed out of the car, and Musa was about to lock it when Haqqanis stopped him, leaned in and popped the trunk.

Now what? Musa thought as Haqqanis walked to the trunk. Musa walked halfway back to see what he was doing and gasped when Haqqanis pulled out a suicide bomber's vest and started to pull it on.

"What the hell! Haven't you set up enough bombs to blow up the entire park? Why do you need the vest?!"

Haqqanis hesitated for a moment, then his lips twisted into an acerbic smile and he pulled it off. Musa started to sigh in relief when abruptly Haqqanis turned to him and said softly, "You're right! You put it on!"

CHAPTER SIXTY-TWO

Musa né Raphael felt his guts twist and fall into his nether regions as Haqqanis held out the suicide bomber vest for him to put on.

"No! Why should I! I have done naught to deserve this treatment," he returned angrily.

"Ah, 'tis true you've done nothing and words come easily to your lips ... too easily I think. Time to prove yourself, Musa. See this small box?" With those words Haqqanis held up a small box. "This contains the control that blows up the vest when pushed." Haqqanis opened the box and inside was a black control stick the length of a hand that could be gripped, while at the top was a red button. "I will give you the box and its contents if you put on the vest."

Musa looked at him, considering, while in his ear the whisper was so emphatic it almost seemed to be shouting, "No! No! Do not put on the vest! He is trying to trick you! Don't put it on, Raphael!"

At that moment Raphael wasn't listening to the voice in his earpiece, he was listening to his heritage, all the Scots who had come before him who had laughed and jeered in the face of danger and death. He gave Haqqanis a savage grin as he put the vest on and took the box from him.

"We're wasting time. Point out the way and lead on," was all he said.

Haqqanis starred at him in surprise and a sudden admiration rippled across his face and was gone. Haqqanis found the trail and soon they were climbing, really climbing, for it was a steep, cliff trail. Musa was sweating and surprised at just how heavy a suicide bomber's vest really was. As he managed to pull himself up from tree to tree he thought to himself, *Well this is another fine mess I've got myself into ... no wait, that was Laurel and Hardy who used that line. And if I get myself out of this mess, I'll never live it down if, that is, they even let me stay on the team. But if I hadn't put the damn vest on I believe he would have killed me right there and then and I wouldn't be able to get the cell phone from him and then all would have been lost ... people would die and the team disbanded. And time is running out and I don't know whether they have disarmed all the bombs ...* It was a steady stream of consciousness running through his mind as he climbed with the weapon of his death wrapped around him.

At last they reached the top of the trail which led upwards through a heavily shaded forest and stepped out into the brilliant day. Musa, sweating profusely from the climb, welcomed the fresh breeze which had greeted them as they climbed out of the trees and onto a grassy flat area. He gazed around—they were on Pacific Point. He could feel the end game rushing towards them.

They could hear park employees still testing the speakers below them, although up here it wasn't as cacophonous as it was below.

"Are you going to try to get ahold of Abed and Yesal from up here?" Musa asked.

"There isn't much point while they are still checking those speakers and the merry-go-round. Yesal and Abed were to make sure no one touched what we've set. They're doing their job."

And that was when the speaker check stopped, the gates opened and people started to rush in.

Haqqanis checked his watch as a mirthless grin lit his face. "Soon ... soon all the unbelievers' laughter will turn into screams and the very ground they run upon will shiver with explosions."

CHAPTER SIXTY-THREE

"What the fuck is he doing?" Bilidou muttered to himself.

They had seen Raphael, Haqqanis and Afridi leave the house from their vantage point in the old YMCA parking garage and had driven back down through the parkade and had made their way out and onto the street. Trey was still snickering over Jim's call to the park employees to do speaker checks on all the speakers about fifteen minutes before. They had known from listening to the conversation which came through the tiny transmitter in Raphael's ear that when Haqqanis had made the calls to the by-then deceased Abed and Yesal, the background noise was such that he couldn't really hear them to identify their voices but just enough to to understand the Pashto language they spoke. So Haqqanis had decided it was safe to return to the park.

"The crazy, wild, danger loving, risk taker of a Scot!! I swear if he doesn't get himself blown to bits, I'm gonna kill him myself!" Bilidou muttered harshly.

"Why, what's happened, what did he do?" Trey asked, his voice filled with alarm.

"I think Haqqanis just tricked him into wearing a suicide bomber's vest!" Bilidou said.

"Oh shit, he didn't, did he?"

"Oh yeah, he did," Bilidou returned, shaking his head, then added, "I think it might have been a trust issue, and if Raphael didn't put it on, I suspect Haqqanis may have killed him right by where they parked the car. He gave Raphael the supposed remote control, but I think it's a fake. I think he's going to kill him after all the fireworks. My guess is Raphael knows or suspects that anyway."

Of a sudden Bilidou's phone rang, pulling him out of his dark worry about Raphael as he saw it was Sid Banks's phone number.

"Sid, tell me, ya got some good news for me?" Bilidou asked.

"I think so, Jim. I think we got all of the IED's," Sid said.

"You, think so?"

"Well, here's the thing. Of course we've disarmed all the IED's we knew about. But we were never sure about how many others he planted. We did find the other one that he planted in the playground, and we've gone over the park with a fine-tooth comb, so to speak, and found four more. And believe me, he found some pretty ingenious ways to hide them. It must have taken quite awhile to set them. I wouldn't be surprised if it took him all of one night to do it, which, from what you told me, was the only time he wasn't being monitored. So yes, I think we got them all, and that's as far as I can call it. The safest bet is a head shot and put the bastard down before he pulls out the cell phone."

"Ok, Sid, I understand. If worst comes to worst, we were planning on that course of action anyways. We have an operative with him and a sniper is set up in close proximity just in case," Bilidou said grimly.

"Yep, 10-4, I kinda figured. My boys are still going to keep lookin' in a discreet way, but we all think we got them all. Talk at you later," Sid return and turned his cell off.

Bilidou glanced at his watch and saw there was only fifteen minutes 'til the park opened. He put in a call to Rick, filled him in on what the bomb squad had found and what they thought.

"Man, oh man! I hate the phrase 'I think,' but I know Sid and those guys on the bomb squad and I trust them. The park opens on time. Your guy is still with the terrorist and he knows what to do?"

"Yes, sir, and we have a sniper on him as well," Bilidou heard the phone turn off.

CHAPTER SIXTY-FOUR

"You really can see the park, the ocean and the peaks from up here. It's so open. The sun enhances all the brilliant colours, the sounds and smells of freedom. My heart, my soul feel liberated, unfettered from the constraints of constant pain and torment. I remember the sensation of being young again. Remember when we were in university, there was time to laugh then, to gaze at pretty girls, to be in love. Can't you feel it, Adnan?" Zarak Afridi said as he breathed in draughts of the fragrant, ocean-washed air. "Why, you can hear the children laughing, even up here. Life was beautiful then."

"Soon you will hear them screaming. Those times are long past and I have not thought of them in a long time, and you would be wise to forget about about them as well. What is wrong with you today? Too long under the torture of Interpol has turned you into a childish, babbling idiot ... you, who used to take great joy in blowing up or assassinating our enemies? You, who also used to say 'kill all the children too, for if allowed to live will grow into the infidels, the unbelievers, our enemies.' What has happened to my friend with whom I have fought so many battles?" Haqqanis said in a harsh voice that dripped venom as he looked at Afridi through narrowed, hate-filled eyes.

Afridi had actually been driven back several steps by Haqqanis' acrimonious, grinding speech and had even put up his arms as if to fend off the words that had seemed like physical blows.

Raphael had almost felt sorry for Afridi ... almost.

Afridi's broken mind and body seemed to enrage Haqqanis beyond all reason and he continued to move in on the crumpling Afridi, his words driving him into the ground.

Musa, who had wisely backed out of the way and out of the line of sight watched Haqqanis' face with a certain enthralled fascination. This was a man who had never seemed to lose control, always in charge, always knowing everything down to the last detail and above all calm ... all the traits of a master bomb maker. And here he was almost leaning over the cowering, grovelling Afridi, his face almost the deep purple of beets, spittle flying from his mouth at every brutal word he wielded like punches on the completely broken body of Afridi who was, by then, weeping and pleading.

Then suddenly, completely out of the blue, Haqqanis, while still screaming at Afridi, reached under his baggy shirt and pulled a handgun out of the waistband of his pants and shot Afridi not once but five times! There was a shocked stillness, even the birds had stopped singing.

CHAPTER SIXTY-FIVE

"What the hell! What the hell just happened?! Bilidou asked of no one in particular as he gazed around. Then he heard the slight crackle of his portable. He keyed his portable and listened to his earpiece.

"Is Raphael ok?" he asked quietly into the portable. He knew his sniper had a complete view of what was happening.

"10-4. Haqqanis just shot and killed Afridi. Weirdest fuckin' thing I've ever seen and heard. And while I got you, why ... oh, fuckin' why, is Raphael wearing a suicide-bomber vest?!"

"It's a long story that has a lot to do with Raphael's personality," Billidou returned.

"Hmm ... I'll leave that alone for now."

"We still clear on the rules of engagement?"

"Crystal."

The conversation on his portable ended although Bilidou stared at the portable radio for a moment longer while he considered his sniper's temperament.

Then he looked up and said to no one in particular, "It's a good thing we've been recording everything 'cause there is some shit even I wouldn't believe if it wasn't being recorded."

There were grunts of agreement from both Carstairs and Das-Groot.

CHAPTER SIXTY-SIX

Musa was standing off to the side and watching the blur of events which had happened so quickly he hadn't had time to really digest them. One minute he had been watching two supposed friends and then one had turned on the other because he had brought up happy reminiscences of their youth. The verbal brutality with which Haqqanis had hammered Afridi had stunned him, and then after Afridi was down and out, utterly broken, to pull a handgun and shoot him not once but five times!

But even more shocking was Haqqanis attitude immediately after the event. Haqqanis' face, which had been deeply flushed with anger, had almost returned to its normal pallid colour, and he ran his fingers through his thick black hair, as some had fallen over his brow while he had raged at Afridi, and those slender fingers that had pushed his hair back were rock solid, no tremble of rage within them. His face, which had been twisted into a rictus of wrath, was now calm, almost peaceful as if nothing untoward had happened. He calmly tucked his handgun back into the front waistband of his pants before he turned and smiled briefly at Musa.

"Musa, would you mind getting that piece of garbage out of my sight," Haqqanis said with a dispassionate voice before turning to look down at the park.

Musa had to grit his teeth to keep his mouth from dropping open in shock as he moved to grab the now bloody, lifeless body of Afridi. He dragged him behind a bush and then walked back to where Haqqanis stood watching the park.

"I think it's almost time to set chaos free. Perhaps let a few more people onto the killing fields," Haqqanis said as his right hand fondled the pocket on his shirt that held the cell phone.

"And I want the bombs that are on timers to go off just as I set off the remote control ones so these infidels run from the explosions of some right into the explosions of others. It takes a 'Master's touch' you know to set off bombs at the perfect time so those who have managed to run away from one danger and think themselves safe, only for another bomb to go off where they think safety lies. It drives some quite mad before they die. It is quite entertaining to see some running around in circles not knowing where to turn," Haqqanis said lightly, almost as if he was a professor giving a lesson.

Raphael, having seen and then heard what had just transpired up on Pacific Point, had shed the remnants of his 'Musa' character as he looked with loathing and revulsion at the figure standing beside him.

"Have you seen what time it is, Adnan?" Raphael asked in a low, harsh voice.

Abruptly, Haqqanis looked at his watch, then shook his wrist and looked again. Then whirled on Raphael. "What have you done!!"

"My job! I don't hear any explosions ... do you?! Raphael said in a hard, low voice.

Haqqanis reached into his shirt pocket and grabbed for the cell phone just as Raphael leapt upon him with the same intent. And the two were in a sudden wrestling, grappling match as each tried to trip the other while maintaining their own balance. They twisted around each other trying to gain the advantage. Raphael couldn't reach his handgun without giving up some leverage and his grip on the cell phone which was still in Haqqanis' pocket. Haqqanis couldn't reach his handgun for the same reason, but he might be able to reach something else! He squirmed, twisted and reached over and then under Raphael's upper arm and managed to grab something which had been tucked away in his shirtsleeve and ripped it out with a grim laugh.

"See!! I have the real remote control for that vest you wear!" Haqqanis gasped as they continued to struggle as he flashed a breathless grin, his teeth bared in a snarl.

Raphael started to laugh as with one hand still grasping the deadly cell phone, he gave a mighty jerk and he heard the cloth pocket rip and the cell was in his hand. He swung and twisted wildly around and viciously struck Haqqanis in the face with his elbow directly under the nose with all his might going in an upward motion! It was a blow meant to disable or kill by driving the nose cartiledge up into the brain. Haqqanis screamed as his one hand flew up to his face, then he faltered, fell back and sprawled on his back and lay still.

Raphael bent over him his hands on his knees as he tried to get his breath. After a few moments he was able to talk into the earpiece. "I have the cell phone ... Haqqanis is either unconscious or dead!"

He stood up and took several more deep breaths as he looked at the cell phone. And then he looked to where he thought there might be a sniper in order to give the all clear sign when he heard and felt a sudden movement behind him. He whirled around and there was Haqqanis struggling to his feet, the bottom half of his face awash in bright red blood. He was holding what looked to be the remote control for the suicide bomber vest!

"I'm not dead yet, infidel!" Haqqanis said in a voice that was muffled by the hand he held over his nose and mouth to try to hold back the flow of blood from his nose.

CHAPTER SIXTY-SEVEN

Lula had watched the entire fight from where she was proned out upon the flat top of an ancient rock face just within the trees. From where she lay with a small metal triangle holding the nozzel end of the AK-47 off the rock, she had had a clear line of sight through the attached high-powered scope between the trees and had watched all that had gone on atop Pacific Point plateau. She had been given orders to shoot if she had a clear line of fire.

Unfortunately, due to the positioning of the three on the flat area, she had no clear line or she would have been able to take out Haqqanis and end all the drama much quicker. But a miss could mean the end of the one who was dearest to her. The shooting of Afridi and what had come before had shocked her, but again no clear line. Then Raphael had gotten into the fight with Haqqanis, both grappling over the cell phone, and she had been sure Raphael had killed him.

She had seen Haqqanis rise, as if from the dead, and he had had the remote control for the suicide-bomber vest in his hand!

Lula had watched as Raphael had manoeuvred him around. Her stomach was clenched as she managed to control the surge of adrenalin by slowing, deepening her breath, focussing on the sight, waiting for the perfect shot, the shot that would take out the bad guy before he could push the button and blow Raphael to bits. She heard the murmur of Raphael's voice as he slowly moved around, holding out the cell, obviously taunting Haqqanis as he took one slow step backward then another, with Haqqanis stepping in to take the cell from him. Just two more steps ... come on Raphael

... just ... one ... more! And then Raphael was holding out the cell and Haqqanis was reaching for it as he raised the remote control.

Her eye pressed to the scope, her finger on the trigger of the AK-47 and there, at the back of the head ... the occipital notch ... pulling back so gently on the trigger ... she felt a slight thump ... a hiss, and the bullet was away. A spray of blood and brain matter. She waited for the explosion that would mean she had failed in her task, but the only sound she heard was the singing of birds off in the distance.

CHAPTER SIXTY-EIGHT

Raphael had been utterly taken aback and horrified when he had heard a sound and whirled around only to seen Haqqanis rising from the ground like one of the undead. The blow to Haqqanis' nose should have killed or incapacitated him, and there he was starting to stand! From the amount of blood that was flowing down over the lower part of his face and splashing onto his shirt, Raphael suspected that Haqqanis was haemorrhaging out from the cartilage which the blow had driven into his brain, and it was only a matter of minutes before he was dead. The only reason he had managed to stand was because of the rage and adrenalin which were still coursing through his damaged brain.

That thought was of little comfort for Raphael as he knew it took just a nanosecond to push the button on the real remote control. He also realized Haqqanis was not in the proper position for the kill shot which would prevent him from pushing the little button and blowing them both to little bits. In one of those flashes of brain instinct, or survival, it occurred to him, if ever there was a time for him to talk, this was it. Working on the concept that bullshit baffles brains, or at least what was left of them, he held the cell phone just out of Haqqanis' reach.

"Come on, Haqqanis! I'll trade you the remote control for this cell phone. Just think, you might still be able to blow up a bunch little kiddies before you die," Raphael said as he waved the cell phone just beyond Haqqanis' reach and took another step back.

"Curse you, I will blow you up ... it will be worth it!" Haqqanis slurred in broken English.

"But then you won't get the cell phone 'cause both our bodies will be joined in bloody bits. We'll both be dead and joined for eternity and won't we have a jolly time with Allah and God!?" Raphael said, a demented grin on his face as he took another step back, forcing Haqqanis to step in and make a grab for the cell.

"Gimme that cell, godless infidel. And you wonder why we called for a jihad?! Haqqanis slurred as he took another stumbling step towards Raphael.

Of a sudden Haqqanis held up the remote control and mayhap feeling the ebb of life and the too-strong pull of death said, "We shall go into death together!!"

It was the first time that Raphael had felt actual fear ... not fear of dying but the fear of all he was going to miss ... and Lula. He closed his eyes, and then he heard a soft hiss and a loud bang!

He opened his eyes and there was a partially headless Haqqanis toppling to the ground, the remote control falling from his lifeless hand. He leapt sideways and managed to catch the remote control before it hit the ground. As he lay on the ground by the corpse, he stared at the remote control in his hand and began to laugh, a wild, crazy laugh which only stopped when he heard her voice.

CHAPTER SIXTY-NINE

"Sweet Jaysus, Raphael! I might have known you would be the only one to laugh at a time like this," a husky female voice said.

Raphael looked over to where she was standing, dressed in cami gear and holding an AK-47 sniper rifle in her hands. He gave her a wild, fierce, lusty look, the very same look the victorious Scots had worn, no doubt, after the Battle of Bannockburn. It was said that there were many a wee bairn born nine months after that particular battle.

"You look like a shield maiden for all the ages, my warrior, my everything. I shudda known that it would be you who took the shot." He strode to where she was standing holding the sniper rifle that finally put Haqqanis down then stopped abruptly as he realized what he was wearing. But his yearning for her was clearly and painfully written on his face. Lula had also started to move towards him in a stumbling walk, the tension between the two was like two magnets pulling towards each other. And yet there was one part of his brain that seemed to shout out to him.

He put up his hand and said, "This is not a Sunday morning going-to-church vest. We have to wait 'til it's been removed, and yet at this moment I almost don't care. All I want to do is sweep you into my arms and cherish you and hold you forever."

Lula looked at him and took one more unsteady step before she stopped and whispered in a husky voice, "But we always seem to be waiting."

Just as she had said those words they heard crashing and cursing coming from the small trail that led up to the plateau, and then there was a final crash, as Bilidou with Carstairs behind him broke through the heavy bushes and ended up on the edge of the plateau.

Bilidou saw Haqqanis' body first and then looked over to where Raphael and Lula were standing and studied their faces for a brief moment. Sensing the tension between them, he shouted, "Shit! Get those bomb guys up here before the heat sets off that suicide vest."

PART THREE

Upon the ancient silk road
The great Alexander Rode.
The Hindu Kush spread wide before him
The Himalayas a crown upon its upper rim.

His Quick-Silver gaze
Beheld Mount Tirich Mir ablaze.
A glorious crystalline peak
With a deep green valley at its feet.

Alexander lingered within the green Vale
And did spread his seed like any male.
Till he heard the siren's song
Of a battle on Jhelum River strong.

Quick-silver the colour of their eyes
The Falash still in the vale abide.

— "From Whence They Came," RW Wells

CHAPTER SEVENTY

The rest of the day had been consumed by a discreet clean-up of the scene up on Pacific Point. First, before all else, the bomb squad had removed the suicide vest that Raphael had been wearing for at least two hours. It had been then put in a special one-inch steel-lined bomb carrier, which members of the bomb squad had brought up, so even if it did explode, it could do no damage. Then the two bodies had been bagged and tagged, then removed. Finally, Raphael had given the bomb guys the cell phone, which contained the phone numbers that would complete the circuit on any remaining bombs in the park. The bomb squad, assisted by Ident members, would take it apart to determine what, if any, bombs remained unidentified and therefore a major threat to the park.

Both Raphael and Lula had given sighs of relief when the suicide vest had been removed. Raphael had seen the look on Bilidou's face everytime he had looked at the vest and knew he was in for a very strongly worded interview when he and Sergeant Bilidou were alone. It was something he was not looking forward to and, in the hopes of getting it over with quickly, he had even approached Bilidou while they were still up on Pacific Point. But Bilidou had cut him off by saying they had done a good job and there would be a debriefing in the next day or two when everybody, including the bomb squad members, could get together and go over all the good points of the operational plan and the questionable or bad points. Now was the time for the clean-up and a possible choir practice afterwards.

Jim Bilidou had looked at Raphael's worried expression and taken pity on him and added, "Don't worry, Raphael. Without you this wouldn't have worked as well as it did. Having said that, there are some real rough edges we have to work on for the next time."

Raphael had looked at him for a moment before he gave him a small smile of relief, then he returned to where Lula was standing and Bilidou saw them talking quietly together. He watched them for a few minutes and felt a small twist of envy, for although they never touched each other, it was as if they were in a world of their own ... maybe not so much a world but a feeling they were so closely connected, like you couldn't think of one without the other. They were both, in and of themselves, excellent operatives but even better when they worked together. *Oh hell, he was turning into a romantic in his old age*, he thought as he rubbed the back of his neck. He was weary. Hell, they were all weary. *Maybe a quick choir practice tonight at the gas garage might do everybody good.* He looked up again at Raphael and Lula and thought to himself, *I wonder if I will ever know everything that happened up here on the point.* He had heard from both Lula and Raphael the short version which would be extended, of course, at the debriefing ... but still.

"Dare I ask what you're thinking?" Trey asked as he walked up behind him.

"Well, first off I was thinking that a choir practice at the garage tonight, just so everybody involved can release some of the pent-up energy and dregs of adrenalin from all the shit that has gone on, might be a good idea. Of course, we'd invite the bomb guys. They did and are doing a great job, considering what little information they had to go on. And second, I was wondering ..."

"Let me guess, Raphael and Lula. Those two are so ... oh, I don't know ... sympatico with each other. But it doesn't seem to blind them when it comes to other members of the team ... it seems to add to their empathy towards other team members. My wife and I used to have something like that, but as we have gown older, had kids and, well to be honest, we never worked together so we live in the big wide world and there are lots of people in our world and not enough time to ourselves, although, I think I will try to make more time," Trey reflected as he considered Raphael and Lula before he turned back to Bilidou. "And shit, yeah, I think a choir practice would be an excellent idea. I think there's enough money in the slush funds for pizza and beer, enough even if we should invite the bomb guys. I've never known them to turn down a beer, and they certainly deserve one or two."

"Ok, sounds like a plan. I gotta phone Sid anyway 'cause the Ident guys are over in the garage dealing with the two deceased terrorists that got shoved into garbage bins 'til this was all over. We still gotta get them out of the park without anybody seeing us removing two stiffs. That certainly might put a damper on the fair and draw the attention of the Fifth Estate. We sure don't want any of those vultures swarming around and asking questions," Bilidou said.

"Ya know, Jim, when you're tired you really do wax poetic," Trey said and burst out laughing.

"Yeah, well go fornicate yourself," Bilidou said with a easy smile as he pulled out his cell phone and called Sid Banks, sergeant of the bomb squads.

"Yoh."

"Hey, Sid, Jim Bilidou here. So how's it goin' over there? They taking those two stiffs out discreetly?"

"Yeah, good thing too 'cause they were just starting to stink a bit. I think terrorists rot quicker than normal folks. They're gonna take them out like normal trash so nobody notices."

"Great! Say, we were wondering if you and your guys would care to join us for some pizza and beer at our garage later. Everyone did a great job, and we can talk and laugh at the garage with no civilians listening in," Bilidou said.

"Hey, sure my guys would like that."

"That's great, plain clothes and their civvy vehicles and what's said in there remains there," Bilidou added.

"Sounds good. We're just cleaning up in here. All the IED's have been removed for proper disposal. Say, did you guys retrieve the bad guy's cell phone?" Sid asked.

"We did, and it's on its way to you. Between your bomb guys and Ident, it's hoped we can ensure that we found all the IED's."

"Alright then. Sounds like things are on their way to being completed. Look forward to seeing you in a bit," Sid returned before he shut off his cell.

CHAPTER SEVENTY-ONE

They drove along Coast Drive towards the enclave which held many old mansions as well as some diplomanic residences. The atmosphere inside the vehicle was taut with the symmetry of their feelings for each other, their need to be together after a day where death had been so near. Yet neither had spoken since they had gotten into the car—there was no need to for theirs was a truly symbiotic relationship. They both felt the pleasant but persistent pressure, the surging urge that had been building every time they had been together. They both understood their time was at hand and they both felt the contentment, the serenity of that thought.

Lula laughed lightly before she said, "That was quite a choir practice tonight."

"Yes, but I think Trey bought too much beer. Good thing beer keeps so it can be put away in the fridge. But the pizza was gone. I think everybody was so stoked and I guess exhilarated by how everything went ... no bombs went off and nobody got dead except the bad guys. Most just had a beer or two, just enough to loosen the tongues so everybody was comparing notes. I think Sid's bomb squad is who we will be working with from now on," Raphael added.

"Yes, I saw Jim, Trey, Sid and Wilmer kind of sitting off in a corner, deep in conversation, and I'm pretty sure they were talking about that very thing. I think it's wise to have one of the bomb squads tied in with us so we aren't constantly explaining. I mean one of our main jobs aside from actual police work is gathering intelligence on and taking down terrorists. We already have a team of immigration officers we are working with although we didn't have to use them this time. Killing the terrorists seemed more expedient during this operation," Lula replied acerbically.

"Oh, don't ever kid yourself. The immigration officers will be getting all the info from this operation to see how our terrorists got into the country, whose associated with them and, of course there is Ahmed Khan to deal with. He's flagged as a major money man for the Talibad. I must admit, though, that I'm glad to have that earpiece out of my ear. Wearing it was like having big brother watching, total lack of privacy," Raphael said with a shake of his head.

"Yes, I can understand from even that short time with you up on Pacific Point when you were trying to do sign language. Between that and the suicide-bomber vest, it was very uncomfortable being around you," Lula said with a shutter.

"You're telling me ... how do you think I felt?" Raphael said softly then added, "But now is our time. The real debriefing is day after tomorrow."

He looked over and smiled at her, and she returned it with a look of complete understanding. Nothing more needed to be said.

They pulled off the road and into the entrance of the enclave. At this time of the night there were only a few street lights and the full moon to light the way to Cambpbell's Keep. All the houses were in darkness.

"What the fuck!"

"What's wrong, Raphael!"

"There are lights on in the house!"

Lula looked and saw that Campbell's Keep was indeed lit up.

Raphael parked back away from the house under the branches of a huge old elm tree, and as he stepped from the car, he pulled his undercover handgun from his shoulder holster and quietly closed the car door. Lula followed suite.

Raphael signed for her to stay close to the fence and work her way forward while he worked his way around the opposite side of the house to where the front door was. Both moved silently from shadow to shadow until Lula was on one side of the great, oaken front door while Raphael was on the side of the door where the door knob was. Lula watched as he tried the door knob. It was unlocked!

Raphael signed for her to go in low while he went in high once he had the door open.

Raphael gently pushed the door opened, and on the count of three they both moved in fast, both moving as a team towards the great room, and of a sudden there was a woman's scream and the shout of a man!

CHAPTER SEVENTY-TWO

"Grandmother! Grandfather Campbell. What! Why are you here? I ... we could've shot you!"

Raphael's grandmother desolved into tears and collapsed onto the huge sofa in front of the fireplace while James's visage, which was normally stern, took on an even sterner look and his face flushed red in anger.

"We have been trying to get ahold of you for the last three days and nobody seemed to know where you were although I got the sense, when I talked to your inspector, that he knew exactly where you were—he just couldn't or wouldn't tell us but did take our message. Alright, alright, Clair! You can stop the hysterics. The prodigal son, or rather grandson, has returned to the fold," James Campbell said stiffly as he looked his grandson up and down with something akin to disapproval and then turned his gaze to Lula, who was just putting her handgun in her shoulder holster and missed the look he gave her.

Raphael, however, did catch the dismissive look he gave Lula, and he felt the ire rising up in his throat like bitter bile as he looked directly at his grandfather and thought, as he often did, why did this man, his grandfather, dislike him so much. He knew that he had disapproved of him joining the police force, but it was more than that. There had always been a feeling of antipathy towards him even when he was a child. He had felt it and not just towards him but towards his mother and father as well, particularly towards his mother. Raphael gave an inward shrug of indifference as he studied his grandfather, then finally he spoke with a studied, cool tone.

"Well, Grandfather, why is it you have been trying so hard to reach me? Certainly, if you wanted to take the care of Campbell's Keep back, you could have just dropped me a note and I would have happily moved out. I cannot think why else you would have tried contacting me, and I know you are aware of the fact that mother and father are out of the country on a diplomatic mission," Raphael said in a cool, polite tone.

Lula, who was standing by Raphael's grandmother in an attempt to comfort her, was shocked by Raphael's tone. She studied both men, the older stiff with formality, while Raphael was relaxed looking as he stood waiting on an explanation from his grandfather. But Lula knew Raphael far better than most people and sensed that his words and pose were meant to irritate his grandfather. He appeared to have succeeded for his grandfather seemed, if possible, even more apoplectic. His stance had stiffened even further and his face was so flushed that Lula thought he might start bleeding from his nose or his eyes.

"You two stop that nonsense right this moment! Honestly, just like your father, Raphael, and you, James ... why ... why must you act like a bull elk ready to butt heads with both your son and grandson over stupid things which have never really meant anything to anybody. Just you and your stupid pride, which have driven away all that is precious in this life," Clair, who had recovered from seeing guns pointed at her, said in a low firm voice and then added "Honestly, the infamous Campbell temper and pride have driven a terrible wedge in this family. Enough is enough!"

Both men looked at her in shock. Never before had she spoken with such firmness, such strength.

"Raphael, I will tell you why we have been so desperate to contact you. We have received word through the consulate in Kabul that the medical and military caravan which your mother and father were travelling with has not arrived in Kabul and there was talk of some explosions near a village that is an al Qaeda stronghold. We've been trying, through our contacts, to get more information, but the most I can tell you right now is there are searches going on and they found some of the vehicles which had been in the convoy had been blown off the road and their occupants killed. Your mother and father were not among the dead.

Raphael went white and took a step back and fell to the sofa. While his grandfather continued to stand, although his shoulders had slumped down, his head was bowed and suddenly he looked his age.

"I think you must be the young police woman that Stuart has spoken so highly of. Lula, right?" Clair asked her before she turned back to the two men.

"Oh, for God's sake, sit down before you fall down, James. We must get this sorted out."

"I have it already sorted out, Grandmother. I'm going over to Afghanistan. I can probably get a plane out tonight to Germany and from there I will get a plane into Pakistan. I will keep in touch. You will have to give me your contact's name and how I can get in touch with him. I'm going up to pack right now. Lula come up with me, will you?

Lula was stunned by what she had just heard and looked at Clair who had simply smiled in relief as she gazed at her grandson. Even his grandfather, who apparently held some sort of anger towards both his son and grandson, had grunted and said it was about time someone took action.

Lula had followed Raphael up to his bedroom, and although she was alarmed by the scene she had just witnessed downstairs and Raphael's sudden plans to leave the country without so much as a by your leave, she remained quiet with the thought that she could calm him down. They could sort this out properly without interference from neither his bristling, angry grandfather nor his obviously concerned and kindly grandmother, or so she thought.

As they entered Raphael's bedroom, he gently closed the door and before she could get a word in he had scooped her up in his arms and his lips met hers in a deep kiss which took her breath away and for the moment wiped away any thought of objection to either the kiss or his plans. They lingered in the warmth of the kiss and the embrace for what seemed like an eternity, and yet it was not enough. *Would it ever be enough?* she thought.

When they finally came apart, both felt the chill of being apart and as she gathered her scattered thoughts, Raphael stepped back, turned and went to an old, large dresser and started pulling out some clothes. Then he went to another chest of drawers where, from the top drawer, he started pulling out some paperwork including his passport. The sight of the passport brought her back abruptly to reality.

"You can't be serious about leaving Canada and heading to Afghanistan?!" she asked in stunned incredulity and then added, "After what we have just been through with some of the former denizens of that misbegotten, ravaged country, surely not?"

Raphael, who had just pulled out a worn knapsack from the back of his closet, turned and looked at her. There was a look in his eyes as he studied her like he was trying to memorize all the features of her face and suddenly she was afraid and her hand went to her throat as she whispered,

"No, Raphael, I'll come with you. I have only to pack a small bag and we are gone."

Raphael shook his head before he said softly, "No, my beloved. I will be going to places where a woman is naught but property and even with all your expertise, it is just as likely you would be killed, and that I will not risk. Plus, I need you here. Someone must take care of my grandparents. Even though there is an antipathy between my grandfather, my father and me, a blood feud of sorts, they still need to be taken care of. And besides, if I'm lucky I need not go into Afghanistan, just to the Hindu Kush area. The last thing my father said to me before they left was if there was trouble, look to the Falash. I may, with luck, be only a few days and bring them both back with me. Keep your phone with you at all times. If I have to bribe someone, my grandparents have money ..." He left the rest unspoken.

"What about the debriefing? What about everything that has happened here?" she asked, desperate to distract him from his mad plan and hold him here.

"That is another thing I must ask of you. Although I hate adding this burden to those I've already asked you to bear. I leave it to you to tell or not tell Jim Bilidou why I had to leave. If you decide to tell him, add also I will bring back as much intelligence as possible. I will be making my way to the Falash tribe in the valley beneath Tirich Mir in the Hindu Kush. And this is very important and only for his ears if you decide he is safe. I have a Pakistani passport in the name of Naveed Malik, and it is the identity I will be using," Raphael said as he looked into her desperate eyes.

"But how ... when?" Lula stuttered.

"When I learned my parents were going back to Afghanistan on a diplomatic mission, I got a bad feeling so I contacted some friends of ours in Pakistan and they arranged for the passport, just in case ...," he said with a shrug of his shoulders.

"You had all this planned and never said anything to me? To Jim or Trey?" she said briefly.

"I was hoping I would never have to use them. Lula, it was just a precaution, and I know I'm risking everything. What would you do?" he asked.

She studied him for a moment before her shoulders slumped. "Shit! There are times when I hate it when you are right, but probably the same thing," she returned.

She watched him pack for a few minutes and was surprised when he pulled out a fairly large suitcase and packed it carefully with a couple of suits, shirts and other things which a businessman might carry. Then she saw him remove a decorated knife from a small drawer, wrap it in a small towel and put it in the suitcase.

"What's the knife for?" she asked.

"It was a gift from a friend, a Falash tribesman who had said at the time, ten or twelve years ago, that I would be back and to be sure to bring the knife with me. It may the only way for them to recognize me," he said as he closed the large suitcase and grabbed the small knapsack.

"You're going to need more than a knife where you are going."

"I can get any other weapons I need on the border between Pakistan and the Hindu Kush."

"I don't know if I'm going to be able to stand being without you," Lula said as a small tear trickled down her cheek.

Raphael dropped the bags and caught her to him hard, almost bruising her, and this time the kiss was one of desperation and the searing thought of being without her for even a minute, never mind a day or a week.

"Oh God, I promise I will be in touch, and I will be back as soon as I can be," he murmured before they kissed, their bodies almost melding together in urgent longing.

Then he broke away, grabbed his bags and was gone, leaving her desolate and despairing.

CHAPTER SEVENTY-THREE

Raphael managed to catch the last flight out for Frankfurt, Germany, with a connecting flight to Islamabad, Pakistan. He flew first class, which allowed him to stretch out so he could get some badly needed sleep although for the first couple of hours, Morpheus, the god of sleep, did not find him as his mind raced, like a rat running through a maze. Even the hum of the 747 jet engines, which usually soothed him, only added to the cacophonous thoughts which were dancing through his mind. He kept seeing the face of his mother and father ... were they still alive ... mixed with Lula's face and the faces of the dead terrorists and the police operation. Finally, out of sheer desperation, he called forth the inner stillness as he focussed his thoughts on the tip of Tirich Mir, the lofty peak where the snow did not melt, yet was so pure and white that it took on a blue-white colour at certain times of the day.

He considered the picture of that high mountain and felt a calm peace seeping into his mind and pushing back all the worry, all the faces, until there was nothing but drifting sleep. If there were dreams, they were not strong enough to cause him to wake.

A pretty stewardess woke him as they entered Pakistani air space and were preparing to land in Islamabad. His mouth felt like a thousand camels had spent the night sleeping in it, and as he rubbed his face he felt the five-day stubble. He longed for a hot shower and shave but he knew that while the shower was just a short distance away, the stubble would remain and thicken into a beard, for most men in the Hindu Kush area of Afghanistan and Pakistan wore beards.

Once the plane had landed and taxied to the terminal, he and the other passengers deplaned. As he stepped out, he was hit full force with the hot, moist air that was Pakistan in the summer. It felt like a hot, wet blanket had been thrown over him, and he felt the beads of sweat forming on his brow as he made his way to the customs and baggage area of the terminal.

In the customs area, he started to explain to a customs agent about his business plans with an old friend of the family. When he mentioned his friend's name, the customs officers immediately expedited his time in customs and bowed him out of the customs area. As he grabbed his suitcase, he looked around and immediately spotted a driver holding up a card with his name on it. Raphael identified himself to the driver and was immediately led to a shiny black limo parked outside the arrival doors. Many of the passenggers from his flight, who were still in customs, sent looks of envy his way as the limo pulled away.

The sights, the smells and the noise of Islamabad struck all his senses at once. He had to smile at the persistent flashbacks to when he was young and had spent many a holiday here with his parents. It always felt like he was coming home.

He caught the limo driver's eyes watching him in the rearview mirror.

"We go to the house of Karim Chaudhry?" Raphael asked in Urdu.

"Assuredly, we will be there in but a few minutes," the limo driver responded with a polite smile.

Raphael returned the smile and then turned back to gazing out the car window at the hurley-burley, the hustle and bustle of the ancient city. They were driving through one of the wealthier sections of Islamabad, and most of the mansions were contained within walls of brick and clay with guards at the elaborately decorated cast-iron gates. Raphael knew diplomats of other countries lived in this area, and as the limo pulled up to a particularly large wall, the driver honked the horn and a massive gate, seemingly of its own volition, opened wide and they drove in.

There standing on the tiled steps that led up to the colonnaded, massive carved oak doors of the mansion were Karim Chaudhry and his exotically beautiful wife, Azra. *Hell, what it really was was a palace,* Raphael thought as he looked up admiring, as always, the graceful beauty of the red marble Corinthian columns with the superb tile work which encased each pedestal. Karim and Azra looked like they were really part of an ancient Persian tale of a prince and his beloved princess come to life.

"Oh, Raphael, it is so good to see you even though it is under these terrible circumstances," Azra said in flowing, accented English.

Karim frowned slightly before adding, "Rest assured, Raphael, I have had my men out searching and it was they who found a part of a convoy. But, alas, those they did find were dead and the rest of the convoy has disappeared into the wildness of the Hindu Kush."

Raphael, whose face had been full of hope that his parents might have already been found, felt hope seeping away and foreboding rushing back in.

"Come in. There is no sense us standing out here in the heat. At least we can make plans in comfort," Karim added as he saw how weary Raphael was.

CHAPTER SEVENTY-FOUR

Karim had suggested that Raphael rest for a little while and then refresh himself with a shower before dinner after which they would discuss plans, and Raphael had readily agreed. Karim had also told Raphael that the clothing he had requested was already laid out for him.

When Raphael rejoined Kirim and Azra a couple of hours later, they were both amazed, for Raphael had changed into the clothing he had requested. The long-sleeved cotton, collarless shirt was a light tan, almost cream colour and extended to a little less than mid-thigh. He wore a dark brown short vest over the shirt, and his pants were baggy and of the same material as the shirt. He also had a thick wool long shawl rolled up and looped over his left shoulder, with the ends tied in a knot which rested upon his right hip. Looped over his right shoulder he had a leather bandole-ro-type belt with loops for holding ammunition which was buckled and lay against his left hip. And the final touch were the heavy sandals whose soles were from retired rubber tires.

Azra was the first to recover from the shock of seeing him dressed thusly and her light laughter made Raphael smile.

"Oh, Raphael, you look too much like a young tribesman ... a handsome young tribesman of the Hindu Kush, either going to meet a lady love or to hunt either man or beast," she declared as her hand went to her throat and her laughter settled down into a faint smile.

Karim studied him longer, his face grim as his eyes met Raphael's. "You do look like a tribesman but of the Falash tribe, and you have to know that the Taliban hunt them again, although from what I hear, far more Taliban are turning up dead while the Falash have disappeared like wisps of smoke. The Falash have pulled back into their secret places, only making sorties out to hunt and kill the Taliban. I fear you may find the wrong tribesman while looking for the other."

"Karim, there is naught else I can do but look for them. Father told me before they left to look to the Falash if something went wrong. I have no choice—I have to find them and I feel in my heart of hearts they still live," Raphael said with a shrug of his shoulders.

Karim threw a comforting arm around Raphael's shoulder before adding, "If it be Allah's will, you will find them. But come, we will eat and talk for some small time before it grows dark and you must leave us. I had heard from your father that you had become a police officer in your country and that the work you have done is very special. He was most proud when I spoke to him last."

During dinner on a tiled patio overlooking a forest of deodar cedars and date palms, Raphael told his father and mother's old friends a few of the funnier escapades of becoming a police officer in Canada. So the dinner took on a light tone and there were even bits of laughter. But each knew there were two missing from the table and that Raphael would be leaving as soon as the deepest dark of night came.

After dinner Kamir and Azra led Raphael into a small library at the rear of the mansion. The library was dimly lit as Kamir led Raphael to a small table and pulled off a cloth which had been covering the top of the table and the items upon it.

"I think you will be needing these where you are going," Kamir said as he indicated the weapons laid on the table.

Raphael walked up and saw an old and weathered AK-47 which looked like it had been used in many battles over many years. Beside it was a semi-automatic handgun and a large wicked looking knife. For each weapon there were large piles of ammo. Raphael looked up and smiled his thanks.

"I had thought to buy weapons when I crossed the border, but these will cut down on the time I thought I would have to use finding weapons," he said with gratitude.

"I know you already know this, but I must reinforce it," Kamir said. "The area where you go is churning with jihad and hatred. If you must put some bandit or terrorist down, make sure you kill him, for should he survive, he will send out the call and a hundred will replace him, and the hunter will become the hunted. Also, I'm sending Ahmed with you. He is trustworthy and will get you to a caravan that goes close to where the Falash are. Grease the palm of the caravan leader—not too much mind you. Whisper my name in his ear and he will take you where you need to go. There is a secret pocket sewn into the back of the vest and hidden there is your passport under the name Naveed Malik and money, both in coin and paper. Let no other eyes spy what you carry, for they will think nothing of killing you for it. Your weapons are of the best quality and have simply been made to look old. Lastly, Raphael, my heart screams for you to go naught, to stay here safe and my friend, your father, would also say thus. But it is as needs must. Bring them back!" Karim said in a low, grim voice. Azra stood slightly back as a tear trickled down her cheek.

Raphael simply nodded his head although his sight was slightly watery as he looked to the doorway to where Ahmed stood waiting.

CHAPTER SEVENTY-FIVE

Raphael met his guide, Ahmed, by a small secret back door that led out behind the servant quarters and they disappeared down a dusty track by some deodar cedars. Even this late at night Raphael could still hear the sounds of the distant city, for Middle Eastern cities never really went to sleep. In the end as they went further from the city, the sound died to a dull thumping sound and then finally to the quiet of the night. Still they walked on, keeping to the track that Ahmed seemed to know even in the depths of the dark. At one point Ahmed had waved his arm in a warning gesture and as Raphael had ducked down into slouching walk, he could see off in the distance the flickering light of a campfire and dark figures moving around it. He could feel Ahmed's tension as they moved further away from the city and into the wilderness of the Hindu Kush.

There came a time when Ahmed indicated they could stop for a few minutes and rest. Both pulled out their water bottles and took small sips.

"Hizhoner is in better shape than I expected and we have made better time, for we are very near the border and should cross it tonight. Therein lies the danger, for there are patrols which watch and report and then there are other eyes which look to see, so we go a secret way. Thee must be very careful where thou places thy feet. Raphael merely nodded at the whispered direction from Ahmed. It had suddenly come to him that Ahmed, his guide, had also been his limo driver earlier.

Raphael followed Ahmed down into a dried-out creek bed with high crumbling banks on either side. At one point they had to duck down under some dried-out bushes as a

Pakistani border patrol had walked upon the banks above them and both had barely breathed as the night was so quiet that even a deep breath might have been heard.

Finally, they had made it across the border and into the area where the caravan would likely be coming in the early morning. Raphael settled under a spindly tree, feeling safe enough to relax slightly while Ahmed sat with his back against a large boulder, and as they waited for the first light of dawn, he spoke in a hushed voice.

"We have made good time so you can rest for a small length of time until the caravan arrives. I will assist you with getting a position on the caravan, and then I must return to my master. I heard what he has said to thee and it is good advice. Be wary of all 'til thou finds the ones thy knows," Ahmed whispered.

Raphael merely nodded his head wearily as he thought to himself, *If Ahmed only knew it was all I could do to keep up with him, and I was too winded to talk with him.*

Raphael did manage to doze on and off for a time 'til he saw the sky starting to lighten in the east, and off in the distance he saw the ragged peaks of the lower end of the Himalayas turning from deep purple to lavender as the sun started its climb into the sky. It was only then that he heard groans, grumbles, growls and the loud snorts of camels complaining about their lot in life, and in amongst the sounds of camel despair he could hear the clicking of buckles, the grind of ancient leather saddles and the light chitter-chatter of females talking interspersed among the harsh calls of the camel drivers trying to get their camels to move along.

He smiled to himself as he thought of the time long ago when his mother, father and he had made their final escape from the lands of the Hindu Kush by way of a caravan, and now here he was returning. And who knows—maybe it was by the same caravan.

CHAPTER SEVENTY-SIX

Jim Bilidou was annoyed. It wasn't just that, he also felt a growing sense of unease.

Everybody who had worked the terrorist and bomb-maker operation had been given a couple of days off to decompress before the official debriefing. All those, with the exception of two, had called in to confirm the date and time; even the police chief had called in. But still no word from them, who were two of the main operatives. He had called them on their civilian phone numbers and even on their emergency phones ... nothing, nada, zilch, although he had left messages which had become firmer and more strident as the debriefing grew closer.

He looked at his watch. "Fuck!" ... two hours 'til the big debriefing and he still hadn't gotten ahold them. Out of a feeling of complete desperation, he tried Lula's emergency number one more time and let it ring.

Just as he was about to click off the cell phone, he heard the sound of the phone being picked up ... then silence.

"Lula? What the hell! ... Talk to me!" Bilidou said in a low, anxiety-ridden voice.

"Ah, Jim? ... Uh, hi ..."

In those few words he heard the reluctance, the caution, the disinclination in Lula's voice, and his unease swung into a feeling of intense worry.

"What's going on Lula, and where is Raphael"? Bilidou asked as he felt his guts clenching. "You and Raphael are going to be at the debriefing, right?"

Again a silent hesitation on the other end of the phone. Bilidou decided to take "the bull by the horns."

"Where are you?! he asked in a voice that brooked no more evasions or prevarication.

"Ah ... I'm at Raphael's parents' place," Lula said in a voice littered with pieces of resignation.

"Is Raphael there?" he asked.

"Ah ... no. He had to go out of town on an emergency," Lula returned stiffly.

"I'm coming over!" Bilidou said and switched his phone off.

'Now what!?' he thought as he strode quickly to his car.

He drove across the Narrows Bridge and onto the freeway without having to play bumper-car rush hour and managed to dodge several cars which were doing more sightseeing than driving the speed limit. He was blind to the beauty of the city by the ocean, his mind immersed in thoughts of the upcoming meeting and what was going on with two of his operatives. He actually made it to Raphael's place within fifteen minutes.

He stormed up to the door and rather than sedately ringing the doorbell, he hammered on the doorknocker which was more in keeping with his mood of the moment. The door swung open after the barrage of knocking and there stood Lula, her face pale and grim as she faced him.

"You better come in," she said tersely as she turned and walked down the hallway to the great room.

Bilidou followed her as he felt his anger starting to bubble up from his belly. He watched as she sat in one of the huge, leather chairs and looked up at him, her face a calm mask. *And that's just what it is, a mask*, he thought. *I can almost see the fine cracks in the mask ... What the hell is going on?*

"Lula, what the hell is going on ... and make it quick 'cause we've got a debriefing to go to!"

Lula studied his face for a few moments before she sighed and finally told Jim Bilidou what had happened.

"You actually thought he might be back from Afganhistan before the debriefing?" Bilidou asked in sarcastic wonder.

"Well, a girl can hope ... dream, can't she? And look, Jim, from the moment when Raphael learned from his grandparents that his parents had gone missing, it took him exactly fifteen minutes to pack and he was gone, and nothing I said could dissuade him. I did get a call from him when he got into Islamabad but nothing since," Lula returned, the strain of the last few days finally breaking through the mask of calm she had been wearing.

"I wish you two had called me. I might have been of help and maybe even gotten him over there quicker, but it is what it is. He's over there now, and we will just have to wait to hear from him. So throw on some different attire. We have a debriefing to go to, and we'll figure out what to say and do about the absent Raphael on the way over there," Bilidou said with a shake of his head.

CHAPTER SEVENTY-SEVEN

The last thing on Raphael's mind was the debriefing, although he had spent a considerable length of time earlier thinking of Lula while rocking back and forth on a grumbling camel. He had even spent some time thinking of all that had happened in the last few weeks. He suspected that he might be in some trouble for taking off without even a by your leave, but there was no use worrying about it now. He needed to focus on staying on this "ship of the desert" through the stormy ride. Funny thing, as a child he had thought it so much fun riding a camel.

The first day with the caravan had been nerve-racking, and he had kept a low profile as they had stopped at various villages to do some trading. But the closer he got to the Falash territory, the more he remembered and then he saw it, Tirich Mir, looming up above him, and he knew he was close to the Falash.

Abdul, the caravan leader, who had been watching this strange young man, saw him smile when they came into view of the great mountain. He did indeed seem to know the area, and yet there was a curiosity about him which made Abdul nervous and suspicious. Yes, the young man had paid him an adequate sum to join them, not too little and not too much, plus he had whispered a certain name into Abdul's ear, but still his Urdu was almost too perfect and his skin colour was paler than most who lived beneath the sun of the desert and the mountains. He would bear watching, what with all the crazy Taliban running around shooting everybody who were not like them or because of the jihad they had declared. What people needed now was some peace to live in and not be constantly suspicious of those around them. These Taliban and al Qaeda were a blood-crazed lot and would not hesitate to destroy him and his caravan if they thought he, Abdul, had brought such a one to spy upon them. Yes, he would have to be very watchful when it came to this young man. And if it came to choice between him and the caravan, Abdul knew exactly which way he would choose.

Raphael had caught the looks of speculation and suspicion Abdul had sent his way and had understood Abdul's dilemma. But for all of that, he still had to reach the Falash. He tried to stay out of Abdul's way by staying near the rear of the caravan and assisting the women with the packing and unpacking of the overnight gear, which was important to the comfort of those travelling the ancient, silk and spice trails.

They had passed through many villages. In those places Raphael had tried to make himself invisible for he sensed that some were terrorist strongholds where the iman spoke the language of fatwa and jihad and the women were in purdah while the men were armed and grim. Even the women of the caravan were discreet and unnoticeable as possible when near those certain villages.

There had come a time when, for a couple of days, they had not been near any villages and the whole caravan had seemed to relax. There had been much joking and gossiping after setting up camp for the evening. Raphael had offered to go out and hunt some wild bush-buck he had seen by a small stream earlier in the day, and all had agreed as they were running low on fresh meat; even Abdul had nodded and smiled in agreement.

Raphael had set out early in the evening just before dusk had started to paint the clouds and mountains with a touch of pink and lavender. The air held a fresh, clean smell which was refreshing, given that the hot, dry day had been laden with the smell of complaining camels and the sweat of the men and women who had moved among them. It was pleasant to be out here alone with his thoughts as he hunted the wild bucks he had seen earlier in the day. He knew he would be leaving the caravan in the next day or two, and it would be nice to leave them some fresh meat.

He felt excitement rising up within him at the thought of seeing Shandi again after all these years and wondered if he would remember him. He had tucked the knife Shandi had given him in a secret pocket sewn into the inside of his baggy pants by the waistband. He had not forgotten how the Taliban actively hunted the Falash in an effort to commit genocide against them for their religion and way of life. He felt if he found Shandi he would somehow find his mother and father with him or at the very least Shandi would know where they were.

Raphael came close to the stream where he had seen the buck and hunkered down behind a low boulder to await the bush-bucks' arrival at the stream for their evening drink. Sure enough, after a brief wait, he saw them—three large bucks, their coats a dusty-brown colour which blended into the surrounding area. They almost appeared as ghosts or spirits as they made their way gracefully to the stream. Raphael admired them from his position and would have rather simply watched them than have to kill one. But the caravan did need the meat, and it was the least he could do.

Of a sudden he heard a sound like a rock being knocked loose, then a harsh whisper, and he froze. He sensed someone or two were hunting him, and he remembered the warning he had gotten just a few days ago about the the hunter becoming the hunted. He could hear the bucks' startled grunts, and then the splash they made as they alerted to the sound of men coming their way.

He turned to make his own escape and when he stood up, he came almost face to face with a bearded man who was almost as startled as he was. Raphael easily overcame him and left him unconcious upon the rocks before he started squirming and twisting amongst the rocks, boulders and twisted roots of the ancient stream bed in an attempt to escape whoever these men were, who, apparently, had been following him. He had moved quite a distance down the stream bed before crouching amid some roots of ancient shrubs and tried to quiet his breathing as he listened for the sounds of being followed. He had known, instinctively, whoever had followed him did not have his best interests at heart.

Silence ... even the breeze had died down. Perhaps he had lost them, whoever they were. Should he stay where he was? Or should he try to get more distance between the followers and himself? He waited, but after a while he could feel his muscles starting to stiffen up. If he didn't move soon, his ability to move at all would be severely compromised. Now or never ...

He stood and suddenly saw a swift movement to his right coming towards him! He tried to duck! Too late! He felt the blow to his right forehead and the massive pain blossoming out from the initial contact area, and then there was nothing, just a spiralling blackness enfolding him in pain.

CHAPTER SEVENTY-EIGHT

Water flung on his face brought him up from the depths of darkness where his conciousness had lain, although he was still dizzy and his thoughts were confused. He was being held up by two men while a third had grabbed him by his hair and brutally brought his head up so his face could be seen. He heard another man raving and yelling in such a harsh voice it caused his head to ache even more. He managed to open his eyes, and once his vision had cleared he saw a bearded man harranging the caravan leader in Urdu. Abdul, in a pleading voice, was denying any knowledge of him. For a flickering moment their eyes met and Raphael understood that should he acknowledge Abdul in any way, these men would lay waste to the caravan, killing everyone and everything.

Raphael groaned loudly enough that he drew the attention of the terrorist who strode to where he was being held and looked into his face.

"So you are awake, eh?" he snarled.

Raphael gave a low moan in response and was promptly slapped across the face.

"Do you know this man?" the terrorist asked Abdul as he pointed to Raphael.

Abdul shook his head vigorously before saying in a humble, almost begging way, "Nay, nay, your worship, we know him naught."

"He comes with us then, and we will dispose of him properly as we do with all Falash. And you, leader of the caravan, be on your way before I give a second thought to how you are out here and we find a Falash so close to where you camp."

Abdul nodded as he backed away, and then hurried back to decamp and move on in the night.

CHAPTER SEVENTY-NINE

He sat crosslegged on a small granite outcropping that overlooked the secret, hidden valley which held the last of the Falash tribe. He had sacrificed a small goat in the proscribed manner earlier in the evening and then had climbed up the steep hill to the outcropping while chanting certain mantras. He felt the inner stillness starting to seep into him, bringing with it the calm and peace which allowed him to think clearly as he gazed up at Tirich Mir, using it as a focus point.

It was quiet and peaceful up here so he was able to let his mind wander free of all the hindrances of responsibilities, which at times had seemed overwhelming. His father had died during a raid on a Taliban encampment, and he had become leader of the Falash tribe, with all its additional worries. Even now he still felt the pain of that loss, although time had dulled it somewhat and no doubt there would come a time when thoughts of his father would bring more smiles of knowing his father and less sighs of the pain of losing him. There was also the thought that his father had died fighting the Taliban, and there was honour in that.

As his mind wandered amongst the problems and new anxieties, the quiet and calmness of this place helped him find solutions that might not have come to him while he was down amongst the noise and constant questions of his people. His biggest concerns at this moment were the two people who were, at this moment, hidden in the village of the Nuristani tribe. He had known both of them and had it not been for the Taliban and al Qaeda actively trying to destroy his people and by extension the two who were hidden, he would have taken great pleasure in seeing them, although one of them was injured.

Of a sudden, while he was in the midst of the inner stillness, he felt ... sensed ... the one who had been missing from his world for a long time and whose presence had given him great joy was somehow near. Yet he also sensed there was great danger surrounding him.

He stood up abruptly to head back to the village and saw one of the villagers working his way up to where he stood. He knew just by the way the villager moved and the expression on his face that he carried news of some importance.

"Shandi! Shandi! Come down, there is a man here ...," the villager, Badeed by name, was trying to say as he ran up the hill.

"Badeed, slow down before you fall down. I'm coming down," Shandi Cershi said as he stepped down off the outcropping.

Shandi climbed down to where Badeed was standing, trying to get his breath back.

"Alright, tell me what is going on and why are thee in such a hurry?" Shandi asked.

"It is Abdul, the caravan leader. He is waiting by the village to talk to you," Badeed replied after he had caught his breath.

Shandi simply looked at Badeed and nodded, but within his heart of hearts he sensed who it was that Abdul wanted to talk to him about.

"I will go and talk to this Abdul while you go to the village and get Pazir. Once I finish talking with this Abdul, you follow him discreetly and make sure he leaves no trail for others to follow," Shandi said. Badeed nodded and gave him a grim smile.

"Assuredly, and if he is leaving a trail?"

"Dispose of him."

"As you wish," Badeed said before leaving Shandi to go find Pazir.

Shandi circled around the village to the spot where Abdul waited and found him sitting by himself, his back against an old tree. As soon as he saw Shandi, he rose to his feet and bowed his head.

"I understand you wish to speak with me?" Shandi asked.

"Yes, I have a tale to tell you. It may or may not mean anything to you, but it may save a man's life who seemed to be looking for the Falash," Abdul said as he watched Shandi's face.

"Tell the tale then, and I will decide."

Abdul proceeded to tell all he knew of Raphael, or as he knew him, Naveed.

Shandi had listened and had at first started to smile, for this indeed was the one whose spirit he had felt. But then, as Abdul had told of his capture by the Taliban, Shandi's face had turned grim and he had asked in a harsh voice, "And why didn't you try to save him?"

"Those terrorists all had guns and would have killed me and mine right down to the chickens if they thought we knew him. I have come to tell you only because he could have given us away and he didn't, so I, we, owe him our lives. And he still may be alive, as it was only hours ago they took him and thee might have a chance of saving him. I have an idea where they may have taken him. It is a small village to the west of here which has been overrun by the Taliban, and I have heard this is where they take all their prisoners who they think are spies or those who in their eyes have not followed the holy precepts of their iman. They are a rough and ignorant bunch who seem to take pleasure in killing, and I have heard even stoned a poor women to death for not obeying her husband."

"This is good thing you have done this day. I think I know of this village, and in truth they have killed some our people just for being Falash. As to the one you spoke of, I do indeed know him as a friend," Shandi returned and then added, "Do you wish to come with us as we track down these terrorists?"

"Alas. No. Were it just me and my men, I would be tempted to join you, for I have no use for these terrorists. But I have woman and children with me, and I dare not risk it. I do wish you happy hunting though and that you find your friend safe," Abdul said.

"And to you as well. It might be even better if you move quickly out of the area as we plan on visiting that particular village and do some cleaning," Shandi returned with a fierce grin.

Abdul nodded his head in understanding.

After Abdul was out of sight, Shandi signalled to where Badeed had been waiting.

"Abdul seems safe but he has given me some information which we must act on immediately. There is a nest of vipers in a small village near here that we must dispose of as they are spreading their venom near and far, and also indiscriminately killing innocents. Tell Pazir to bring the rest of the men. It is time we do some cleaning, but I think we must hurry so no more are killed."

Badeed's visage took on a fierce look as he bowed to his chief before turning and quickly making his way back to the village to gather men and weapons.

CHAPTER EIGHTY

He stumbled on the uneven ground, his hands bound behind him, and he would have done a face plant had rough hands not yanked him upright so he would not miss his date with the wall ahead of them. He glanced at the wall and saw the bullet-pocked surface coated with dried blood stains, and had a pretty good idea what the old wall was used for these days. He looked down at his dusty, sandal-clad feet, the soles of which were made out of old tires that had outlived their original purpose ... retired tires. His feet just kept walking because when he hesitated he felt the nozzle of an AK-47 push against his back through his loose bleached cotton that protected against the heat somewhat. Yet, that nozzle at his back felt cool. Interesting, in a fuckin' "for we that are about to die" kinda way. Only there was no "we;" it was just him walking, walking to the wall.

He didn't want to look at where his walk would end, so he studied the harsh, hard and unrelenting dirt upon which he walked, maybe for the last time. He could see that some-one had hacked and worked the ground into rows, no doubt pouring their sweat and waning hope into the land where gradually fecundity had dried up and blown away in this last century. Rain had become a stranger that rarely passed this way, and then only to provide cruel, false hope.

Oh shit. In these last moments of life, he was playing mind games to distract himself from what lay ahead, never mind distracting himself enough so that he didn't meet the end of his life babbling and crying like a fucking baby. And wouldn't you fucking know it, his ability to write finally comes to life! And wouldn't you know it, he was going to be leaving behind writing that was as bad as an old syphilitic whore commiting one final act of coitus on some ancient john who couldn't get it up with a tire jack, never mind the second coming.

That last little bit of ignoble thought caused him to burst into laughter, and that was how he met the wall. His laughter abruptly stopped as he stood facing that which he dreaded. Rough hands turned him around and held him steady for a moment until he got his balance. He felt the urge to thank them and thought, *Yep, typical Canadian. Even though these assholes are about to shoot me, I wanna thank them for a small courtesy.*

One of those soon-to-be parts of his firing squad pulled back the hood of his robe, revealing what some would consider a handsome face with classic cheekbones riding high over a soft, dirty beard, a Roman nose, lips that any woman would find interesting, a broad, high forehead wearing a large purple and red bruise on the right side, topped off with a curly, shaggy head of deep brown hair. It was the eyes though that helped him pass for one of the nomads of the area; they were large with long eyelashes (the envy of any woman) and the irises were of the unique sea-foam grey colour of a storm-tossed sea, or as some would say, the colour of quick-silver.

He stood there watching the firing squad arrange itself in some semblance of order, and his mind games continued: *Well shit! This really sucks. Just when I'm finding myself, I get shot. Maybe my dear, sainted mother named me Raphael after an archangel for a reason. Now would be a good time for me to spread my wings and get the flock outta here. Alas, I feel no stirring of wings on my back,* he thought. He saw them lifting their rifles and heard the shots fired and a starburst of pain in his head, then falling ... falling ...

CHAPTER EIGHTY-ONE

They had to crawl the last two hundred feet or so to the very edge of the village. As they were making their way through the scrub brush and low boulders they were close enough to hear the iman exhorting the male villagers to lay waste to more unbelievers as it was quickest way to paradise. And then they heard shots and a woman's wailing scream as others jeered. In fact, all the noise from the centre of the village hid the sound of their approach, and they were able to move quicker.

It had turned out to be relatively easy for Shandi to gesture to his men to take up positions around the village centre, for the focus of the villagers was on what was occurring at the wall in the centre of the village as men dragged out an older man and stood him against an old, blood-stained wall. Then five or six men lined up facing the wall, and as a crowd of villagers cheered, the order was given, shots ran out and the man collapsed like a broken doll at the bottom of the wall. They watched as the corpse was dragged away and tossed on a pile of corpses who had already met the wall.

Shandi watched as the next man was pushed out of a hut. Something about him was familiar, the way he walked, and as he drew closer to the wall, the sudden laugh. It was a laugh he had heard before, a long time before, but it was his laugh. There was much taunting and mocking from the crowd until one of the men beside the soon-to-be victim of the wall pulled off the victim's hood and all could see the young, handsome man who stood before the wall wearing a ferocious grin upon his face.

It was him! Who else would stand before a firing squad and face death with a laugh. It was then Shandi gave the signal and his men raised their weapons, and just as the order to shoot was given by the terrorist, his men also fired!

When the gunsmoke cleared, all who had been part of the firing squad lay dead upon the ground. But, alas, the young man also lay motionless on the ground by the wall. Shandi cursed his luck and ordered his men to lay waste to those who had been involved in the monstrous destruction even as the iman screamed at the village men to destroy the intruders. The villagers, caught off guard, were confused and started firing at each other while Shandi and his men easily picked off those involved.

Shandi dodged back and forth as he tried to reach the wall where his friend lay and finally had to shoot the iman, who had grabbed a weapon and was trying to ward off the intruders. Once the iman lay dead, the villagers' confusion was complete, with no one to guide them. Shandi made it to the wall, ducked down and lifted his friend's head and upper torso. It was only then that he heard a groan and saw that a bullet had only grazed the side of his head.

"Thanks be to Allah, and the gods that reside on Tirich Mir that you should have such a hard head, my friend!" Shandi said with a laugh before he gestured for one of his men to help him carry his friend to the edge of the village.

Once his friend was safe with one of his men guarding him, Shandi returned to the village, and with brutal joy, he and his men finally cleansed the village of the Taliban terrorists who had taken up residence there.

CHAPTER EIGHTY-TWO

He felt the grinding bumps that seemed to be shooting up through his body and striking his forehead like small, almost continuous explosions of pain. He couldn't understand why he should be feeling like this when the last thing he remembered was going to shoot some bushbuck down by the stream, unless, of course, one of the bucks took umbradge at the thought of becoming someone's dinner. He started to grin at that thought when a particularly large bump caused whatever he was riding in or on to jar him even more violently. It felt like Canada Day fireworks going off in his head, and he groaned at the crushing pain.

He heard a voice which seemed to be ordering something to be stopped and, mercifully, whatever he was in or on halted. A flap of the of material or a blanket lifted and a grinning face appeared in the opening.

"How are you doing, my old friend? For a while I thought you had left this world and gone on to paradise," a warm, happy voice which seemed to match the smiling face asked.

The face seemed somehow familiar although he was having a hard time thinking past the pain and yet, what was it about the face ... older looking but familiar? The throbbing and pounding in his head seemed to be lessening now that the rough motion had stopped and his mind started to clear somewhat.

"Somehow, I think ... wasn't I just in front of a firing squad?" he asked in a confused voice.

"Yes, indeed, you were and we liberated you only just in the nick of time or perhaps just beyond the nick of time, for a bullet grazed your skull and had knocked you senseless," the smiling face responded.

"So that is why my head feels like it is about to explode?"

"Assuredly. And it would seem, from what I'm told, your head has received at least one other blow this day."

Shandi watched as Raphael raised one slim hand up to his forehead and lightly touch the bandage. Even that small movement caused Raphael to wince in pain.

"Perhaps you might try riding on a horse rather than being dragged behind one for a time? It might go easier on you and we can talk as we ride," Shandi asked.

Raphael looked up at him with a certain amount of relief and nodded his answer.

Raphael stumbled as he exited the roughmade contraption they had been dragging him in while he was unconcious. But in the end, the fresh air and relatively easy gait of the horse proved more beneficial to his recovery than being bumped and dragged around behind the horse.

As they rode together with Shandi's men walking or in some cases riding around them, they finally had a chance to talk although the first words which Raphael spoke caused some surprised laughter as Raphael asked, "Chief Cershi, it appears that somehow you saved me, and where is my friend Shandi?"

As Raphael heard a few snickers and some bursts of laughter around him, he realized he had made a mistake and that was when he really looked at the person riding next to him.

"Shandi, is that really you? But you look so much like your father. Please forgive me—I meant no disrespect."

Shandi burst into laughter at Raphael's discomfort before saying, "And none has been taken. Many have commented over the years about how much alike my father and I were. Alas, he was killed in a firefight with some Taliban just in this last year. As to how we found you? We've actually been expecting you because of your parents. And as luck would have it, Abdul, the leader of the caravan you were with, found me and told me you had been taken by the Taliban. It would seem we arrived just in time."

Raphael felt deep shock and dismay, for the elder Cershi was good man and great tribal chief who had convinced Raphael's father, while they were hiding out with Falash tribe, that Raphael should go to school with the village children and learn the ways of a warrior with Shandi, his son.

"I am so sorry, Shandi. Your father was a good man who I always remembered with respect. It would seem from your words that you somehow knew my mother and father recently returned to Afghanistan on a diplomatic mission. Then you may know their truck convoy was attacked by terrorists. My father had said, just before they left, to 'look to the Falash' if anything were to happen to them. That is the reason I came looking for you and your father to see if you had heard anything or might have an idea about what had happened to them," Raphael explained, apprehension written plainly on his face.

"I have good news and concerning news for you. First off, we found your parents. They are alive and we have hidden them within the Nuristani people tribal area. Right now they are safer with them than us, given the Taliban and al Qaeda seem determined wipe the Falash people off the face of the earth at this time. But as you know, we are very hard to kill," Shandi said with a fierce laugh, and those who were within earshot joined in.

Raphael was so relieved that he very nearly fell off his horse before he recalled there was a second part to the news concerning his parents, and with some trepidation he asked his old friend, "And what is the second piece of news?"

"Your father was injured in the fight to get away from the terrorists and has been unconscious from the head injury he sustained. They are both safe for now, but we must move them soon, for the terrorists have been looking for them. And then there is also your father's injuries. Although having seen you getting shot in the head by a firing squad and survive, I'm hoping you inherited such a hard head from your father," Shandi said lightly.

Raphael smiled at the remark although his mind was racing as he tried to figure out how to get to his parents without jeopardizing them, the Nuristani or the Falash people.

Shandi could feel the tension building within his friend and see the strain on his face He was also mindful of the fact that Raphael had also been injured.

"Come, come, we will figure this dilemma out together once we are back at my village. There will be many who remember you from before. So we will sit and eat, then you must rest before we work this problem out."

Raphael nodded reluctantly, and then smiled at Shandi thinking how he had pulled both him and his parents out of a disaster not just this time—Shandi's father and the Falash people had been instrumental in saving them the first time years before. He owed these people so much.

CHAPTER EIGHTY-THREE

They sat slightly back from the other villagers who had initially been sitting and standing around a fire pit, although soon someone had started to play on a type of flute while another villager began to beat softly on a drum. Both Shandi and Raphael continued talking in low voices as others began to dance and sing as they moved around the fire in the centre of the village.

It was the first time in a long time Shandi had allowed any type of fire because he understood the danger. They had been hunted by the terrorists for many months, but this night was special. Not only had the Falash finally dealt with the Taliban who had taken over a village close to them then started using it as a staging area for actively hunting his people, he and his warriors had managed to rescue his friend who had been away from them for a long time. Shandi, however, was wise enough to set out sentries to make sure none came too close to the entrance of the hidden valley inside which the village lay.

Many of the villagers remembered Raphael and were happy to see him, especially some of the young women who had been awkward little girls when last they saw him and now were tall, graceful young women. And not a few were very lovely with their embroidered scarves draped over their blue-black hair and their grey eyes looking him up and down in their bold way.

When Shandi saw this, he burst out laughing and then teased Raphael about how welcome he would be in the village as the husband of a Falash wife. Raphael actually thanked the gods that it was dark enough that no one could see him blushing or Lula was with him, for she would not have been pleased about Shandi's comment.

"There are some very beautiful women here, and I'm surprised you've not taken a wife, Shandi," Raphael replied with a slight smile.

"There is one to which I am bonded, but we cannot do the final, formal rites 'til the year of mourning is over. No doubt you will meet her later. For now you and I must discuss how we are going to get you and your parents out of here. With your father's injuries, and given all the terrorist activity in the area, the way overland is out. I don't mind telling you, my friend, the danger becomes worse each day," Shandi said, the laughter leaving his face only to be replaced by a look of anxiety.

"I, too, have been thinking of a way out that won't endanger the Falash or the Nuristani people, and I think I might have come up with a plan. But it requires a phone of some type. If I can set this in motion, I think not only can I get my parents out but perhaps we can be rid of many of the terrorists in the area, or at the very least create such noisy destruction that they flee of their own accord, and whatever small bands are left you can dispose of in an appropriate fashion," Raphael returned.

"If your plan can truly do what you say, I am interested. What type of phone do you require, for I don't think a cell phone will work in these mountains?" Shandi asked in an undertone.

"I'm thinking of some type of satellite phone. Would there be such a phone in the area which we can beg, borrow or steal?" Raphael asked, his mind racing with the beginnings of a wild, crazy plan.

"A satellite phone?" Shandi returned as Raphael nodded. "Aaahhh ... let me think ..."

Raphael, who had been watching Shandi, saw him suddenly looked uncomfortable. He seemed almost hesitant and his eyes looked off down the valley as if he was considering something.

"What's wrong, Shandi? What have I said that makes you so uneasy, my brother? If I have misspoken, have said something which makes you so ill at ease, I'm sorry," Raphael said, a perplexed look sliding onto his face.

"No, no it is not what you say, it is what I know that may shock you," Shandi said as he looked up.

"What? I don't understand what you mean. I know you are in a war zone where certain groups are trying to destroy your entire race and you must defend yourself in any way you can and do whatever you must to survive," Raphael replied.

"Yes, you are right. But what if a certain tribal leader knew a certain farmer, high up in another hidden valley, and this farmer grew a cash crop in order to feed his family, and what if the Americans would burn his crop if they knew about it? And as a result of this cash crop, the farmer not only helped his family but also the Falash and Nuristani people, providing weapons and at times food. This certain farmer also has a satellite phone for ... for business ... and, of course, he can be trusted. What would you say?" Shandi asked as he watched Raphael's face, which at first had a perplexed look on it but within a few moments the baffled look disappeared to be replaced by a smile of understanding.

"I would say this certain farmer was a kind and thoughtful person, and I would wonder if he would let us use his phone. In these high valleys, it is hard to see what is going on, as you know well. I would, though, tell my farmer-friend that the Americans are busy with other matters right now. But there will come a time when they might turn their gaze to what the farmers in the area are growing. And this farmer-friend should not get too greedy and watch for the time when the war slows down as that would be when they will take an interest in what is grown, especially colourful flowers," Raphael said, and Shandi had listened to what Raphael said and nodded his head in agreement and relief.

"You are very wise, my friend. And, yes, I believe he would let us use his phone. In fact, he would probably come down for a visit and bring it with him, which would be best for he would not want to burden us, or rather you, with the knowledge of where he lives," Shandi returned with a broad grin that matched Raphael's.

"And when may we look forward to this visit?" Raphael asked.

"Tomorrow afternoon, I think."

"Then we must be ready with the rest of the plan."

CHAPTER EIGHTY-FOUR

After the discussion about the satellite phone, Shandi called in one of his men who was related to the farmer and gave him a note to take to the farmer. Shandi had explained how urgent it was that the farmer get the note and for the runner to come back with him. The runner assured Shandi they would both be back by noon the following day.

With that done Raphael explained the rest of his idea to Shandi. Shandi had listened and, at first, was amazed, even doubtful that Raphael might be able to get his hands on such things until Raphael briefly explained his own job and who he ultimately worked for. Then Shandi, convinced of the possibility of the plan, added in his own thoughts. They both went over and over what they had come up with 'til it sounded doable, hinging, of course, on timing and if they could get the equipment and the manpower to handle it.

Finally, Raphael got up and stretched as he looked over and saw the fire had burned down to crackling embers. Then he looked up at the sky and saw a slight easing of night's hold on the sky to the east above the peaks, although Tirich Mir, the grandest peak in the Hindu Kush, was almost directly above them and still held the night close. He thought he saw a flash at its very top, like a single star was resting there. He let the mountain fill his senses and felt the inner stillness seeping through him, bringing with it peace and calm as he sent a silent prayer up to the gods of the mountain.

Shandi watched him for a time and then also looked up. He too saw the brilliant flash and sent his thoughts up and up to mix with Raphael's. It was quiet and the pre-dawn breeze brought with it the smell of fresh snow from atop the peaks. There was a certain contentment they both felt.

There was no need for anymore words between friends, and after a time they both went to their respective huts to grab some sleep before all the action started.

CHAPTER EIGHTY-FIVE

After a few hours sleep, Raphael woke to sunshine streaming through the window of his hut. He stretched and when he touched his forehead, he found his headache from the bullet graze and the earlier blow had, for the most part, gone and all he felt was a slight tightening of the skin around the graze in his scalp. He hoped his luck, as far as injuries went, held up, for by rights in the last couple of weeks, he shoulda ... coulda been dead.

With that cheery thought rebounding through his head, he left the hut only to find Shandi waiting outside for him with some food and what appeared to be rolled-up maps. As he ate Shandi unrolled one of the maps, and Raphael could see it was a topographical map of the area.

"Where did you get these maps!? These are just what we need!" Raphael said around a mouthful of food.

"My father had helped the Canadian soldiers with certain coordinates in the area and guided them to other areas that were not known to al Qaeda or the Taliban but were excellent spots for the soldiers to use as sniper and watching posts. Just before a major in the intelligence unit was being sent home, his deployment over, he came to my father and gave him these maps, for he thought we might be able to use them at some time," Shandi returned.

"They are exactly what we need. With these all we have to do once we get to where my mother and father are is call in the coordinates off these maps. What a relief! I have been racking my brain about how we were going to get the proper coordinates," Raphael said with a big grin as he poured over the maps as Shandi pointed out on one of the maps where the Nuristani had hidden Raphael's parents.

"Once we get the phone and I call in, how long do you think it will take for us to get to that particular place?" Raphael asked.

"Well, we must go on horse back for approximately four hours before we come to a village where we have an old truck hidden away, and then it is at least another four hours by truck, and then another hour on foot up into the Valley of the Caves," Shandi responded as he pointed out the route on the map.

Raphael nodded before adding, "Alright, how many men should we take with us, and do you think we have enough weapons?"

"Assuredly, we have enough weapons, for the Canadian major who left us the maps also left us with weapons to add to our collection. As to the men we need, first you must make the call to your friends to see what they can do from their end, and then we will make the determination about manpower."

"So now we await the arrival of the certain farmer we discussed last night. Waiting is always the hardest," Shandi said, and Raphael simply nodded his agreement as he watched the trail they would come in on.

Raphael felt his headache starting to ramp up and he wondered if it was just the injuries he had sustained or a combination of head wounds, stress and speaking Urdu mixed with Pashto, Farsi and Persian for the last several days. He even speculated to himself about his ability to speak English after all this time. Maybe Shandi was right—maybe he should take a Falash woman as a wife and just stay here. And wouldn't that have Lula seeing red ... He could just see her storming the battlements, as it were, to rescue him from some Falash woman.

"You are quiet my brother, and yet you have a smile on your face. Are you alright?" Shandi asked.

"Undoubtedly. I was just thinking of my woman back in Canada, my warrior woman," Raphael said.

"Aaaahhh, we must talk about her sometime, but not now for I see the certain farmer coming down the trail."

Raphael looked up and saw the farmer, an older man with a long bushy, grey beard, riding a small mountain pony coming down the trail which led into the village. Now, as Shanti had said, they would find out if his friends could do anything. All Raphael could hope for was that Jim Bilidou had enough pull or favours owed to him to help get them the equipment and manpower to pull off the plan.

CHAPTER EIGHTY-SIX

When Shandi had assisted the certain farmer, by the name of Mukhtar, from his horse, Raphael noted he carried a large canvas bag shaped like a briefcase. Once they got Mukhtar settled, introductions were made, and as they drank sweetened tea, Raphael explained the situation to Mukhtar and why they needed the satellite phone. Mukhtar had listened to their plan with great intensity as he puffed on a pipe and sipped the tea.

Once Raphael and Shandi were finished talking, Mukhtar sat silently for a few minutes before he asked, "And what if I said no to this plan?"

"I would be very disappointed and perhaps even angry, but by some means I would get back to Pakistan and with the help of my friends there arrange some type of plan to get my parents out. But I think the time grows short, for the terrorists look for them and get closer every day," Raphael answered.

"You could rob me of this satellite phone, do away with me and no one would be the wiser," Mukhtar said as he watched them.

"I, that is we, would be the wiser. You have gone out of your way to help us in the past. We are not bandits creeping through the night like those that hunt us. If you say no, we will respect your decision and find another plan," Shandi said as Raphael nodded his head in agreement.

Mukhtar studied them some more before he said, "If I lend you the phone, when will it be returned?"

"Hopefully, within a matter of two or three days if all goes well," Raphael said.

"Inshallah, it is done then." With that Mukhtar pulled the canvas case onto his knees as he was sitting and opened it revealing a large phone with separate key pad within. "If you know the number, then simply push the right keys."

Raphael gently picked up the phone from Mukhtar's lap and saw that it was an "analog" satellite phone, meaning it was a military phone which definitely met their needs, for it was almost impossible for others to tap into it. He set it on the table where they had laid out the maps, took in a large breath of air and then punched in Bilidou's emergency number. He heard faint beeping noises at first and then an actual mechanical ringing sound as he held the phone to his ear. He let the phone ring and ring. The longer it rang the more depressed he felt. What was he going to do if this didn't work? Just as he was about to hang up, there was a loud clicking sound and he heard a voice!

"Hello ... hello!"

It was a voice he recognized immediately.

"Jim! ... Jim Bilidou! Is that you?

"Raphael! Where the hell are you?"

Raphael laughed out loud. Yep, that was definitely Bilidou's voice. "I'm here in the Hindu Kush with the Falash. We know where my mom and dad are! Fuck, these satellite phones are incredible! You sound like you're right next door," Raphael said.

"Well, since we seem to be playing the 'guess where I am' game, it's my turn. Guess where I, actually we, are?" Bilidou responded.

"Uh ... Ok, where are you?"

"Well, myself and four of your teammates are in Kandahar," Bilidou responded.

There was a stunned silence on the line for a brief time, almost like someone had dropped the phone then picked it up.

"What the fuck!?" were all the words Raphael could rally together, he was so stunned. He just stood there with the phone to his ear, and for a brief moment he was incapable of any more speech.

"Raphael ... Raphael, are you there? What did you do, drop the phone?" Bilidou asked.

CHAPTER EIGHTY-SEVEN

Jim Bilidou looked at the other members of the team he had brought with him and grinned before he said, "I think that's the first time I've seen Raphael at a loss for words. Do you want to speak to him," he asked one of the team members and got a negative head shake. "Alright, but he's gonna find out sooner than later." Bilidou got back on the phone. "Raphael have you recovered enough to talk to me?"

"Fuck, yes. I thought you were still back in Canada. Man, oh man, am I ever glad you're here! It makes the plan so much simpler, I hope," Raphael said jubilantly as his mind still whirled with the thought that some of his teammates were this close.

"Ok. Now tell me what you're planning and how can we help. I heard you say your mom and dad are still alive, which is fantastic because they are top diplomats. Your father is ... or was ... returning as ambassador with, of course, your mother, but they are also agents for our and a few other intelligence services, so it's pretty much carte blanche with what we need to get them out of the area alive," Bilidou said.

Raphael, upon hearing those words, turned to Shandi, grinned at him and gave him a thumbs up.

"Ok, Jim we're working on a version of the KISS plan. The area through here is swarming with Taliban and al Qaeda. However, having said that, the Falash have lived in the area since at least Alexander the Great so they know every stone, every village. My mother and father are hidden in an area held by the Nuristani tribesman, who are friendly with the Falash, and we have the coordinates to where they are hidden. We can't get them out overland because of my father's injuries, but this is what we think will work, and not only will it get my parents out but there is the added plus we can maybe do a search and destroy on some of the terrorist bases." Then Raphael laid out the plan and what was needed.

Jim Bilidou listened, made some notes and asked only a few questions. When Raphael was finished, he asked a few more questions and added in some suggestions of his own.

"I think you're right about the 'Keep-It-Simple-Stupid' plan. Less can go wrong, and I think with a little begging and pleading we can get the equipment and manpower we need, and maybe a bit more, as the Americans are really nervous about your parents being captured, bless their hard little hearts. So when do we want this to go down?" Bilidou asked.

"It will takes us a day to get there from here as we are travelling by horseback, old truck and, as my granny used to say, 'Shanks' mare' [on foot]. So, day after tomorrow at dawn. We have a borrowed satellite phone so we can keep in touch," Raphael returned.

"Sure you don't want us ta pick ya up on the way?" Bilidou asked.

"No, that would alert the terrorists to where the Falash village is. My blood-brother and friend is the leader of the Falash. He knows all the trails, has the contacts, the ground manpower and weapons, plus he plans on doing a kind of mop-up operation after we've done the scoop and are out of the area. We need this to be a complete surprise, and it's best at dawn," Raphael said.

"'Kay. I'll be in touch with the details on equipment. Be careful, eh?

"Hey, I always am," Raphael and heard a snort of sarcastic derision.

"Not since I've met you. You and me are gonna have a chat about that when we get back," Bilidou said as he heard wild laughter in reponse.

"10-4 and out," Raphael said as he got his laughter under control.

CHAPTER EIGHTY-EIGHT

Raphael continued grinning as he put the phone in its holder withinin the case and then looked to where Shandi was standing.

"Looks like it's going to be a go, my brother, and perhaps you can meet some of my friends from Canada. I guess now we should talk about how many from this village should be going on the raid?" Raphael said.

"Yes, I can feel the excitement building up from my belly at the thought of really fighting back against our enemies instead of these small skirmishes and hit-and-run fights we've had to do to prevent them from finding where our main village is. It will be good to fight these cowards, who call themselves terrorists, in the open again. It is the time when I must decide who we take with us and who stays behind to protect the village and our lands," Shandi said in return.

At that moment Mukhtar interrupted Shandi. "I, too, am tired of all this fighting between those who used to be friends and are now foe. I, too, would like to go, to fight for my lands."

Both Raphael and Shandi looked at each other, and it was very plain to Mukhtar what that look meant.

"You think me too old. But I tell you, I am not! I can shoot every bit as well as you two can, plus while you are busy with other things, I can work the satellite phone. It will be my last battle on this earth, and I would like go to paradise knowing I have done one worthy thing," Mukhtar said in a voice filled with fervour.

Shandi, Raphael and a few of the men who had started to gather around all looked at each other, some with slight smiles on their faces and some gazed at Mukhtar with respect written plainly on their faces at the request. But all were silent 'til the quiet was broken by a slight, polite cough from Shandi and all looked to him.

"Mukhtar, what of your farm, and who will take care of it while you are gone? You are right—you are a good shot, for I have seen you win many a contest and even once won out over my father a long time ago. But there is one thing you cannot win out over and that is time. We must all submit to the ravages of time, for the longer we live upon the earth, the more she takes from us. And all the more bitter, we don't notice 'til we need to use a skill and find time has stolen it from us. We must leave on the morrow before dawn breaks, and there is four hours of hard riding before we drive for a ways, and then we must finally walk the last bit up steep trails. Can you honestly say you won't slow us down? For we must be in a place by a certain time or all is lost," Shandi asked.

Mukhtar dropped his head and pulled at his beard as he thought. After a few moments of contemplation, he looked back up at Shandi, and Shandi could see his deep grey eyes were rimmed with unshed tears of disappointment and shame as he said, "My sons guard my farm but, alas, you are probably right. However, I would like to be of some use, so if you wish I will stay here and help guard the village so you may take one more fighter."

"I would be honoured, Mukhtar," Shandi returned and bowed his head.

Shandi had already decided who would be best to go and those who would stay and guard the village. Then came the time when Shandi and two other men went to the place where weapons and ammunition were hidden, and those were handed out. Raphael noted the Falash had a large number of AK-47's with plenty of 7.62 NATO ammunition to go with them as well as glock semi- and fully automatic handguns. Raphael thought to himself that the Canadian major who had supplied them had been extremely generous. It would be nice one day to meet this major and thank him for his generosity.

Once all the weapons and ammo had been handed out, those men who were going into the Nuristani lands went to the corrals to pick out the horses they would need while Shandi discussed guard duty with those who would be staying to protect the village and the valley. Shandi had asked Mukhtar to oversee those doing guard duty in the hills around the village as he knew Mukhtar had extensive knowledge of that area, given what he grew as a farmer.

By the time everything had been set up, it was getting late in the day and dusk was slowly moving in.

When everything had been done, Raphael called Bilidou on the satellite phone and let him know that they were leaving early next morning, and Jim in turn told Raphael he had gotten everything on his wish list. It was a short conversation, and Raphael had told him they would contact him when they reached the Valley of the Caves the next evening.

Just one more night and a day if all went well.

CHAPTER EIGHTY-NINE

It was still dark when they left the village the next morning. All the horses—sturdy mountain horses—had their hooves muffled in heavy canvas, and the metal parts of their saddles and bridles had been carefully wrapped as well, so they made no sound.

The Falash considered their horses a part of their identity—a warrior—and as such treated them as a family member. A young man was paired with a young horse and together they learned the warrior's way, and they were watched by the elders as they trained. Any sign of cruelty by either horse or rider was viewed as a failure although both were tried with others. If that too met with failure, it was considered the gods had deemed other paths were more suitable for both horse and rider. In this wild country, there were many places where a horse could go where motor vehicles could not. Horses were an integral part of the warrior sect, and as such the warriors took great care and pride in them. Their horses had also been trained not to whinny or snort when geared up for battle. Fortuitously, Shandi had not only his own horse but had inherited his father's horse which, when introduced to Raphael, seemed to accept him.

Men, like their horses, also did not speak while on the trail that lead to battle. All orders had been given out while they were still in the village and only hand signs were used while on the trail. Those warriors who were going had checked to make sure nothing they carried made sound or would flash when the sun touched it. They all also wore garments that were dull brown and grey, their weapons were wrapped in similar colours so they blended in with the surrounding country. There were outriders to the front and sides who watched to make sure they did not run into friend or foe, for if word got out that a large group of men had been seen, it would be questioned and draw their enemies to them like bees to honey. So even though they travelled paths unknown to most and rarely travelled by a few, they still took the precautions, for they knew what was at stake. Their horses moved at a quick gait which, while not exhausting the horses, would get them to their goal swiftly.

Raphael, who had not ridden in some time and knew he was going to be stiff by the time this ride was over, gave a mental shrug as he thought, *As needs must.* Then he looked at the men surrounding him and felt a surge of gratitude wash over him as he thought how they had dropped everything, risked their lives and all to help him. It was just at that moment Shandi turned to look at him and gave him a fierce, savage grin. Raphael very nearly laughed out loud, for he too felt the ferocity and the wildness surging through him. He also knew there was another reason as well for these men to come with him. This was their chance to take revenge on those who were trying to wipe them and their way of life out of existence.

Luck was with them, for they made it to the village where they would trade their horses for the truck an hour earlier than they planned. The old garage where the truck was being stored was on the very outskirts of the small town, and the owner was waiting for them. They all followed him to a hidden corral, and they could see that both feed and water for their horses were already there. All the saddles and bridles were removed from the horses and hidden in the garage while the owner spoke quietly with Shandi as Shandi listened and nodded his head.

Shandi gathered the men around him and spoke quietly. "The two who have been assigned to watch over the horses 'til we return will hide within the garage. The truck, I am told, although old, is in good condition and filled with gas and carries extra containers of gas. I've been told all has been quiet in this area of the Hindu Kush, so perhaps our luck will hold. If we are stopped, all who are hidden in the back must be quiet while Raphael, who will be known as Naveed, and I will do the talking. If you hear Naveed or me say in a loud voice, 'But it is only farm workers in the back,' it means we will have to fight our way out. Let us hope it does not come to that." All the warriors nodded their heads in understanding.

Those who were going on went out back of the garage where the old truck was parked. When Raphael first saw the truck, he was struck dumb and then, unbidden, the thought came to him this truck was not just old it was ancient and was possibly built around the time Ford was coming out with the first cars in America. The truck was large and the back was covered with canvas and could easily fit twenty to twenty-five men, but it was going to be a tight squeeze for the thirty-five men who were going with them. He was very glad that he was riding up front with Shandi, for it was going to be a hard, hot, bumpy, jarring ride for those in the back. As Raphael looked around, he could see the same thought written on the faces of some of the men.

Apparently Shandi had the same thought, for he turned to the owner and said, "Are thee sure this truck will get us to where we are going?"

"Assuredly. It has been up and down the road and track many times with no trouble," came the reply.

Shandi looked at Raphael, who merely shrugged. They had no other choice.

Shandi sighed and climbed up into the driver's seat, which had been covered in an old horse blanket while Raphael climbed up onto the passenger side and very nearly impaled himself on an old, rusty seat spring which had worn through the original seat cover. The owner, seeing his predicament, tossed up a thick, dusty, old blanket to cover the spring, and Raphael sat very gingerly upon the passenger seat.

The other men in the group seemed to brighten up at the thought that they would not be the only ones suffering discomfort in the old beast of a truck.

Shandi asked for the keys and was told there were no keys, just a toggle switch. He shook his head as he switched the toggle switch on and the engine, with a mighty belch of black smoke, roared to life. He put it in first gear and it jumped ahead, but after the first lurch the ancient truck settled down and things went fairly smoothly after that although shifting from one gear to the next was a little rough, and they could hear the odd groan from the back. Shandi managed to find the road they were supposed to be on, although Raphael thought calling it a road was definitely hyperbole as it was more of a rough track. But it was safer not to say anything because Shandi might suggest he should spend some time in the back of the truck.

They had managed to get almost three-quarters of the way to the place where they would park the truck when four men carrying rifles stepped out from behind some large boulders, pointed their rifles at them and ordered them to stop. One even went so far as to lift his rifle up and start taking aim at Shandi.

"I'm afraid to stop this cursed truck for I fear it won't start again," Shandi shouted to Raphael above the noise of the engine as he saw the four men. It was then as he glanced with alarm at Raphael that he saw Raphael already had his handgun with silencer attached, lying on his lap out of sight of those wanting them to stop.

"Do you see any others besides these four? Raphael asked.

Shandi shook his head.

"Slow down like your going to stop. I'll take them out—they're on my side."

As Shandi started to slow down, Raphael quickly raised his handgun and shot four times. All four men dropped to the ground ... dead. All four had suffered headshots.

Shandi glanced over a Raphael and saw cold, hard resolution written plainly on the face of his friend and said nothing as he gripped the steering wheel tighter.

"I'll come back with some men and hide the bodies once we get to where we park this damn thing," Raphael said as he lay the handgun back in his lap.

"What do you think, bandits or terrorists?" Shandi asked.

"I don't know, but they were getting ready to shoot, and we can't risk any of ours getting shot."

Shandi nodded his head.

They found the cave where they were to hide the truck another klick up the track and pulled it inside the huge, cool cave and turned the truck off. Everybody got out of the truck and some groaned as they stretched to loosen stiff, banged-up bodies, the result of riding in the back of the old truck which apparently had no suspension springs left to ease the ride.

"Asadi, you come with Raphael and me. We must go back and hide those bodies. Pazir, set out some guards as there may be others around. Make sure everybody has had some water and is ready to go when we get back. We still have some steep hills and a cliff to climb," Shandi ordered as some started asking about the shooting.

"Wait 'til we get back and I will tell you all about it," Shandi added as he and the two others left the cave.

Raphael, Shandi and Pazir hiked back to where the bodies were and found them exactly where they had been shot.

"Well, at least this might mean there were no others with them as the bodies have not been touched. Also, I used a silencer," Raphael said.

"Raphael, it wouldn't have mattered if you had used a bazooka, the truck was so loud nobody was likely to hear although it was good shooting on your part," Shandi said with a smirk.

"True, in the rush I hadn't thought of that," Raphael returned.

"These have the look of bandits. Look they have old guns and they are somewhat rough and ragged, not like terrorists at all."

"Let us hope you are right, for then it is likely no one will come looking for them," Raphael grunted as dragged one of the bodies over to a shallow grave dug out neath the side of a large boulder.

Within a matter of twenty minutes, they had disposed of the bodies so they were well out of site and cleaned up the area so no one, unless they looked very closely, would know anything untoward had happened there. Then they worked their way back to the cave where the others waited, erasing as much sign of their passing as possible just in case the bandits had friends who might look for them.

The others were waiting for them and after drinking some water and stuffing food in their mouths, they started on the final stage of their journey, and as they went Shandi told them the tale about how Raphael had shot the four bandits with just four shots each in the head. All the men were impressed, for shooting a handgun from the rough beast of a truck and hitting what you were trying to aim at was quite a feat, and those around him slapped Raphael on the back and congratulated him. All Raphael could do was smile at them as he focussed on climbing the narrow trail which led up to the caves.

They were almost there.

CHAPTER NINETY

For the most part, the climb up the steep hills was breathtaking in two ways, Raphael thought. The scenery was stunning in an untamed, rough and colourful way with some of the sandstone walls around them a deep terracotta red while others a deep black with pockets of greenery throughout, and the second was it was literally breathtaking as the trail on which they were climbing was in the lower end of the Himalayas and was so steep in some parts one had to stop to get one's breath back. As they climbed further up, the trail widened so they could walk comfortably two abreast.

It was during one of those times that Shandi and Raphael walked side by side. Shandi had looked at his friend, really looked at him for the first time since he had been back here with them. He saw much written on that face which was perhaps written on his own as well, certainly the loss of innocence, the sweet naivety of youth. They had been replaced by a hard intelligence and an understanding of how the world worked, hence the cold, ruthless, almost cruel look when he had shot those four bandits. A very faint shadow of that expression remained within those quick-silver-coloured eyes. But on the face were also the faint lines which indicated he smiled and laughed much, which had not changed from when they had been boys together. Raphael had always had an easy laugh which he used as much at some of his own bonehead stunts as those around him. Yes, some things had changed about his friend, yet some remained the same, Shandi thought.

"We've had almost no time to talk about our lives since we parted some twelve years ago, but I have thought of you often. I admit there were times when I felt as if our spirits touched when I was looking up at Tirich Mir and thinking of inner stillness," Shandi said with a quiet smile.

Raphael returned the smile before he cast his gaze around 'til off in the distance, almost lost in a blue haze, he saw Tirich Mir before he said, "I, too, have thought of you, our mountain and being a warrior. I joined the police department in the city where I live. The police there are considered warriors unlike some of the places here where the police can be corrupt. There, in Canada, it is so different. The way of thinking can be so tame compared to here. They do teach a kind of inner stillness although it is not called that. Like here, there are monsters, and like you we try to search them out and destroy them. Just before I came back here I had been on a mission during which we had searched out and destroyed some very bad monsters," Raphael said in a voice which was slightly breathless due to lesser amounts of oxygen in the high mountain air. It had also affected, in a very minor way, the edges around how he thought.

Intrigued by what Raphael had just said, Shandi asked him, "And what are your monsters called?"

"The Taliban, al Qaeda and some others like serial killers, murderers, drug dealers, gang bangers, gun runners and others of their ilk. Evil can be anywhere," Raphael responded in a voice that seemed almost lost in a dream.

Shandi looked abruptly at Raphael and realized he might be suffering from the lack of oxygen this far up within the mountain range, and it could be starting to affect thinking patterns. They must take a break. Shandi signalled for everybody to take a break and catch their breath. At first Raphael was resistant 'til Shandi finally got him to understand that his thought processes weren't functioning properly, no doubt, from lack of oxygen. Finally, after very nearly getting into an argument with his friend, it sunk in, especially when he realized he was becoming combative towards him, and he sat down.

It took about twenty minutes of sitting quietly before Shandi judged Raphael ready to go on, but Raphael had been anxious the whole time. They were so close.

They came to a curve in the pathway approximately half-way up the cliff side, and Shandi indicated they needed to stop while he went forward to where the path disappeared around the corner. They could hear Shandi calling out to someone in Urdu and then a very faint response as Shandi vanished around the corner and was gone for what seemed a long time although it was but a few a short few minutes. When he returned he had a smile upon his face, and with him he had brought the Nuristani who had obviously been guarding the pathway.

Raphael let out a long sigh as Shandi waved his arm at him to come forward and follow the guard. Raphael greeted the guard with a broad smile and thanks in the Urdu vernacular before he started to follow him. As they rounded the curve, Raphael could see the opening to a large cave approximately fifty feet away and, although he started out in his long-legged stride, he quickly broke into an excited run. As he entered the cave, he was in a full run and finally came to a abrupt stop as the cave broke into several smaller caves. He turned round and round wondering which one, until a Nuristani boy who was by some equipment stood up, smiled and pointed to one of the caves.

CHAPTER NINETY-ONE

He rushed into the smaller cave, and at first he wondered where his mother and father were. There were only two older Nuristani crouched in the corner. One—by her dress, a female—had one hand at her throat while in her other hand she held a handgun which was pointing at him. She was leaning over an older man who was lying on a small cot with a bandage around his head. Where were his parents? They were suppose to be here. The man in the other room must be mistaken. These weren't his mother and father! But wait ... that hand to throat gesture was so familiar but her hair was almost all silvery white and she looked like ... old and tired, yet familiar ... the way she held the gun. Father, always saying she would break her wrist holding it like that ... wait. He looked closer. The light in here wasn't good, and the quick vision he had had of when they were actually old was gone, and in its place his beautiful mother and his father whose head was half covered by a large bandage, but those blue eyes were open.

"Mother, you shoot that handgun when you're holding it in such a way, you're going to break your wrist!" Raphael said as he rushed forward and scooped his mother up in his arms and gave her a bear hug. As he hugged his mother, he looked down at his father and saw him smile as a single tear oozed down his cheek.

"Raphael! My darling boy, you found us. I've been so worried ... what with your father! Oh, my darling boy, you must put me down now so I don't shoot you! The safety is off on the gun," Martha Wentworth Campbell said in a shakey voice as Raphael gently set her down.

Raphael knelt beside his father and grabbed the hand his father offered and then grinned at him although he was alarmed at how weak his father's grip was, and with his other hand, he reached up and touched his father's bandaged head. He had barely touched it and he could see his father wince in pain.

Raphael's mother knelt beside him and wrapped an arm around him as he held his father's hand.

"I've been so worried about your father. We managed to escape the attack on our convoy. I don't know how, but your father got us to a small Nuristani village where the chieftain recognized your father and they hid us in the village for a short time while they sent out word to Shandi Cershi. It was decided we should hide out in these caves as it was safer for both the villagers and us. Oh, Raphael, no sooner did we get here than your father collapsed and has been unconscious ever since, until just an hour ago when he suddenly regained conciousness and the first words out of his mouth were 'Raphael's coming!' and here you are!" Martha said as she continued holding on to Raphael.

"I can see we are going to have some very long talks about everything that has happened in the last several weeks to each of us. But for now, you remember Shandi, my friend from when were here before? Well I want to reintroduce him as he has grown as much as I have in these past years," Raphael said as Shandi came in with a smile upon his face.

"Shandi ... Shandi, is that really you? Stuart Campbell said in a weak voice. "You look so much like your father. How is he by the way?"

Shandi merely shook his head and saw the pained look of understanding flicker across his face. "We have much to talk about, but first Raphael and I must finalize plans for getting you out of here."

CHAPTER NINETY-TWO

Raphael hugged his mother again and grinned at his father before he left with Shandi and went out into the main section of the larger cave.

"Ok, I'll bite. Just how are we going to get my parents out of this cave and to a proper spot for the scoop and run?" Raphael asked in an undertone, for the caves bounced the echo of voices around if they spoke any louder.

"Before I answer your question, I want to show you something the Nuristani have kept secret, except for the chieftain of the Falash, for many generations. Since you are considered one of the Falash, they have allowed us to see and use this," Shandi said as Raphael looked at his friend with a puzzled expression.

Shandi smiled at Raphael and said, "Follow me," before walking through the large cave, which was the bright, almost terracotta red sandstone and into another smaller cave of similar coloured stone. In the centre of the smaller cave there was a large beam of sunlight which seemed to be coming through an opening at the top of the cave. Curious, Raphael walked over too and looked up at where the beam of sunlight was.

"Now I'm going to show you something astonishing," Shandi said and went to the back of the cave and, in what seemed almost magic, started walking up the back wall of the inner cave.

"What the hell ...!" Raphael said as he walked over to where Shandi had seemed to be walking up the wall.

And then he saw it! A broad pathway which went up the wall all the way to the smooth, large round opening in the top of the cave. The path was the same red sandstone as the walls, and when the sun was shining and the beam of sunlight filled the cave, the path became almost invisible. Raphael eagerly followed Shandi up the path and through the hole at the top. They emerged on a broad, flat plateau which overlooked the lower mountain ranges and cliffs. Raphael's mouth dropped open in wonder at what he saw around him. He was speechless and Shandi laughed at him as he held out his arms and whirled around.

"Do you think this will do for the scoop and run?" Shandi asked.

"You, my friend, are a fuckin' genius! Why didn't you tell me about this before?" Raphael returned in a voice filled with wonder.

"This is considered a place of great magic and a place to worship Allah. I had to have a long talk with the iman of the Nuristani to even be allowed to hide your parents in the caves below, and luck was with us for the iman recognized them as the ones who did a great service for the Nuristani several years ago which saved them from the genocide and jihad which was being planned for them.

The iman and the Nuristani people have agreed this one time to our scoop and run with your parents, but those who come for the rescue must swear on all that is holy to them to never repeat or tell where this sacred place is," Shandi said with great solemnity.

"That I can promise. This is a place which can only be used once," Raphael repeated.

"I brought the satellite phone. We should call in the coordinates now."

"Say, what about the map with the coordinates on it?" Raphael asked.

"The map of which you speak will never again see the light of day," Shandi said.

They sat cross-legged on the stone as Raphael called Bilidou and gave him the coordinates and confirmed who and what was involved in the mission.

The sun was setting over the Hindu Kush. They sat on the warm stone and watched the fiery display of clouds matched only by the majestic landscape as the mountains and deep valleys dimmed from brilliant reds and purples to lavender 'til finally the night held sway. Then they walked back down through the hole and along the path inside the cave.

They returned to the cave where Raphael's parents were and sat for hours talking of old memories and making new ones.

CHAPTER NINETY-THREE

Raphael stood on the plateau by the hole. It was still night but he could see to the east a faint hint of lighter blue was fighting its way to the tips of the mountains. The air was clear but there was a hint of a chill in it, a small warning ... winter was coming. Off in the distance, he thought he could hear the faint thump, which some might think was thunder over some distant plain, but he knew better.

"Ok, let's bring them up," he called down into the hole that led to the cave below.

He looked up again and saw the sky had lightened even further and the thumping sound seemed closer. As he watched, the sun tore a small laceration in the night's blackness. As the tear grew larger, more light seeped in and across the sky, enough to silhouette the giant bird which almost looked prehistoric with the first beams of sun hitting it, and on either side its young, smaller versions of itself.

The thumping sound was right above them now and with it a windstorm of epic proportions which blew loose cloth and hair as the Black Hawk helicopter, running on silent mode, set down while the two Apache helicopters remained in the air guarding the bigger helicopter. He watched as his mother and his father, who was on a stretcher, were rushed to the Black Hawk. As they were being placed in the helicopter, the gunner who had been manning the M60 stealth-belt machine gun leapt out of the helicopter and ran towards him. The gunner had his helmet on and yet looked, in the way he moved, somehow familiar. Then as the gunner drew closer, he took off his helmet to reveal a woman with auburn air, who laughed in amusement at his stunned look.

"I, that is, we, agreed, Oh hell, Lula, you shouldn't be here. But I'm glad anyway," Raphael said as he wrapped his arms around her briefly and gave her a quick hug. He looked up and saw someone else getting out of the Black Hawk who looked remarkably like Jim Bilidou.

As he came up to him, he looked around and after greeting his wayward, prodigal police officer-team member, he asked, "So where is Shandi Cershi? We've got some flying to do."

"Time for you to jump on the Black Hawk, Raphael. Shandi is coming up on one of the Apaches with me to help point out some of the Taliban and al Qaeda enclaves that have been killing off the Falash and Nuristani.

Raphael introduced Shandi to Bilidou before he climbed up on the Black Hawk helicopter and Lula took up her position of side gunner, and they lifted off.

He watched as Shandi and Bilidou climbed on the Apache which had just landed, and he had a sudden and unexpected twist of envy in his belly. He wanted to be out there with them.

The adventure was not over—it had just begun.

Turn the page for an excerpt from the second book in the
Stand on Guard series

✦━━━━➤✦◀━━━✦◀➤━━━━✦

Exigent Circumstances

RW Wells

✦━━━━➤✦◀━━━✦◀➤━━━━✦

Coming Soon!

Chapter 1

He stepped into the room, his room, and was embraced by the comforting arms of darkness which, to him, felt subtle and somehow sensuous as he was drawn gently over and into his chair. He could still hear the muted sound of the television which was spewing out one of the endless game shows his mother—she who gave pain-racked birth to him as she constantly reminded him—watched with such avid intensity.

It was odd, but there was an ancient movie which ran at the back of his mind's eye of her when he was very young. It showed a slender, laughing, pretty woman who hugged and played with him while in the background was a smiling man—his father, he thought. Then one day the father was gone and it seemed that with him he took all the laugher and love, and from that day his mother had seemed somehow to devolve ... to shrink, to pull into herself.

He hated bugs, particularly beetles. When he found one, he would squash it or torment it first before killing it, and his mother had started looking more and more like a squat, fat little beetle. There she would sit in her special chair which was covered in a chenille throw that absorbed all the beetle juice that squirted out of her mouth every time she talked to him. All the toxic rhetoric about how men left, took happiness with them, and someday he would leave too. She did say she loved him, she fed him and made sure he went to school, but her heart wasn't in it, for her heart had been wrenched out when his father left.

He was one of the invisible at school, smart in a quiet way, but it was like there was a grey haze of invisibility around him. He was not popular, nor mediocre; he was not victim material and bullies who thought to terrorize him would look into his face, and they would meet those pale blue, ice-cold eyes, and they would back away from what they read in that calm, icy gaze. So he wandered through his young life unnoticed and ignored, and that was alright with him. Even the teachers would go for long periods ignoring him, not because they were cruel, it was just so damn easy to forget the boy who always sat at the back of the class. He got good marks and when teachers thought to talk to him, his answers were monosyllabic and inoffensive. Plus there was a vagueness surrounding him, and soon their attention turned to the rabble-rousers, the victims, the popular kids and the bullies, which was also ok with him.

He had found his own world when he was in junior high. His mother, in a rare moment of motherly love and perhaps guilt, had bought him a computer and in the computer was where his real life lurked, waiting for him and only him. His life within his world had initially been filled with heroic avatars, his creations, and others who talked to him and had adventures. There was no loneliness in his life. And as he grew older, his computer grew with him, and he delved into the web world until he found the dark web, and there he found some very different friends who showed him that some of the outside life was wrong. They showed him images, violent images of how to change the world. He felt the power of that thought, and he met a new friend named Ahmed Khan whose words were like liquid gold which rolled off his tongue and made perfect sense. Ahmed showed him the weapons of war and promised to train him in their use.

He would sit in his dark room and simply punch in his password to his real life. He could see his reflection on the computer screen as numbers and letters, and the red flashes from explosions flickered beneath the screen. The plain freckled face and the icy eyes reflected back, as he stared into glass, were only a disguise that hid the power within.

ACKNOWLEDGEMENTS

To my basic fan base, that being my sister Heather, who's always believed in me, and my boy/nephew Cooper and Randy. Tree-hugger Sue (you always could and still might). My best friend Martha, and all the laughter we have shared over the years. Doc P., and your invaluable medical advice about some homicides, rates of decomposition and all that interesting stuff, and your ability to laugh at the ridiculous. Sapper Kyle, of the Canadian Combat Engineers, who did tours overseas in some of the most tragic areas in Europe. His information on I.E.D.'s added so much to this latest tome. And then there's the "Grunt," who fought in the war in Vietnam and introduced me to the "Occipital Notch" that a snipper aims for.

And last but certainly not least, to Craig, Island Blue Book Printing, who introduced me to the ladies of Behind the Book, who have been and are amazing. Where would I be without you?